I0824034

EGYPTIAN MYTHS AND TALES

EGYPTIAN MYTHS AND TALES

STORIES OF THE GODS AND GODDESSES

This edition published in 2025 by Sirius Publishing, a division of Arcturus Publishing Limited,
26/27 Bickels Yard, 151–153 Bermondsey Street,
London SE1 3HA

ISBN: 978-1-3988-6109-1
AD012282UK

Printed in China

CONTENTS

INTRODUCTION

Most people's ideas about ancient Egyptians have arisen from the fact that nearly all we know about them has come from their tombs. Those who think about the ancient Egyptians often remember their great buildings, such as the Pyramids and some of the temples, which housed their famous tombs and mummies. A glimpse onto the walls of these tombs reveals images illustrating an idealistic ancient Egyptian life before death, as they are riddled with scenes of festivity and merriment. Music and singing were important pieces of ancient Egyptian culture, and some of the oldest songs in all the world are the verses that the workmen used to sing at their work – the fisherman as he hauled his nets, the farm-servant as he drove the oxen round and round to tread out the corn. They were very fond of sports of all kinds – fishing and fowling and hunting; and when their work or their sport was done, they enjoyed large feasts, with plenty to eat and drink, with garlands of roses to fasten on their heads, and sweet scents to fill the rooms with pleasant odour, and musicians, dancers, and acrobats.

Beyond the merriments of life, most other nations of old days had most unpleasant ideas about the other world to which people go after their life here is done – the Greeks thought of it as a dim, shadowy, gloomy abode, where the ghosts of even the greatest heroes wandered miserably and aimlessly about; the Babylonians and Assyrians called it The Land of No Return, where people live on dust and mud

and dwell in darkness; the Hebrews called it The Pit, and dreaded nothing so much as going down into it. However, in the ancient Egyptians' heaven, folks ploughed and sowed and reaped the most wonderful corn, whose stalks were three yards long with ears a yard more, and sailed, fishing and fowling, in little papyrus canoes, over beautiful lakes and canals, and then played draughts and enjoyed a glass of beer under the shade of the sycamore-trees in the evening.

But how is it that ancient Egyptian tales have come down to our times? Some of them tell us of things that happened, if they ever happened at all, about 5,000 years ago.

A great deal of the information that has come down to us from the days of ancient Egypt has lasted so long because it was carved in stone upon the walls of some great building. The ancient Egyptians had a form of writing called 'hieroglyphic,' or 'sacred writing.' It is made up of hundreds of little pictures – an eagle for an *a*, a lion for an *m*, and so on. And when they had anything to write, they carved it in this picture-writing, sometimes filling in the picture-letters with brightly coloured pastes, so that the whole story blazes with all sorts of colours.

However, it wasn't everybody who could afford to build a temple when they wanted to publish a poem. So most ancient Egyptian books, and all ancient Egyptian storybooks, were written not in hieroglyphic, but in one or other of two simpler forms which we call 'hieratic' or 'demotic'; and they were written not on stone, but on papyrus. The papyrus, from which our word 'paper' comes, was a reed with a long, fleshy, thick stem, which grew plentifully in ancient Egypt. They used to split up the inside of the stem into broad, thin layers, which, when pasted crosswise over one another, were strong enough to bear writing upon.

Then the scribe, or writer, took his palette, which had holes for black ink and for coloured inks, and his pens, which were really little brushes made of reeds with their ends bruised, and painted in the letters on the papyrus. Then the papyrus,

when it was finished, was rolled together. It was then put into a case, and when the owner of it wanted to read he took it out of the case and unrolled a little of the beginning. As he went on he rolled up on the one side and unrolled on the other until he got to the end.

Now, these rolls of papyrus were very costly to make, so that not everyone could afford to have them; and they were very easily destroyed, so that great care had to be taken of them. Sometimes they were prized so much that when the owner of the roll died he left orders for his favourite roll or rolls to be buried in his coffin with him. And there the papyrus has lain, beside the mummy of its old owner, for hundreds upon hundreds of years. Some years ago a lady's grave was discovered, and when her coffin was opened, they found a papyrus roll with part of Homer's great poem, the 'Iliad,' written upon it. Scholars have been able to read these scrolls and to translate what is written on them into English and French and German, and nearly all the stories that follow in this book were written on papyrus.

When we come to read the stories, we may look at them in two ways. The first is the way that only cares for the story itself – that is only anxious to find out what happened to the doomed prince, or how the shipwrecked sailor was saved, or how the ghost made the wizard prince give back the magic roll. In these tales, we can see the seeds from which some of our own favourite stories have sprung.

We can also read these stories to learn about the land of ancient Egypt itself: the people who lived in it, their manners and customs, what they thought and what they believed, and about the other lands and peoples which lay around Egypt. From the central myth of creation to stories about the gods' vengeance, death, and redemption, they give you pictures of all kinds of Egyptian life.

The belief in the efficacy of magic colours almost every one of the tales to the very last. You see Senosiris, the reincarnation of an old Egyptian sage, as he confounds an Ethiopian wizard before the Pharaoh and his court, and the goddess

Isis's healing powers as she draws a scorpion's poison from her son's body. Or you get a glimpse into the sinister realm of court intrigue, with its atmosphere of suspicion, jealousy, and sudden death. The stories are riddled with strange dangers and marvels laying in each protagonist's path – talking serpents, and vanishing islands, and vanquished gods. Stories like that of Tahuti, the doomed prince, and the Sphinx reveal aspects of Egyptian belief systems, while other stories, such as the story of the peasant and the workman, feature the lives of the working class.

The stories which are here narrated cover, from first to last, a period of about 2,000 years; and they are a faithful recreation of the changing manners, customs, and beliefs of one of the world's first civilizations.

THE GODS OF EGYPT

The group of beliefs which constituted what for convenience' sake is called the Egyptian religion in an existence of some thousands of years passed through nearly every phase known to the student of comparative mythology. If the theologians of ancient Egypt found it impossible to form a pantheon of deities with any hope of consistency, assigning to each god or goddess his or her proper position in the divine galaxy as ruling over a definite sphere, cosmic or psychical, it may be asked in what manner the modern mythologist is better equipped to reduce to order elements so recondite and difficult of elucidation as the mythic shapes of the divinities worshipped in the Nile Valley. But the answer is ready. The modern science of comparative religion is extending year by year, and its light is slowly but certainly becoming diffused among the dark places of the ancient faiths. By the gleam of this magic lamp, then – more wonderful than any dreamt of by the makers of Eastern fable – let us walk in the gloom of the pyramids, in the cool shadows of ruined temples, aye, through the tortuous labyrinth of the Egyptian mind itself, trusting that by virtue of the light we carry we shall succeed in unravelling to some extent the age-long enigma of this mystic land.

One of the first considerations which occur to us is that among such a concourse of gods as is presented by the Egyptian religion it would have been surprising if

confusion had not arisen in the native mind concerning them. This is proved by the texts, which display in many cases much difficulty in defining the exact qualities of certain deities, their grouping and classification. The origin of this haziness is not far to seek. The deities of the country multiplied at such an astonishing rate that whereas we find the texts of the early dynasties give us the names of some two hundred deities only, the later Theban Recension (or version) of the *Book of the Dead* supplies nearly five hundred, to which remain to be added the names of mythological beings to the number of eight hundred.

LOCAL GODS

Another cause which made for confusion was that in every large town of Upper and Lower Egypt and its neighbourhood religion took what might almost be called a local form. Thus the great gods of the country were known by different names in each nome or province, their ritual was distinctive, and even the legends of their origin and adventures assumed a different shape. Many of the great cities, too, possessed special gods of their own, and to these were often added the attributes of one or more of the greater and more popular forms of godhead. The faith of the city that was the royal residence became the religion *par excellence* of the entire kingdom, its temple became the Mecca of all good Egyptians, and its god was, so long as these conditions obtained, the Jupiter of the Egyptian pantheon. It might have been expected that when Egyptians attained a uniformity of culture, art, and nationhood, their religion, as in the case of other peoples, would also become uniform and simplified. But such a consummation was never achieved. Even foreign intercourse failed almost entirely to break down the religious conservatism of priesthood and people. Indeed, the people may be said to have proved themselves more conservative than the priests. Alterations in religious policy, differentiation in legend and hieratic texts emanated from time to time from the various colleges of priests, or from that

fount of religion, the sovereign himself; but never was a change made in deference to the popular clamour unless it was a reversion to an older type. Indeed, as the dynasties advance we behold the spectacle of a theological gulf growing betwixt priests and people, the former becoming more idealistic and the latter remaining as true to the outer semblance of things, the symbolic, as of old.

The evolution of religion in ancient Egypt must have taken the same course as among other races, and any hypothesis which attempts to explain it otherwise is almost certainly doomed to non-success. Of late years many works by learned Egyptologists have been published which purport to supply a more or less wide survey of Egyptian mythology and to unravel its deeper significances. The authors of some of these works, however admirable they may be as archaeologists or as translators of hieroglyphic texts, are for the most part but poorly equipped to grapple with mythological difficulties. To ensure success in mythological elucidation a special training is necessary, and a prolonged familiarity with the phenomena of early religion in its many and diverse forms is a first essential. In the work of one foreign Egyptologist of standing, for example, a candid confession is made of ignorance regarding mythological processes. He claims to present the 'Egyptian religion as it appears to an unprejudiced observer who knows nothing of the modern science of religions.' Another Egyptologist of the first rank writes upon the subject of totemism in the most elementary manner, and puts forward the claim that such a system never existed in the Nile valley. But these questions will be dealt with in their proper places.

Beginning with forms of the lower cultus – forms almost certainly of African origin – the older religion of Egypt persisted strongly up to the time of the Hyksos period, after which time the official religion of the country may be found in one or other form of sun-worship. That is to say, all the principal deities of the country were at some time amalgamated or identified with the central idea of a sun-god.

The Egyptian religion of the Middle and Late Kingdoms was as much a thing of philosophic invention as later Greek myth, only, so far as we have the means of judging, it was not nearly so artistic or successful. For, whereas we find numerous allusions in the texts to definite myths, we seldom find in Egyptian literature the myths themselves. Indeed, our chief repository of Egyptian religious tales is the *De Iside et Osiride* of the Greek Plutarch – an uncertain authority. It is presumed that the myths were so well known popularly that to write them down for the use of such a highly religious people as the Egyptians would have been a work of supererogation. The loss to posterity, however, is immeasurable, and, lacking a full chronicle of the deeds of the gods of Egypt, we can only grope through textual and allied matter for scraps of intelligence which, when pieced together, present anything but an appearance of solidity and comprehensiveness.

CREATION MYTHS

There are several accounts in existence which deal with the Egyptian conception of the creation of the world and of man. We find a company of eight gods alluded to in the Pyramid Texts as the original makers and moulders of the universe. The god Nu and his consort Nut were deities of the firmament and the rain which proceeds therefrom. Hehu and Hehut appear to personify fire, and Kekui and Kekuit the darkness which brooded over the primeval abyss of water. Kerh and Kerhet also appear to have personified Night or Chaos. We find in the account of the creation story now under consideration the admixture of the germs of life enveloped in thick darkness, so well known to the student of mythology as symptomatic of creation myths all the world over. A papyrus (*c.* 312 B.C.) preserved in the British Museum contains a series of chapters of a magical nature, the object of which is to destroy Apep, the fiend of darkness, and in it we find two copies of the story of creation which detail the means by which the sun came into being. In one account the god

Ra says that he took upon himself the form of Khepera, the deity who was usually credited with the creative faculty. He proceeds to say that he continued to create new things out of those which he had already made, and that they went forth from his mouth. 'Heaven,' he says, 'did not exist and earth had not come into being, and the things of the earth and creeping things had not come into existence in that place, and I raised them from out of Nu from a state of inactivity.' This would imply that Khepera moulded life in the universe from the matter supplied from the watery abyss of Nu. 'I found no place,' says Khepera, 'whereon I could stand. I worked a charm upon my own heart. I laid a foundation in Maāt. I made every form. I was one by myself. I had not emitted from myself the god Shu, and I had not spit out from myself the goddess Tefnut. There was no other being who worked with me.' The word Maāt signifies law, order, or regularity, and from the allusion to working a charm upon his heart we may take it that Khepera made use of magical skill in the creative process, or it may mean, in Scriptural phraseology, that 'he took thought unto himself' to make a world. The god continues that from the foundation of his heart multitudes of things came into being. But the sun, the eye of Nu, was 'covered up behind Shu and Tefnut,' and it was only after an indefinite period of time that these two beings, the children of Nu, were raised up from out the watery mass and brought their father's eye along with them. In this connexion we find that the sun, as an eye, has a certain affinity with water. Sacred wells famous for the cure of blindness are often connected with legends of saints who sacrificed their own eyesight; the allusion in those legends is probably to the circumstance that the sun as reflected in water has the appearance of an eye. Thus when Shu and Tefnut arose from the waters the eye of Nu followed them. Shu in this case may represent the daylight and Tefnut moisture.

Khepera then wept copiously, and from the tears which he shed sprang men and women. The god then made another eye, which in all probability was the moon.

After this he created plants and herbs, reptiles and creeping things, while from Shu and Tefnut came Geb and Nut, Osiris and Isis, Set, Nephthys and Horus at a birth. These make up the company of the great gods at Heliopolis, and this is sufficient to show that the latter part of the story at least was a priestly concoction.

But there was another version, obviously an account of the creation according to the worshippers of Osiris. In the beginning of this Khepera tells us at once that he is Osiris, the cause of primeval matter. This account was merely a frank usurpation of the creation legend for the behoof of the Osirian cult. Osiris in this version states that in the beginning he was entirely alone. From the inert abyss of Nu he raised a god-soul – that is, he gave the primeval abyss a soul of its own. The myth then proceeds word for word in exactly the same manner as that which deals with the creative work of Khepera. But only so far, for we find Nu in a measure identified with Khepera, and Osiris declaring that his eye, the sun, was covered over with large bushes for a long period of years. Men are then made by a process similar to that described in the first legend. From these accounts we find that the ancient Egyptians believed that an eternal deity dwelling in a primeval abyss where he could find no foothold endowed the watery mass beneath him with a soul; that he created the earth by placing a charm upon his heart, otherwise from his own consciousness, and that it served him as a place to stand upon; that he produced the gods Shu and Tefnut, who in turn became the parents of the great company of gods; and that he dispersed the darkness by making the sun and moon out of his eyes. After these acts followed the almost insensible creation of men and women by the process of weeping, and the more sophisticated making of vegetation, reptiles, and stars.

We have references to other deities in the Pyramid Texts, some of whom appear to be nameless. For example, in the text of Pepi I we find homage rendered to one who has four faces and who brings the storm. This would seem to be a god of wind

and rain, whose countenances are set toward the four points of the compass, whence come the four winds.

THE 'COMPANIES' OF THE GODS

In the Pyramid Texts we find frequent mention of several groups consisting of nine gods each. One of these companies of gods, or Enneads, was called the Great and another the Little, and the nine gods of Horus are also alluded to. It is not known, however, whether this group is in any way connected with either of the others. We also read in the Pyramid Texts of Teta of a double group of eighteen gods which recur in the text of Pepi I. These eighteen gods may simply be the Great and Little companies of gods taken together. In the texts of Pepi I and Teta, however, we find a third company of nine gods, officially recognized by the priests of Heliopolis, and all three companies are represented by twenty-seven symbols representing the word *neter* (god) placed in a row.

Although these companies of gods are spoken of as containing nine deities, that is owing to their designation of *Pesedt*, which signifies 'nine'. The Little company in reality contains eleven gods, but nine was their original number, and, as Sir Gaston Maspero says, each of them, especially the first and last, could be developed. A local company such as that of Heliopolis might have the god of another nome or district embraced in it in one of two ways; that is, the alien god might replace one of the local gods or be set side by side with him. Again, strange gods could be absorbed in the leader of the *Pesedt*. When a fresh god was admitted into a company all the other deities who were connected with him were also included, but their names were not classed beside those of its original members.

These three companies of gods were fully developed by the period of the Fifth Dynasty, and there is little doubt that the Egyptian theology owed the formation of this pantheon to the caste of priests ruling at Heliopolis.

To the third *Pesedt* they gave no name. The gods of the first company are Tem, Shu, Tefnut, Qeb, Nut, Osiris, Isis, Set, Nephthys. Occasionally Horus is given as the chief of the company instead of Tem. In the text of Unas we find the names of the gods of the Little company given, but they are for the most part quite unimportant. The third company is rarely mentioned, and the names of its gods are unknown. Earth as well as heaven and the underworld had its quota of deities, and it is considered highly probable that the three companies of gods are referable one to each of these regions. The members of each company varied in different periods and in different cities. But the great local god or goddess was always the head of the company in a given vicinity. As has been said, he might be joined to another deity. At Heliopolis, for example, where the chief local god was Tem, the priests joined to his name that of Ra, and addressed him in prayer as Ra-Tem. Texts of all periods show that the chief local gods of many cities retained their pre-eminence almost to the end. The land of Egypt was divided into provinces called *hesput*, to which the Greeks gave the name of *nome*. In each of these a certain god or group of gods held sway, the variation being caused by racial and other considerations. To the people of each nome their god was the deity *par excellence*, and in early times it is plain that the worship of each province amounted almost to a separate religion. This division of the country must have taken place at an early epoch, and it certainly contributed greatly to the conservation of religious differences. The nome gods certainly date from pre-dynastic times, as is proved by inscriptions antedating the Pyramid Texts. The number of these provinces varied from one period to another, but the average seems to have been between thirty-five and forty. It would serve no purpose to enumerate the gods of the various nomes in this place, as many of them are obscure, but as each deity is dealt with the nome to which he belongs will be mentioned. Several nomes worshipped the same god. For example, Horus was worshipped in not less than six, while in three provinces Khnemu was worshipped, and Hathor in six.

THE EGYPTIAN IDEA OF GOD

The word by which the Egyptians implied deity and, indeed, supernatural beings of any description was *neter*. The hieroglyphic which represents this idea is described by most Egyptologists as resembling an axe-head let into a long wooden handle. Some archaeologists have attempted to show that the figure resembled in outline a roll of yellow cloth, the lower part bound or laced over, the upper part appearing as a flap at the top, probably for unwinding. It has been thought possible that the object represents a fetish – for instance, a bone carefully wound round with cloth, and not the cloth alone.

We are ignorant of most of the gods worshipped during the first four dynasties, chiefly because of the lack of documentary evidence, although some are known from the inscription called the Palermo Stone, which alludes to several local deities. Some portions of the *Book of the Dead* may have been revised during the First Dynasty, and from this we may argue that the religion of the Egyptians, as revealed in the later texts, closely resembled that in existence during the first three dynasties. It is only when we come to the Fifth and Sixth Dynasties that we discover material for the study of the Egyptian pantheon in the Pyramid Texts of Unas, Teta, Pepi the First, and others. By this period the first phase of Egyptian development appears to have been entered upon. At the same time it is plain that the material afforded by the Pyramid Texts contains stratum upon stratum of religious thought and conception, in all probability bequeathed to the pyramid builders by innumerable generations of men. In these wondrous texts we find crystallized examples of the most primitive and barbarous religious elements – animistic, fetishistic, and totemic. These texts are for the most part funerary and, in consequence, relate chiefly to deities of the underworld.

DEITIES OF THE PYRAMID TEXTS

In order to understand this earliest fixed phase of religious thought in Egypt, it is necessary to pass in brief review the deities alluded to in the Pyramid Texts, and for the moment to regard them separately from the rest of the Egyptian pantheon. In doing so we must beware of definitely labelling these conceptions with such names as 'water-god,' 'thunder-god,' 'sun-god,' and so forth. Despite the labours of the last half-century, the science of mythology is yet in its infancy, and workers in its sphere are now beginning to suspect that mere variants or phases of certain deities, which are by no means separate entities, have in many cases been credited with an individual status they do not deserve. The deities of the Greek and Roman pantheons are doubtless good examples of gods whose attributes are finally fixed. Thus one may say of Mars that he is a war-god, and of Pallas Athene that she is a goddess of wisdom, but these were merely the attributes possessed by these deities which were most popular and uppermost in the public consciousness. Recent research has proved that most of the Greek and Roman deities are traceable to earlier forms, some of which possess a variety of attributes, others of which are more simple in form than the later conception which is developed from them. Again, many deities which exhibit some particular tendency are necessarily connected with other natural forms. Thus many rain gods or goddesses are connected with thunder and lightning. Possession of the lightning arrow frequently implies a connexion with hunting or war. All moon-gods are deities of moisture, and preside over birth. Some deities of rain preside also over the winds, thunder and lightning, the chase and war, general culture, and so forth. A sun-god, as lord of the vault of heaven, can preside over all the meteorological manifestations thereof. He is god of growth, of wealth, because gold possesses the yellow colour of his beams, of travelling, because he walks the heavens, and he rules countless other departments of existence. From polytheism may evolve in

time a condition of monotheism, in which one god holds complete sway over mankind – that is, one deity may become so popular, or the priestly caste connected with him so powerful, that all other cults languish as his spreads and grows. But, on the other hand, polytheism, or the multiplicity of deities, may well spring from an early monotheism, itself the child of a successful fetish or totem, for the attributes of a great single god may, in the hands of a people still partially in the animistic stage, become so infused with individuality as to appear entirely separate entities. In dealing, then, with the gods alluded to in the Pyramid Texts, several of which are obviously derivative, we must recollect that although in a manner it is necessary to affix to them some more or less definite description, it will be well to bear in mind the substance of this paragraph.

We are not at present finally considering the natures or characteristics of the deities mentioned in the Pyramid Texts, but merely affording such a brief outline of them as will give the reader some idea of Egyptian religion in general during the early dynasties.

The goddess Net, or Neith, who is mentioned in the Pyramid Texts of Unas, is a figure in which we descry a personification of moisture or rain, because of her possession of the arrow, the symbol of lightning. The hawk-headed Horus, probably originally a hawk totem, is one of the manifestations of the sun-deity, from whom he may have evolved, or with whom he may have been confounded. Khepera, also found in the Unas Texts, is another form of the sun. His possession of the beetle glyph is symbolical of the manner in which the sun rolls over the face of the sky as the Egyptian beetle or scarabæus rolled its eggs over the sand. Khnemu, the ram-headed, whose name signifies 'the moulder' or 'uniter,' was probably the totemic deity of an immigrant race who had achieved godhead, and perhaps monotheism, or at least creatorship, in another sphere, and who had been accepted into Egyptian belief with all his attributes. Sebek, the crocodile-god, Ra and Ptah, two other

forms of the sun-god, Nu, the watery mass of heaven, are also alluded to in the Pyramid Texts of Unas and Teta, as is Hathor.

AMEN'S RISE TO POWER

Many hymns of Amen-Ra, especially that occurring in the papyrus of Hu-nefer, show the completeness of this fusion and the rapidity with which Amen had risen to power. In about a century from being a mere local god he had gained the title of 'king of the gods' of Egypt. His priesthood had become by far the most powerful and wealthy in the land, and even rivalled royalty itself. Their political power can only be described as enormous. They made war and peace, and when the Ramessid Dynasty came to an end the high-priest of Amen-Ra was raised to the royal power, instituting the Twenty-first Dynasty, known as the 'dynasty of priest-kings.' But if they were strong in theology, they were certainly not so in military genius. They could not enforce the payment of tribute which their predecessors had wrung from the surrounding countries, and their poverty increased rapidly. The shrines of the god languished for want of attendants, and even the higher ranks of the priesthood itself suffered a good deal of hardship. Robber bands infested the vicinity of the temples, and the royal tombs were looted. But if their power waned, their pretensions certainly did not, and even in the face of Libyan aggression in the Delta they continued to vaunt the glory of the god whom they served. Examining the texts and hymns which tell us what we know of Amen-Ra, we find that in them he is considered as the general source of life, animate and inanimate, and is identified with the creator of the universe, the 'unknown god.' All the attributes of the entire Egyptian pantheon were lavished upon him, with the exception of those of Osiris, of whom the priests of Amen-Ra appear to have taken no notice. But they could not displace the great god of the dead, although they might ignore him. In one of his forms certainly, that of Khensu the Moon-god, Amen bears a slight likeness to

Osiris, but we cannot say that in this form he usurps the *rôle* of the god of the underworld in any respect. Amen-Ra even occupied the shrines of many other gods throughout the Nile valley, absorbing their attributes and entirely taking their place. One of his most popular forms was that of a goose, and the animal was sacred to him in many parts of Egypt, as was the ram. Small figures of him made in the Ptolemaic form have the bearded face of a man, the body of a beetle, the wings of a hawk, human legs with the toes and claws of a lion. All this, of course, only symbolizes the many-sided character of him who was regarded as the greatest of all gods, and typified the manner in which attributes of every description resided in him. The entire *Pesedt* or company of the gods was supposed to be unified in Amen, and indeed we may describe his cult as one of the most serious attempts of antiquity to formulate a system of monotheism, the worship of a single god. That they did not achieve this was by no means their fault. We must look upon them as a band of enlightened men animated by a spiritual fire, which burned very brightly among the sadly material surroundings of Egypt. But, like all priestly hierarchies, they possessed the inherent weakness of ambition and the love of overweening power. Had they relegated politics to its proper sphere, they might have been much more successful than they were; but the true cause of their ultimate failure to conquer entirely the other cults of Egypt lay in the circumstance of the very ancient and deep-seated nature of these cults, and of the primeval and besotted ignorance of those who supported them.

THE ORACLE OF JUPITER-AMMON

No part of Egypt was free from the dominion of Amen-Ra, which spread north and south, east and west, and had ramifications in Syria, Nubia, and other Egyptian dependencies. Its most powerful centres were Thebes, Hermonthis, Coptos, Panopolis, Hermopolis Magna, and in Lower Egypt Memphis, Saïs, Heliopolis,

and Mendes. In one of the oases in later times he had a great oracle, known as that of Jupiter-Ammon, a mysterious spot frequented by superstitious Greeks and Romans, who went there to consult the deity on matters of state or private importance. Here every roguery of priestcraft was practised. An idol of the god was on occasion carried through the temple by his priests, responding, if he were in a good humour, to his votaries, not by speech, but by nodding and pointing with outstretched arm. We know from classical authors that the Egyptians possessed the most wonderful skill in the manufacture of automata, and there is no room for doubt that the god responded to the questions of the eager devotees who had made the journey to his shrine by means of cleverly concealed strings. But the oracle of Jupiter-Ammon in Libya is surrounded in obscurity. Even Alexander the Great paid a visit to this famous shrine to satisfy himself whether or not he was the son of Jupiter. Lysander and Hannibal also journeyed thither, and the former received a two-edged answer from the deity, not unlike that which Macbeth received from the witches.

MUT THE MOTHER

The great female counterpart of Amen-Ra was Mut, the 'world-mother.' She is usually represented as a woman wearing the united crowns of north and south, and holding the papyrus sceptre. In some pictures she is delineated with wings, and in others the heads of vultures project from her shoulders. Like her husband, she is occasionally adorned with every description of attribute, human and animal, probably to typify her universal nature. Mut, like Amen, swallowed up a great many of the attributes of the female deities of Egypt. She was thus identified with Bast, Nekhebet, and others, chiefly for the reason that because Amen had usurped the attributes of other gods, she, as his wife, must do the same. She is a striking example in mythology of what marriage can do for a

goddess. Even Hathor was identified with her, as was Ta-urt and every other goddess who could be regarded as having the attributes of a mother. Her worship centred at Thebes, where her temple was situated a little to the south of the shrine of Amen-Ra. She was styled the 'lady of heaven' and 'queen of the gods,' and her hieroglyphic symbol, a vulture, was worn on the crowns of Egypt's queens as typical of their motherhood. The temple of Mut at Thebes was built by Amen-hetep III about 1450 B.C. Its approach was lined by a wonderful avenue of sphinxes, and it overlooked an artificial lake. Mut was probably the original female counterpart of Nu, who in some manner became associated with Amen. She is mentioned only once in the *Book of the Dead* in the Theban Recension, which is not a little strange considering the reputation she must have enjoyed with the priesthood of Amen.

PTAH

Ptah was the greatest of the gods of Memphis. He personified the rising sun, or, rather, a phase of it – that is, he represented the orb at the time when it begins to rise above the horizon, or immediately after it has risen. The name is said to mean 'opener,' from the circumstance that Ptah was thought to open the day; but this derivation has been combated. 'Sculptor' or 'engraver' have been suggested as the true translation, and as Ptah was the god of all handicrafts it seems most probable that this is correct. Ptah seems to have retained the same characteristics from the period of the Second Dynasty down to the latest times. In early days he seems to have been regarded as a creator, or perhaps he was confounded with one of the first Egyptian creative deities. We find him alluded to in the Pyramid Text of Teta as the owner of a 'workshop,' and the passage seems to imply that it was Ptah who fashioned new boats in which the souls of the dead were to live in the Duat. From the *Book of the Dead* we learn that he was a great worker in metals, a master architect,

and framer of everything in the universe; and the fact that the Romans identified him with Vulcan greatly assists our understanding of his attributes.

It was Ptah who, in company with Khnemu, carried out the commands of Thoth concerning the creation of the universe. To Khnemu was given the fashioning of animals, while Ptah was employed in making the heavens and the earth. The great metal plate which was supposed to form the floor of heaven and the roof of the sky was made by Ptah, who also framed the supports which upheld it. We find him constantly associated with other gods – that is, he takes on the attributes or characteristics of other deities for certain fixed purposes. For example, as architect of the universe he partakes of the nature of Thoth, and as the god who beat out the metal floor of heaven he resembles Shu.

Ptah is usually represented as a bearded man having a bald head, and dressed in habiliments which fit as closely as a shroud. From the back of his neck hangs a Menat, the symbol of happiness, and along with the usual insignia of royalty and godhead he holds the symbol of stability. As Ptah-Seker he represents the union of the creative power with that of chaos or darkness: Ptah-Seker is, indeed, a form of Osiris in his guise of the Night-sun, or dead Sun-god. Seker is figured as a hawk-headed man in the form of a mummy, his body resembling that of Ptah. Originally Seker represented darkness alone, but in later times came to be identified with the Night-sun. Seker is, indeed, confounded in places with Sept, and even with Geb. He appears to have ruled that portion of the underworld where dwelt the souls of the inhabitants of Memphis and its neighbourhood.

The Seker-boat

In the great ceremonies connected with this god, and especially on the day of his festival, a boat called the Seker-boat was placed upon a sledge at sunrise, at the time when the rays of the sun were slowly beginning to diffuse themselves over the earth.

It was then drawn round the sanctuary, which act typified the revolution of the sun. This boat was known as Henu, and is mentioned several times in the *Book of the Dead*. It did not resemble an ordinary boat, but one end of it was much higher than the other, and was fashioned in the shape of the head of an animal resembling a gazelle. In the centre of the vessel was a coffer surmounted by a hawk with outspread wings, which was supposed to contain the body of Osiris, or of the dead Sun-god. The Seker- or Henu-boat was probably a form of the Mesektet-boat, in which the sun sailed over the sky during the second half of his daily journey, and in which he entered the underworld in the evening. Although Seker was fairly popular as a deity in ancient Egypt, his attributes seem to have been entirely usurped by Ptah. We also find the triple-named deity Ptah-Seker-Asar or Ptah-Seker-Osiris, who is often represented as a hawk on coffers and sarcophagi. About the Twenty-second Dynasty this triad had practically become one with Osiris, and he had even variants which took the attributes of Min, Amsu, and Khepera. He has been described as the 'triune god of the resurrection.' There is very little doubt that the amalgamation of these gods was brought about by priestly influence.

Ptah was also connected with the god known as Tenen, who is usually represented in human form and wearing on his head the crown with ostrich feathers. He is also drawn working at a potter's wheel, upon which he shapes the egg of the world. In other drawings he is depicted as holding a scimitar. It has been suggested that this weapon shows that he is the destructive power of nature or the warrior-god, but this is most unlikely. The scimitar of Ptah in his guise as Tenen is precisely the same as those axes which are the attributes of creative deities all over the world. With this scimitar he carves out the earth, as the god of the Ainu of Japan shapes it with his hatchet, or as other deities which have already been mentioned use their axes or hammers. Tenen was probably a primeval creative god, but for that reason was co-ordinated with Ptah.

SEKHMET

The principal centre of the worship of Ptah was Memphis, in which were also situated the temples of Sekhmet, Bast, Osiris, Seker, Hathor, and I-em-hetep, as well as that of Ra. The female counterpart of Ptah was Sekhmet, and they were the parents of Nefer-tem. Sekhmet was later identified with forms of Hathor. She had the head of a lioness, and may be looked upon as bearing the same relation to Bast as Nephthys bears to Isis. She was the personification of the fierce destroying heat of the sun's rays. One of her names is Nesert, flame, in which she personifies the destroying element.

THE SEVEN WISE ONES

We occasionally find Ptah in company with certain beings called the Seven Wise Ones of the goddess Meh-urt, who was their mother. We are told that they came forth from the water, from the pupil of the eye of Ra, and that they took the form of seven hawks, flew upward, and, together with Thoth, presided over learning and letters. Ptah as master-architect and demiurge, carrying out the designs of Thoth and his assistants, partook of the attributes of all of them, as did his female counterpart Sekhmet.

BAST

Bast, the Bubastis of the Greeks, possessed the attributes of the cat or lioness, the latter being a more modern development of her character. The name implies 'the tearer' or 'render,' and she is also entitled 'the lady of Sept' – that is, of the star Sothis. She was further sometimes identified with Isis and Hathor. In contra-distinction to the fierce Sekhmet, she typified the mild fertilizing heat of the sun. The cat loves to bask in the sun's rays, and it is probably for this reason that the animal was taken as symbolizing this goddess. She is amalgamated with Sekhmet

and Ra in a deity known as Sekhmet-Bast-Ra, and as such is represented as a woman with a man's head, and wings sprouting from her arms, and the heads of two vultures springing from her neck. She has also the claws of a lion. She was the goddess of the eastern part of the Delta, and was worshipped at Bubastis, in Lower Egypt. Her worship seems to have been of very considerable antiquity in that region, and although she is mentioned in the Pyramid Texts, it is only occasionally that she figures in the *Book of the Dead*. In all probability she was originally a cat totem, and in any case was first worshipped in the shape of a cat pure and simple. It has been stated that she possesses the characteristics of a foreign goddess, but there do not appear to be any very strong grounds for this assumption. Although she is connected with fire and with the sun, it would appear that she also has some association with the lunar disk, for her son Khensu is a moon-god. Cat-gods are often associated with the moon, chiefly because of the fertility of the animal which typified the ideals of fruitfulness and growth connected with the lunar orb.

NEFER-TEM

Nefer-tem was the son of Ptah and Sekhmet, or of Ptah and Bast. He is drawn as a man surmounted by plumes and sometimes standing upon a lion. Indeed, occasionally he is painted as having the head of a lion and with a body in mummy-shape. In early times he was symbolized by the lotus-flower. He was the third member of the triad of Memphis, which was made up of himself with Ptah and Sekhmet. His attributes are anything but well defined, but he is probably the young Tem, god of the rising sun. He is perhaps typified by the lotus because the sun would often seem to the Egyptians to rise from beds of this plant in the Delta of the country. In later texts he is identified with numerous gods all of whom appear to be forms of Horus or Thoth.

I-EM-HETEP

I-em-hetep, another son of Ptah, was also regarded as the third member of the great triad of Memphis. The name means 'Come in peace,' and was given him because he was supposed to bring the art of healing to mankind. Like his father Ptah, he is depicted as wearing a skull-cap. Before him is stretched a roll of papyrus to typify his character as a god of study and learning; but it is as a god of medicine that he was most popular in Egypt. In later times he took the place of Thoth as scribe of the gods, and provided the words of magic power which protected the dead from their enemies in the Duat. He had also a funerary character, which perhaps implies that physicians may have been in some manner connected with the art of embalmment. He is addressed in a text of the Ptolemies in his temple on the island of Philæ as 'he who giveth life to all men.' He was also supposed to send the boon of sleep to the suffering, and indeed the sorrowful and afflicted were under his especial patronage. Originally, it is likely that he was a medicine-man, who had introduced elementary medicine and means of preserving the bodies of the dead amongst the Egyptians. The supposition is a very likely one indeed, only the medicine-man must have become fairly sophisticated in later times, as is evidenced by his perusing a roll of papyrus. I-em-hetep was the god of physicians and those who dealt in medical magic, and his worship was certainly of very ancient date in Memphis. I-em-hetep was possibly the deified form of a distinguished physician who was attached to the priesthood of Ra, and who flourished before the end of the rule of the kings of the Third Dynasty. In the songs which were sung in the temple of Antuf occurs the passage: 'I have heard the words of I-em-hetep and of Heru-tata-f, which are repeated over and over again, but where are their places this day? Their walls are overthrown, their seats have no longer any being, and they are as if they had never existed. No man cometh to declare unto us what manner of beings they were, and none telleth us of their possessions.' Heru-tata-f was a man of great learning, who,

as we find in the Tale of the Magician given elsewhere in this book, brought that mysterious person to the court of his father Khufu. He also discovered certain chapters of the *Book of the Dead*. It is likely that I-em-hetep, who is mentioned in connexion with him, was also a skilled physician, whose acts and deeds were worthy of being classed with the words of Heru-tata-f. The pictures and figures of I-em-hetep suggest that he was of human and local origin, and he had a great hold upon the imagination of later Egyptians of the Saïte and Ptolemaic periods. He was indeed a species of Egyptian Hippocrates, who had probably become deified because of his great medical skill.

KHNEMU

At the city of Elephantine or Abu a great triad of gods was held in reverence. This consisted of Khnemu, Satet, Anqet. The worship of the first-mentioned deity was of great antiquity, and even in the inscription of King Unas we find him alluded to in a manner which proves that his cult was very old. His position, too, had always been an exalted one, and even to the last he appears to have been of importance in the eyes of the Gnostics. Khnemu was probably a god of the pre-dynastic Egyptians. He was symbolized by the flat-horned ram, which appears to have been introduced into the country from the East. We do not find him referred to in any inscription subsequent to the Twelfth Dynasty. He is usually represented in the form of a ram-headed man wearing the white crown, and sometimes the disk. In some instances he is pictured as pouring water over the earth, and in others with a jug above his horns – a sure indication that he is connected in some way with moisture. His name signifies the builder or framer, and he it was who fashioned the first man upon a potter's wheel, who made the first egg from which sprang the sun, who made the bodies of the gods, and who continued to build them up and maintain them.

Khnemu had been worshipped at Elephantine from time immemorial and was therefore the god of the First Cataract. His female counterparts, Satet and Anqet, have been identified as a form of the star Sept and as a local Nubian goddess. From the texts it is pretty clear that Khnemu was originally a river-god who, like Hapi, was regarded as the god of the Nile and of the annual Nile flood, and it may be that he and Hapi were Nile gods introduced by two separate races, or by the people of two different portions of the country. In the texts he is alluded to as 'father of the fathers of the gods and goddesses, lord of created things from himself, maker of heaven and earth and the Duat and water and mountains,' so we see that, like Hapi, he had been identified with the creative deities. He is sometimes represented as having four rams' heads upon a human body, and as he united within himself the attributes of Ra, Shu, Geb, and Osiris, these heads may have typified the deities in question. It has been considered, however, that they symbolized the four elements – fire, air, earth, and water. But it is a little difficult to see how this could be so. In any case, when represented with four heads Khnemu typified the great primeval creative force.

The Legend of the Nile's Source

The powers that were ascribed to Khnemu-Ra as god of the earthly Nile are exemplified in a story found inscribed on a rock on the island of Sahal in 1890. The king mentioned in the inscription has been identified as Tcheser, the third monarch of the Third Dynasty.

The story relates that in the eighteenth year of this king's reign a famine spread over Egypt because for seven years the Nile had not risen in flood. Thus grain of all kinds was scarce, the fields and gardens yielded naught, so that the people had no food. Strong men tottered like the aged, the old fell to the ground and rose no more, the children cried aloud with the pangs of hunger. And for the little food there was men became thieves and robbed their neighbours. Reports of these terrible

conditions reached the king upon his throne, and he was stricken with grief. He remembered the god I-em-hetep, the son of Ptah, who had once delivered Egypt from a like disaster, but when his help was invoked no answer was vouchsafed. Then Tcheser the king sent to his governor Māter, who ruled over the South, the island of Elephantine, and Nubia, and asked him where was the source of the Nile and what was the name of the god or goddess of the river. And to answer this dispatch Māter the governor went in person before the king. He told him of the wonderful island of Elephantine, whereon was built the first city ever known; that out of it rose the sun when he wanted to bestow life upon mankind. Here also was a double cavern, Querti, in shape like two breasts, and from this cavern rose the Nile flood to bless the land with fruitfulness when the god drew back the bolts of the door at the proper season. And this god was Khnemu. Māter described to his royal master the temple of the Nile god at Elephantine, and stated that other gods were in it, including the great deities Osiris, Horus, Isis, and Nephthys. He told of the products of the country around, and said that from these, offerings should be made to Khnemu. Then the king rose and offered sacrifices unto the god and made supplication before him in his temple. And the god heard and appeared before the grief-stricken king. He said, 'I am Khnemu the Creator. My hands rest upon thee to protect thy person and to make sound thy body. I gave thee thine heart ... I am he who created himself. I am the primeval watery abyss, and I am the Nile who riseth at his will to give health to those who toil. I am the guide and director of all men, the Almighty, the father of the gods, Shu, the mighty possessor of the earth.' And then the god promised unto the king that henceforward the Nile should rise every year as in the olden time, that the famine should be ended and great good come upon the land. But also he told the king how his shrine was desolate and that no one troubled to restore it even although stone lay all around. And this the king remembered and made a royal decree that lands on each side of the Nile near the

island where Khnemu dwelt were to be set apart as the endowment of his temple, that priests were to minister at his shrine, and for their maintenance a tax must be levied on the products of the land near by. And this decree the king caused to be cut upon a stone stele and set up in a prominent place as a lasting token of gratitude unto the god Khnemu, the god of the Nile.

SATET

Satet, the principal female counterpart of Khnemu, was also a goddess of the inundation. The name probably means 'to pour out' or 'to scatter abroad,' so that it might signify a goddess who wielded the powers of rain. She carries in her hands a bow and arrows, as did Neith, typical of the rain or thunderbolt. She was regarded as a form of Isis from the circumstance that both were connected with the star Sept, and in this guise she appears in the *Book of the Dead* as a counterpart of Osiris.

ANQET

Anqet, the third member of the triad of Elephantine, was a sister-goddess of Satet. She wears a crown of feathers, which would go to show that her origin is a purely African one, and she may have been a goddess of some of the islands in the First Cataract. She had been associated with the other members of the triad from very early dynastic times, however, and her cult was fairly widely disseminated through Northern Nubia. In later times her worship was centred at Sahal, where she was regarded as a goddess of that island, and where she had a temple built perhaps in the Eighteenth Dynasty. She had also a shrine at Philæ, where she was identified with Nephthys, as was almost necessary, seeing that Osiris had been identified with Khnemu and Satet with Isis. She is considered a personification of the waters of the Nile, and her name could signify 'to surround,' 'to embrace,' a reference to the embracing and nourishing of the fields by the river.

ATEN

Aten, the disk of the sun, stands in a class by himself in Egyptian mythology. Although he possesses certain broad characteristics in common with other sun-gods of Egypt, yet an examination of this deity shows that he differs widely from these in many respects, and that his cult is indeed entirely foreign to the religious genius of the Egyptian people. The cult of Aten, of which there is little record before the time of Amen-hetep IV, sprang into sudden prominence during that monarch's reign and became for a time the State religion of Egypt. Of its origin nothing is known, and it would appear that under the Middle Kingdom Aten was an obscure local deity, worshipped somewhere in the neighbourhood of Heliopolis. His important position in the Egyptian pantheon is due to the fact that his cult was directly responsible for a great religious, social, and artistic revolution which occurred during the reign of Amen-hetep IV.

With the overthrow of the Hyksos kings and the consequent establishment of the Theban monarchy (at the beginning of the Eighteenth Dynasty), Amen, the local god of Thebes, took the place of honour in the Egyptian pantheon, and was worshipped as Amen-Ra. However, it is known that Thothmes IV did much to restore the worship of Ra-Harmachis. His son, Amen-hetep III, built temples to this deity and to Aten at Memphis and Thebes. In this he would appear to have been supported by his wife Tyi, daughter of Iuaa and Thuau, who, though not connected with the Egyptian royal line, became chief of the royal wives. Possibly she herself was originally a votary of Aten, which would account for the reverence with which her son, Amen-hetep IV, regarded that deity. On the accession of the last-named monarch he adopted the title of 'high-priest of Ra-Heru-Akhti, the exalted one in the horizon, in his name of Shu who is in Aten,' this implying that, according to the view generally current at that period, he regarded Aten as the abode of the sun-god rather than as the divinity himself. In the early part of his

reign Amen-hetep worshipped both Amen and Aten, the former in his role of monarch, the latter in his private capacity, while he also built a great obelisk at Thebes in honour of Ra-Harmachis. Then it became apparent that the king desired to exalt Aten above all the other gods. This was by no means pleasing to the worshippers of Amen, whose priesthood was recruited from the noblest families in the land. A struggle ensued between the votaries of Amen-Ra and those of Aten, and finally the king built a new capital, dedicated to the faith of Aten, on the site of what is now Tell-el-Amarna, in Middle Egypt. Thence he withdrew with his followers when the struggle reached its height. To the new city he gave the name of Akhet-Aten ('Horizon of Aten'). His own name, Amen-hetep, he changed to Akh-en-Aten ('Glory of Aten').

Aten's Attributes

Now as to the attributes of Aten. As already stated, he was a somewhat colourless deity, and is perhaps better to be distinguished by the attributes which are not ascribed to him than by those which are, though in time some of the attributes of Ra, Horus, and other forms of the sun-god were given to him. From his original subordinate position as the abode of Ra – the material disk wherein the sun-god had his dwelling ('Ra in his Aten') – Aten came in time to signify both the god and the actual solar disk. Attempts made to identify him with the Semitic Adonai, the Greek Adonis, have met with no success. Evidence of Aten's early position in the pantheon is to be found in the *Book of the Dead*, where Ra is addressed thus: 'O thou beautiful being, thou dost renew thyself and make thyself young again under the form of Aten.' 'Thou turnest thy face toward the underworld, and thou makest the earth to shine like fine copper. The dead rise up to see thee, they breathe the air and they look upon thy face when Aten shineth in the horizon.'

A Hymn to Aten

During the period when his cult was supreme in Egypt Aten was regarded by his worshippers as the creator, self-existent and everlasting, fructifier and nourisher of the earth and all it contains, measurer of the lives of men. Aten was invested with a cartouche, wherein he is styled 'Lord of heaven,' 'Lord of earth,' 'He who liveth for ever,' 'He who illumineth the earth,' 'He who reigneth in truth'. A singularly beautiful and poetic version of a hymn to Aten, in which he is exalted as the giver of life and fruitfulness to all things, has been found in the tomb of Aï, a high official under Amen-hetep, or Akh-en-Aten. It begins thus:

> Beauteous is thy resplendent appearing on the horizon of heaven,
> O Aten, who livest and art the beginning of life!

He it was who made the Nile in the Duat and conducted it to men, causing its waters to rise; he, also, who sent the rain to those lands which were beyond the reach of the Nile's beneficent flood.

> Thou makest the Nile in the underworld, thou conductest
> it hither at thy pleasure,
> That it may give life to men whom thou hast made for
> thyself, Lord of All!
> Thou givest the Nile in heaven that it descendeth to them.
> It causeth its waters to rise upon the rocks like the sea; it watereth their fields
> in their districts.
>
> So are thy methods accomplished, O Lord of Eternity!
> thou who art thyself the celestial Nile:

Thou art the king of the inhabitants of the lands,
And of the cattle going upon their feet in every land,
  which go upon feet.
The Nile cometh out of the underworld to Egypt.

The Aten hymns, then, ascribe to the deity such attributes as any people might see in their sun-god. All the paraphernalia of the cult of Ra, Osiris, and like divinities are absent. There is no mention of the barques in which they sailed across the heavens; of Apep, the great serpent, and the other enemies of Ra; of the companies of gods and goddesses which formed his train. We find in the cult of Aten no myths such as that of the battles of Horus, nor do the ceremonies and ritual of the domain of Osiris enter into it. All these are without parallel in the Aten-worship. It is easily understood why it failed in its appeal to the Egyptian people.

Aten was not even figured as anthropomorphic, as were Ra and Osiris, but was invariably represented as the sun-disk, with rays emanating from it in a downward direction. Each ray terminated in a human hand, to which were sometimes attached the sign of life, the sign of power, and so on. Reliefs of this period frequently depict the king and queen seated with their children, over their heads the symbol of Aten, one of whose numerous hands presents the sign of life to each member of the royal family.

In short, the cult of Aten was the worship of the sun-god pure and simple, shorn of the picturesque story and ritual so dear to the heart of the Egyptian.

HATHOR

It is no easy matter to gauge the true mythological significance of the Egyptian goddess Hathor, patron of women, of love, and of pleasure, Lady of Heaven, and Mistress of the Underworld. She occupied a very important position in the pantheon

of ancient Egypt, dating as she did from archaic or even pre-dynastic times. We find a multitude of mythological ideas fused in the Hathor conception: she is a moon-goddess, a sky-goddess, a goddess of the east, a goddess of the west, a cosmic deity, an agricultural goddess, a goddess of moisture, even on occasion a solar deity. Though her original status is thus in a measure obscured, it is supposed that she is primarily a moon-goddess, for reasons which follow hereafter.

The original form under which Hathor was worshipped was that of a cow. Later she is represented as a woman with the head of a cow, and finally with a human head, the face broad, kindly, placid, and decidedly bovine, sometimes retaining the ears or horns of the animal she represents. She is also shown with a head-dress resembling a pair of horns with the moon-disk between them. Sometimes she is met with in the form of a cow standing in a boat, surrounded by tall papyrus-reeds. Now in mythology the cow is often identified with the moon – why it is hard to say. Perhaps it may not be too far-fetched to suppose that the horned appearance of the moon at certain seasons has suggested its association with the cow. Mythology is largely based on such superficial resemblances and analogies; it is by means of these that the primitive mind first learns to reason. Or it may be that the cow, naturally of great importance to agricultural peoples, was, by reason of this importance, associated with the moon, mistress of the weather and principle of growth and fruitfulness. The fact that Hathor the cow is sometimes shown in a boat suggests that she was also a water-goddess, and heightens the probability that she was identified with the moon, for the latter was regarded by the Egyptians as the source of all moisture.

The name Hathor signifies 'House of Horus' – that is, the sky, wherein dwelt the sun-god Horus, and there is no doubt that at one time Hathor was regarded as a sky-goddess, or a goddess of the eastern sky, where Horus was born; she has also been identified with the night sky and with the sunset sky. If, however, we regard her as a moon-goddess, a good deal of the mythology concerning her will become

clear. She is, for example, frequently spoken of as the 'Eye of Ra,' Ra, the sun-god, probably possessing in this instance the wider significance of sky-god. She is also designated 'The Golden One,' who stands high in the south as the Lady of Teka, and illumines the west as the Lady of Saïs. That she is mistress of the underworld is likewise not surprising when we consider her as identical with the moon, for does not the moon make a daily pilgrimage through Amentet? Neither is it astonishing that a goddess of moisture and vegetation should be found in the underworld dispensing water to the souls of the dead from the branches of a palm or a sycamore.

Hathor as Love-Goddess

On the same hypothesis we may explain the somewhat paradoxical statement that Hathor is 'mother of her father, daughter of her son' – that she is mother, wife, and daughter to Ra. The moon, when she appears in the heavens before the sun, may be regarded as his mother; when she reigns together with him she is his wife; when she rises after he has set she is his daughter. It is possible that the moon, with her generative and sustaining powers, may have been considered the creative and upholding force of the universe, the great cosmic mother, who brought forth not only the gods and goddesses over whom she rules, but likewise herself as well. It was as the ideal of womanhood, therefore, whether as mother, wife, or daughter, that she received the homage of Egyptian women, and became the patron deity of love, joy, and merry-making, 'lady of music and mistress of song, lady of leaping, and mistress of wreathing garlands.' Temples were raised in her honour, notably one of exceptional beauty at Denderah, in Upper Egypt, and she had shrines without number. She became in time associated or even identified with many local goddesses, and, indeed, it has been said that all Egyptian goddesses were forms of Hathor.

As guardian of the dead Hathor is figured as a cow, issuing from the Mountain of the West, and she is also represented as standing on its summit receiving the setting

sun and the souls of the dead (the latter travelling in the footsteps of the sun-god). In this case Hathor might be regarded as the western sky, but the myth might be equally significant of the moon, which sometimes 'stands on the mountains of the west' after the time of sunset, with horns resembling hands outstretched to welcome the unseen souls. Yet another point is worthy of note in connexion with the mythological aspect of Hathor. When she was born as the daughter of Ra (her mother was Nut, the sky-goddess) she was quite black. This fact admits of several interpretations. It may be that Hathor's swarthy complexion is indicative of an Ethiopian origin, or it may be that she represents the night sky, which lightens with the growth of day. It is still possible, however, to regard her as typifying the moon, which is 'born black,' with only a narrow crescent of light, but which grows brighter as it becomes older. It is unlikely that the keen eyes of these primitive peoples would fail to observe the dark disk of the new moon, faintly outlined with light reflected from the earth.

The Forms of Hathor

Hathor is sometimes identified with the star Sept, or Sothis (Sirius), which rose heliacally on the first day of the month of Thoth. When Ra entered his boat Sothis, or the goddess Hathor, took her place on his head like a crown.

Reference has already been made to the numerous forms of this goddess. She was identified with Aphrodite by the Greeks, and by the Egyptians with a multitude of local deities. The *Seven Hathors*, sometimes stated to be independent deities, were in reality but a selection of forms of the goddess, which selection varied in the various localities. Thus the Seven Hathors worshipped at Denderah were Hathor of Thebes, Hathor of Heliopolis, Hathor of Aphroditopolis, Hathor of the Sinaitic Peninsula, Hathor of Momemphis, Hathor of Herakleopolis, and Hathor of Keset. These were represented as young women carrying tambourines and wearing the Hathor head-dress of a disk and a pair of horns. In the Litanies of Seker other groups

of Seven Hathors are mentioned, while Mariette includes yet a different company under that title.

Briefly, Hathor is a personification of the female principle – primitive, fruitful, attractive – such as is known to most peoples, and becoming more sophisticated as the centuries pass.

HAPI, THE GOD OF THE NILE

This deity was especially connected with the great river whence Egypt drew her sustenance, and as such was a god of very considerable importance in the Egyptian pantheon. In time he became identified with Osiris. The name Hapi still baffles translation, and is probably of pre-dynastic origin. Perhaps the first mention of this deity is in the Text of Unas, where the Nile god is exhorted to fructify grain for the requirements of the dead monarch. In the same texts Hapi is alluded to as a destructive force, symbolizing, of course, the inundations so frequently caused by the River Nile.

In appearance Hapi possesses both male and female characteristics, the latter indicating his powers of nourishment. As god of the North Nile he is crowned with papyrus plants, and as god of the southern part of the river with lotus plants. These two forms of Hapi resulted from the geographical division of the country into Upper and Lower Egypt, and they are sometimes combined in a single figure, when the god is shown holding in his hands both plants. On the thrones of certain of the Pharaohs we often find the lotus and papyrus conjoined with the emblem of union, to signify the sovereignty of the monarch over both regions.

The very position of Hapi made it certain that he would become successful as a deity. The entire country looked to the Nile as the source of all wealth and provender, so that the deity which presided over it rapidly rose in public estimation. Thus Hapi quickly became identified with the greater and more outstanding figures

in early Egyptian mythology. He thus became a partner with the great original gods who had created the world, and finally came to be regarded as the maker and moulder of everything within the universe. We find him credited with the attributes of Nu, the primeval water-mass, and this in effect made him a father of Ra, who had emerged from that element. Hapi, indeed, stood in more immediate relationship to the Egyptians than almost any other god in their pantheon. Without the sun Egypt would have been plunged into darkness, but without the Nile every living creature within its borders would assuredly have perished.

The circumstance, too, that the source of the River Nile was unknown to the Egyptians tended to add a mystery to the character of its presiding deity. The people of the country could not understand the rise and fall of the river, which appeared to them to take place under supernatural auspices.

On the occasion of the annual rise of the Nile a great festival was held in honour of Hapi, and statues of the god were carried about through the towns and villages. It is noticeable in many mythologies that gods of fructification are those honoured by the circulation of their images throughout the region where they are worshipped, and it is a little difficult to see why this should be so. It cannot be said that none but deities with an agricultural significance were thus carried about, but it is noteworthy that these are by far the most numerous to receive such honours.

Counterparts of Hapi

Isis was in a manner regarded as the female counterpart of Hapi, but we also find that in the north of Egypt the goddess Natch-ura was regarded as the female companion of Hapi, and that Nekhebet reigned in the south in a like capacity. The following hymn to Hapi, found in a papyrus of the Eighteenth or Nineteenth Dynasty, clearly shows the great importance of his worship in Egypt: 'Homage to thee, O Hapi, thou appearest in this land, and thou comest in peace to make Egypt to live. Thou art the Hidden

One, and the guide of the darkness on the day when it is thy pleasure to lead the same. Thou art the waterer of the fields which Ra hath created, thou givest life unto all animals, thou makest all the land to drink unceasingly as thou descendest on thy way from heaven. Thou art the friend of bread and of Tchabu, thou makest to increase and be strong Nepra, thou makest prosperous every workshop, O Ptah, thou lord of fish; when the Inundation riseth, the waterfowl do not alight upon the fields that are sown with wheat. Thou art the creator of barley, and thou makest the temples to endure, for millions of years repose of thy fingers hath been an abomination to thee. Thou art the lord of the poor and needy. If thou wert overthrown in the heavens the gods would fall upon their faces and men would perish. He causeth the whole earth to be opened by the cattle, and princes and peasants lie down and rest.... Thy form is that of Khnemu. When thou shinest upon the earth shouts of joy ascend, for all people are joyful, and every mighty man receiveth food, and every tooth is provided with food. Thou art the bringer of food, thou art the mighty one of meat and drink, thou art the creator of all good things, the lord of divine meat, pleasant and choice.... Thou makest the herb to grow for the cattle, and thou takest heed unto what is sacrificed unto every god. The choicest incense is that which followeth thee, thou art the lord of the two lands. Thou fillest the storehouses, thou heapest high with corn the granaries, and thou takest heed unto what is sacrificed unto every god. The choicest incense is that which followeth thee, thou art the lord of the two lands. Thou fillest the storehouses, thou heapest high with corn the granaries, and thou takest heed to the affairs of the poor and needy. Thou makest the herb and green things to grow that the desires of all may be satisfied, and thou art not reduced thereby. Thou makest thy strength to be a shield for man.'

NUT

The goddess Nut was the daughter of Shu and Tefnut, the wife of Geb, and the mother of Osiris and Isis, Set and Nephthys. She personified the sky and the vault of

heaven. A good many other goddesses probably became absorbed in her from time to time. She is, however, the personification of the day sky, a certain Naut representing the sky of night, but this distinction was an early one. She was indeed the counterpart of Nu, and represented the great watery abyss, out of which all things originally came, so that Nut, the spouse of Nu, and Nut, the spouse of Geb, are one and the same being. She is usually represented as a woman carrying upon her head a vase of water, which plainly indicates her character. Sometimes she wears the horns and disk of Hathor, but she has many other guises as the great mother of the gods.

Her most general appearance, however, is that of a woman resting on hands and feet, her body forming an arch, thus representing the sky. Her limbs typified the four pillars on which the sky was supposed to rest. She was supposed originally to be reclining on Geb, the earth, when Shu raised her from this position. This myth is a very common one among the aborigines of America, but in an inverted sense, as it is usually the sky which takes the place of the original father, and the earth that of the great mother. These are usually separated by the creative deity, just as were Geb and Nut, and the allegory represents the separation of the earth from the waters which were above it, and the creation of the world.

According to another myth Nut gave birth daily to the sun-god, who passed across her body, which represented the sky. In a variant account he is represented as travelling across her back. The limbs and body of the goddess are bespangled with stars. In another pictorial description of Nut we see a second female figure drawn inside the first, and within that again the body of a man, the last two conforming to the semicircular shape of the sky-goddess. This is explained as meaning that the two women personify the day and night skies, but it does not account for the male body, which may represent the Duat. Again we read that Nut was transformed into a great cow, and she is frequently represented in this form. The deceased are described in the *Book of the Dead* as relying on her for fresh air in the underworld,

over the waters of which she was supposed to have dominion. She possessed a sacred tree, the sycamore, which was situated at Heliopolis, at the foot of which the serpent Apep was slain by the great cat Ra. The branches of this tree were regarded as a place of refuge for the weary dead in noonday during the summer, and in its shade they were refreshed by the food on which the goddess herself lived.

It was asserted by the priests of Denderah that Nut had her origin in their city, and that there she became the mother of Isis. Her five children, Osiris, Horus, Set, Isis, and Nephthys, were born on the five epagomenal days of the year – that is, the five days over the three hundred and sixty. As in Mexico, certain of these were regarded as unlucky. Nut plays a prominent part in the underworld, and the dead are careful to retain her good offices, probably in order that they may have plenty of air. Indeed, her favour renewed their bodies and they were enabled to rise and journey with the sun-god each day, even as did Ra, the son of Nut. A portrait of the goddess was often painted on the cover of the coffin as a mark of her protection, and this was rarely omitted in the Egyptian burial ceremonies.

TAURT

Taurt is usually pictured as a hippopotamus standing upon her hind legs, holding in her hand an amulet which has not yet been satisfactorily explained. She wears on her head the solar disk and two tall feathers. Occasionally she is pictured in human form with the cow-horns worn by all Egyptian goddesses. She was regarded as the mother and nurse of the gods, and had a counterpart in Apet, the hippopotamus-goddess of Thebes, who was supposed by some Egyptians to have been the mother of Osiris. In later times Taurt was known as Rert or Reret, the female hippopotamus, but she was also identified with Isis, Hathor, Bast, and other goddesses. Her image in faience formed a favourite amulet, which, indeed, was almost as popular as that of Bes. Indeed, figures which appear to have been copied from that of Taurt are to

be seen on Mykenæan wall-scenes, so widespread was her fame. She was supposed to be the guardian of the mountain of the west, through which lay the road to Hades. It would appear that she was certainly of totemic origin. Her popularity seems to have been greatest during the New Empire, and increased greatly during the latter period.

HEKT

Hekt, the frog-headed goddess, was regarded as the wife of Khnemu, although in some degree she may be looked upon as a form of Hathor. Her character has not been made very clear by writers on Egyptian mythology, but the circumstance that she possesses the head of a frog obviously shows her connexion with water, and therefore with the powers of fructification. She appears also to have been associated with the deities of growth. Many corn-gods are deities of resurrection and re-birth. At the festival of a certain Mexican goddess of the maize a frog was placed upon the top of a sheaf of grain as being symbolical of the goddess. It might be hazardous to identify Hekt with the Greek Hecate, who was perhaps a moon-goddess, and as such associated with water. It is noticeable that Hecate is regarded by Farnell as a foreign importation from Thrace. She is, of course, the goddess of the lower world as well, just as Osiris, the moon-god, was god of the Egyptian dead. She was also worshipped at the Samothracian mysteries, which probably had an Egyptian origin. We find that Hecate was also a goddess of fertility.

KHONSU

Khonsu was a lunar deity, and as such was often identified with Thoth. Indeed, at Hermopolis and Edfû the two were occasionally joined under the name of Khonsu-Thoth. The name is derived from the root *khens*, to traverse, showing that he was the traveller who nightly crossed the heavens. He was depicted as a hawk-headed

god crowned with the lunar crescent and the solar disk. Rameses III built him a great temple at Thebes between those of Amen and Mut. He had two distinct forms: Khonsu in Thebes Neferhetep, and Khonsu the carrier out of plans. The Greeks compared Khonsu to Heracles, for what reason it would be difficult to say. Occasionally the Egyptians fused him with Horus, Shu, and Ra, which shows that he could assume a solar character, as is indicated by his hawk-head. It would appear as if Khonsu, originally a moon-god, became also a sun-god when the lunar calendar was merged into or abandoned for the solar method of computation.

MINOR DEITIES

There were hundreds of minor gods surrounding the Egyptian pantheon, and the characteristics of only a few of these can be dealt with. Each hour of the day had its representative deity, as had each hour of the night. The four winds were also represented in the Egyptian pantheon, as in the Greek. The north wind was called Qebui, and is pictured as a four-headed ram with wings; the south wind, Shehbui, is represented as a man with a lion's head, and wings; and the west wind, Huzayui, has a serpent's head on the body of a winged man. The east wind, Henkhisesui, sometimes times occurs in anthropomorphic shape, and, like the north wind, has a ram's head, but he is occasionally figured as a winged beetle with the head of a ram.

The senses were also symbolized by deities. Saa was the god of the sense of touch or feeling. He is depicted in human shape and wears upon his head a sign composed of parallel lines, which as they rise grow smaller. In the Theban Recension of the Book of the Dead he is shown in the judgment scene amongst those gods who watch the weighing of the heart of the deceased. Saa is sometimes shown as sailing with Thoth and other gods in the boat of Ra. In one passage he is alluded to as the son of Geb. He is the personification of intelligence, human and divine.

The god of taste was called Hu. He is also depicted as a man, and is said to have come into existence from a drop of blood which fell from Ra. He became the personification of the divine food upon which the gods and the blessed dead lived.

Maa was the god of sight. He is also drawn as a man having an eye placed over his head, which is also the symbol of his name. Setem was the god of hearing, and in his case his head is surmounted by an ear.

The planets were also deified. Saturn was called Horus, the bull of heaven; Mars was also identified with Horus under the name of the 'red Horus,' but, strictly speaking, was under the guardianship of Ra; the god of Mercury was Set, and of Venus, Osiris. Some of the constellations were also identified with deities. The Great Bear was known as 'the haunch,' and Draco was identified with the hippopotamus Reret.

The days of the month had also patron gods.

CREATION LEGEND

At the beginning the world was a waste of water called Nu, and it was the abode of the Great Father. He was Nu, for he was the deep, and he gave being unto the sun god who hath said: 'Lo! I am Khepera at dawn, Ra at high noon, and Tum at eventide'. The god of brightness first appeared as a shining egg which floated upon the water's breast, and the spirits of the deep, who were the Fathers and the Mothers, were with him there, as he was with Nu, for they were the companions of Nu.

Now Ra was greater than Nu from whom he arose. He was the divine father and strong ruler of gods, and those whom he first created, according to his desire, were Shu, the wind god, and his consort Tefnut, who had the head of a lioness and was called 'The Spitter' because she sent the rain. In aftertime these two deities shone as stars amidst the constellations of heaven, and they were called 'The Twins'.

Then came into being Seb, the earth god, and Nut, the goddess of the firmament, who became the parents of Osiris and his consort Isis and also of Set and his consort Nephthys.

Ra spoke at the beginning of Creation, and bade the earth and the heavens to rise out of the waste of water. In the brightness of his majesty they appeared, and Shu, the uplifter, raised Nut upon high. She formed the vault, which is arched over

Seb, the god of earth, who lies prostrate beneath her from where, at the eastern horizon, she is poised upon her toes to where, at the western horizon, bending down with outstretched arms, she rests upon her fingertips. In the darkness are beheld the stars which sparkle upon her body and over her great unwearied limbs.

When Ra, according to his desire, uttered the deep thoughts of his mind, that which he named had being. When he gazed into space, that which he desired to see appeared before him. He created all things that move in the waters and upon the dry land. Now, mankind were born from his eye, and Ra, the Creator, who was ruler of the gods, became the first king upon earth. He went about among men; he took form like unto theirs, and to him the centuries were as years.

When all the land is black, the sun bark of Ra passes through the twelve hour-divisions of night in Duat. At eventide, when the god is Tum, he is old and very frail. Five-and-seventy invocations are chanted to give him power to overcome the demons of darkness who are his enemies. He then enters the western gate, through which dead men's souls pass to be judged before Osiris. In front of him goes the jackal god, Anubis, for he is 'Opener of the Ways'. Ra has a sceptre in one hand: in the other he carries the Ankh, which is the symbol of life.

When the sun bark enters the river Ûrnes of the underworld the companions of Ra are with him. Watchman is there, and Striker, and Steersman is at the helm, and in the bark are also those divinities who are given power, by uttering magical incantations, to overcome the demons of evil.

The gloomy darkness of the first hour-division is scattered by the brightness of Ra. Beside the bark gather the pale shades of the newly dead, but none of them can enter it without knowledge of the magical formulae which it is given unto few to possess.

At the end of the first hour-division is a high and strong wall, and a gate is opened by incantations so that the bark of Ra may pass through. So from division to division, all through the perilous night, the sun god proceeds, and the number of demons that must be thwarted by magic and fierce fighting increases as he goes. Apep, the great Night serpent, ever seeks to overcome Ra and devour him.

The fifth hour-division is the domain of dreaded Sokar, the underworld god, with three human heads, a serpent's body, and mighty wings between which appears his hawk form. His abode is in a dark and secret place which is guarded by fierce sphinxes. Nigh to him is the Drowning Pool, watched over by five gods with bodies like to men and animals' heads. Strange and mysterious forms hover nigh, and in the pool are genii in torture, their heads aflame with everlasting fire.

In the seventh hour-division sits Osiris, divine judge of the dead. Fiery serpents, which are many-headed, obey his will. Feet have they to walk upon and hands, and some carry sharp knives with which to cut to pieces the souls of the wicked. Whom Osiris deems to be worthy, he favours; such shall live in the Nether World: whom he finds to be full of sin, he rejects; and these do the serpents fall upon, dragging them away, while they utter loud and piercing cries of grief and agony, to be tortured and devoured; lo! the wicked perish utterly. In this division of peril the darksome Night serpent Apep attacks the sun bark, curling its great body round the compartment of Ra with ferocious intent to devour him. But the allies of the god contend against the serpent; they stab it with knives until it is overcome. Isis utters mighty incantations which cause the sun bark to sail onward unscathed nor stayed.

In the eighth division are serpents which spit forth fire to illumine the darkness, and in the tenth are fierce water reptiles and ravenous fishes. The god Horus burns great beacons in the eleventh hour-division; ruddy flames and flames of gold blaze aloft in beauty: the enemies of Ra are consumed in the fires of Horus.

The sun god is reborn in the twelfth hour-division. He enters the tail of the mighty serpent, which is named 'Divine Life', and issues from its mouth in the form of Khepera, which is a beetle. Those who are with the god are reborn also. The last door of all is guarded by Isis, wife of Osiris, and Nephthys, wife of Set, in the form of serpents. They enter the sun bark with Ra.

Now Ûrnes, the river of Duat, flows into the primeval ocean in which Nu has his abode. And as Ra was lifted out of the deep at the beginning, so he is lifted by Nu at dawn. He is then received by Nut, goddess of the heavens; he is born of Nut and grows in majesty, ascending to high noon.

The souls of the dead utter loud lamentations when the sun god departs out of the darkness of Duat.

HOW MEN REBELLED AGAINST RA

Ra was the greatest of all the gods. No other god created him, but he created himself, and was from the beginning; and he was King both of gods and men. But it came to pass that when he had reigned for many ages over the world, men grew weary of serving him, and they said in scorn: 'Behold, His Majesty the God Ra groweth old; his bones have become silver, his flesh gold, and his hair is pure lapis-lazuli.' Thus they spoke in rebellion against him, and His Majesty heard the wicked words which they uttered. Then he called to him all the other gods, and they came to him quickly and silently at the great temple of the Sun in Heliopolis – the swift goddess of love and war, whom Ra calls the apple of his eye, and whom men call Hathor, or sometimes Sekhmet, when she is in the fury of war and destruction ; and the god Shu, who holds up the heavens; and the god of the earth, whose name is Seb; and the goddess Nut, whose starry body arches from east to west across the world, and makes the midnight sky to all the men who live thereon. These and many others came at their Sovereign's call.

Now, when all these gods were come together to the temple of Ka, they made salaam before His Majesty, and said to him: 'Speak thou unto us that we may hear thy words.' Then His Majesty spoke unto Nu, who is the eldest of the gods, the god of the waters that were before the world was made, and thus he said: 'O thou eldest

of the gods, and ye other ancestral gods, behold, mankind, whom I myself created, hold counsel against me. Tell me what ye would do in this strait, and do ye take counsel for me, for I am loth to slay them until I have heard what ye will say as touching this matter.'

Then spoke Nu, the god of the waters, saying: 'O thou who art the greatest of all the gods, thy throne standeth fast, and great is the fear of thee! Only turn thine eye against them who conspire against thee.'

But the Majesty of the god Ra answered: 'Behold, already men flee unto the hills, for their hearts tremble within them because of the evil words which they have spoken; and who shall catch them among the dens and caves of the hills?'

Then said all the gods before His Majesty the King of the gods: 'Send forth thine Eye in the form of the goddess Hathor. Let it destroy for thee these people who have imagined wicked devices against thee; for there is none among mankind who can withstand Hathor when she descendeth to destroy.'

Then went forth the fierce goddess Hathor, whose delight is in battle and in slaughter, and wherever she went, up and down the long valleys that run among the hills, she slew mankind, and her heart exulted in the slaughter. And at night she returned well-pleased, and the great god Ra spoke to her, and said: 'Come in peace, my daughter Hathor! Never will I be parted from thee, who hast avenged me on mine enemies.'

And Hathor answered, with a fierce and cruel joy: 'Long live the King! Blessed he his name who hath given me such a task to accomplish; for this liketh me right well, and when I lay hold of man to slay him, then my heart rejoiceth.'

Then the Majesty of the god Ra answered: 'Verily, I will triumph over mankind as their King, and will destroy them!'

But even while he spoke his blood ran cold because of the dreadful joy which Hathor had in slaying the men whom he had created. So it came to pass that for

many nights Hathor went forth throughout the land of Egypt as far as Henensuten, and her hands were red with slaughter, and she waded with crimsoned feet in the blood of the men whom she had slain.

But Ra looked forth upon the world and, behold, men were dying everywhere, and the great river ran red with blood. Then it repented him that he had sent Hathor forth to destroy, and he would fain have recalled her; but the word of the King of the gods could not be broken, neither could Hathor be obliged to leave the prey which had been given into her hand. Therefore Ra took counsel with himself how he might by subtlety turn aside the heart of his daughter Hathor from the fierceness of her anger against men. Then spoke the Majesty of the god, saying: 'Call to me messengers; let them run like a blast of wind.' They came, therefore, and made obeisance before the Majesty of the great god. Then spoke Ra unto them: 'Run swiftly even unto Elephantine, and bring thence to me abundance of the sleepy fruit that grows there. Hasten, so that it may be here before the dawn.' Then the messengers ran swiftly, like the blast of wind that blows from the desert, and they came unto Elephantine, where the great god Hapi pours the waters of his river in thunder over the rocks that bar its passage. And at Elephantine there grew the crimson clusters of the sleepy fruit, whereof if one eat, or drink of its juice, heavy slumber and forgetfulness falls upon his eyes and brain.

Then the messengers of Ra gathered great plenty of the clusters of this fruit, and brought them back to His Majesty at Heliopolis; and Ra gave them to Sekti, the grinder-god who dwells in Heliopolis, that he should grind them. And while Sekti ground the sleepy fruit, the women crushed much barley, and made beer; and when the beer was ready the juice of the sleepy fruit was poured into it, and, lo! It became crimson, like human blood. And they filled seven thousand jars with the blood-coloured beer. Then came His Majesty the great god Ra, Lord of the Two Lands, with the other gods, to see this beer, ere yet the day had dawned. And when Ra saw

the beer, he said: 'This is excellent! Now will I protect mankind against Hathor by the virtue of this beer.' Then said he: 'Let these jars be carried and emptied over the land at the place where men are being slaughtered; and hasten, that it may be done while yet the night is dark and cool, before the dawning of the morning.' It was done as His Majesty had commanded; and all the country on every side was flooded four palms deep with the beer, whose colour was even as the colour of blood.

Now, when the day dawned came the goddess Hathor, eager once more to slay; but when she looked abroad over the fields, she saw nothing but blood, blood on every hand, so that her feet stood in it, and her face was mirrored back to her crimson from the crimson flood. Then her heart rejoiced yet more, and in the madness of her cruel joy she stooped and drank of the crimson tide at her feet; and it liked her well, and she drank again, and yet again, and the fumes of the sleepy

fruit mounted to her brain, and she went about drunken and helpless, and could no more see to slay man.

Then said the Majesty of Ra unto Hathor: 'Come back to me in peace, O sweet one! Because thou hast done my will, therefore shall drinks be prepared for thee on every New Year's Feast-Day of the sleepy fruit in which thine heart rejoices, and the number of the measures of them shall be according to the number of mine handmaidens the priestesses.' Therefore, even unto this day, on the feast-day of Hathor, sleepy drinks are made by all men according unto the number of the priestesses who wait upon the great God Ra in Heliopolis.

But though His Majesty had avenged him on his enemies and had spared the residue of them, his heart was still sore because of their ingratitude. Then spoke he to Hathor: 'My heart is pained within me with a burning pain. Verily my heart is weary at the thought that I have to live with such creatures as men; I have destroyed some of them, but not nearly as many as I should have done according unto my might and my dignity.'

Then answered the gods that were of his following: 'Be not weary of heart; thou hast but to command, and it is done, for thy might is according to thy desire.'

But the Majesty of the god spoke unto the Majesty of Nu: 'Now, for the first time, I feel my limbs fail; I will not wait until this weakness seizeth upon me a second time.'

Therefore His Majesty the god Nu commanded Nut, the goddess of the starry heavens, to make an abode for the great god Ra, far from the men who had grieved his heart. And Nut raised herself over the earth in the form of a great cow, whose legs stood at the four corners of the world, north and south, east and west; and Ra rested upon her back far above the sinful children of men. But when the earth grew light, and the morning dawned, it came to pass that men came forth into the fields again, and, behold, they saw that Ra, their god, was departed from them, and was

seated afar upon the back of the celestial cow. Then their hearts failed them for sorrow, and they repented them of their evil; and they went forth with their bows and did battle against the enemies of Ra. Then spoke the Majesty of this god: 'Your crime is forgiven you; for the shedding of blood hath brought remission, and the slaughter that ye have done for me atoneth for the slaughter that was purposed against me.' Nevertheless, the great god would not return unto men, for he said unto Nut: 'I have determined to cause myself to be uplifted into the sky. There will I dwell, and not on the earth, for it is full of evil.'

And when the Majesty of the great god Ra had rested in heaven, he spoke and said: 'Let there be set a great field of Rest;' and the Field of Rest appeared. 'I will gather plants in it;' and the Field of Bulrushes appeared; and all the flowers of these fields Ra turned into stars. Then Ra gave it in charge to Shu, the god of the air, and Nut, the goddess of heaven, to give light to all the sons of men who live upon earth. Then, calling to him Seb, the god of the earth, he warned him against the poisonous serpents that are in the world, saying: 'Watch thou the reptiles of the earth and the water, and bid them beware of harming anything. Let them know that though I go hence, I shall still shine upon them. Their father in heaven shall keep watch upon them, and thou shalt be their father on earth eternally. Let heed be paid to those creatures. The men who know my words of power shall charm them, and shall deal as they will with the creatures of the earth, charming those that are in their holes.' Then the Majesty of the god Ra spoke and said: 'Let Thoth be brought unto me;' and Thoth was brought. The Majesty of the god spoke unto him and said: 'Let us go, thou and I, leaving heaven; and I will make a place, great and wonderful, in the Underworld, and in the Land of the Deep. There shalt thou write the names of those who did wicked deeds on earth, and there shalt thou imprison them, even the evil servants whom my heart hateth. And, behold, henceforth thou art in my place: and thou shalt be called Thoth, the Viceroy of Ra.'

Now, when anyone wishes to recite the words of this book for himself, he shall rub himself with oil and ointment, an incense-burner full of incense shall be in his hands, behind his two ears shall be natron, and sweet-smelling ointment shall be upon his lips. He shall be clothed with two new garments, he shall be purified with water of the inundation, he shall wear white shoes upon his feet, and the figure of Truth shall be painted upon his tongue with green paint. Then shall he purify himself seven times in three days; priests and men shall do the like.

THE LIFE BEYOND

TO the earliest dwellers in the Nile valley the earth was not such as we know it to be. It was a long narrow valley surrounded by lofty mountains, that rose in the north to a very great height.

Above the earth was the ceiling of the sky, which, said some, was the face of a man, the sun and moon being his eyes, while his long flowing hair formed pillars to support the roof. Most people, however, conceived the sky as a canopy of iron, 'the heavenly metal,' held up by four towering peaks in the encircling mountains in the north and south and east and west. High up on the mountain slopes was a broad ledge on which ran the celestial Nile, traversing a vast semi-circle from east to west. Along this stream was carried the boat of the Sun-god Ra, known as the boat of Millions of Years, and so long as Ra was in his boat light was given to the earth. In the evening when he reached Manu, the mountain of the west, where the heavenly Nile poured down into a deep abyss behind the mountain range, he passed from sight, and did not reappear until morning, when he emerged near Bakhu, the mount of the east, to repeat his journey, and to shed his bounties on the earth below.

When the river disappeared at sunset, the Sun-god did not continue in his boat, although his spirit accompanied it in its journeyings. Ra passed on to the roof that overcovered the earth, where was the home of the gods and goddesses and those of

mankind who had gained admission into heaven. For this was the heaven they sought to attain to, the land they called the Fields of Peace. Here, seated on a magnificent throne that was ornamented with the heads of lions and the feet of bulls, emblems both of majesty and strength, the mighty Ra dispensed justice, and directed all things in heaven and earth. Around his throne, seated or standing, were the gods of his train, ready to carry out his commands at a nod or a sign from their lord.

Then there were the other great gods, many of whom were scarcely less powerful than Ra himself, each with a number of attendants chosen from the heavenly hosts. Again, far removed in grandeur from these powerful divinities, but equally distant from those they had left behind, were those of mankind who had passed through the valley of the shadow of death, and who, by the help of friendly gods, and the merit of their good deeds on earth, had come forth on the other side, to be admitted to the lands of the blessed.

This land, Aalu, as it was called, was not such a heaven as many early nations have pictured to themselves: there were no shining mansions, no streets of gold, no gorgeous buildings adorned with countless precious jewels. The life hereafter that the Egyptian thought of was but a continuation of his life on earth, without its pains and sorrows. His heaven, therefore, consisted of fertile lands, traversed by endless canals, whose water came from the celestial stream itself. Here grew white wheat and red barley in plenty, the vine and the fig tree supplied him with fruit ; and spreading sycamores yielded ample shade when the heaven-dweller wished to rest.

Yet it was no life of idle ease that he conceived. He had to plough, and sow, and reap, and thresh, just as he had done before. But between this life and that to come was one great difference. There the work was light, and the worker was free from the cares that often beset him here. He need never be anxious about an excessive flood, against which the earthly Nile would keep him struggling for life day and night, nor fear a day when the Nile would yield no water, and his land would be

scorched by the burning rays of the sun. Against these and other like calamities that had harassed him heretofore, the gods made due provision; everything was well ordered by them, and care was unknown.

Not all the earthborn attained to heavenly happiness. Some were unworthy, and many of the weak fell by the way when passing through the dark valley. Only when strengthened by the merit of noble deeds on earth, by respect and honour paid to the gods, and by careful preparation for the long journey after death, could man hope to arrive at last at the Fields of Perfect Peace.

THE STORY OF RA AND ISIS

In those far distant days before history begins, it is said that there lived in Egypt a woman of great knowledge called Isis. She was well skilled in all arts and magic, and her wisdom and learning were equal to those of the gods. This superiority over her fellow-creatures made her desirous of yet more power and honour. 'Why should I not,' she said to herself, 'make myself mistress of all the earth, and become like unto a goddess in heaven? Did I know the secret name of Ra, verily I could accomplish this.'

Now when Ra, the greatest of the gods, was created, his father had given him a secret name, so awful that no man dared to seek for it, and so pregnant with power that all the other gods desired to know and possess it too. That they might not find it out by spells and enchantments it was hidden within the body of the Sun-god himself. But what man dared not, and the gods had failed to do, Isis resolved to achieve.

Every morning Ra came forth from the land of darkness and travelled across the sky in his Boat of Millions of Years. Now Isis had noticed that water fell from his mouth; so she took some of this and the earth on which it had fallen and fashioned them in the form of a sacred serpent, which, by reason of its being made from the spittle of a god, came to life when she uttered over it one of her magic spells. The

serpent she then laid carefully in the path of Ra, in such wise that he should not see it and yet he must pass over it. Thus, indeed, it fell out. On his next journey as he passed by the place where the serpent lay hid, the reptile bit him. The pain was intense, and Ra began to cry aloud. 'What is it?' asked the gods who attended on him. 'Wherefore criest thou thus as if in pain? 'But Ra found no words wherewith to answer them. His limbs shook, his teeth chattered, his face became pale, and his whole body was rapidly being suffused with the poison.

At length the Sun-god called his companions to him. 'Come hither, ye gods,' he cried, 'and hear what hath befallen me. I have been bitten by something deadly. My eyes have not seen it, nor did I make it: it is not one of my creatures. But never have

I felt pain so mortal. I am God, the son of God, and I was travelling through my lands to see them and my people, when the creature arose in my path and wrought me this ill. Go quickly, therefore, to the other gods, and bring those who are skilled in spells and enchantments that they may take away this pain.'

Soon the company of the gods, especially those versed in the use of magical words, were assembled about the boat of Ra; and with them came the woman Isis. In vain did Ra's companions use their talismans and utter their spells; the poison continued to burn within him. Then Isis approached, and said, 'What is this, O Ra? Surely some serpent hath bitten thee; some one of thy creatures hath dared to raise its head against the hand that made it. Tell me thy name, I pray thee, thy secret name, that by its power I may cast out the poison and thou shalt be whole.'

'I am the maker of heaven and earth,' answered Ra, 'and without me was nothing made that is made. When I open my eye, behold, it is light; and when I close it again, then darkness reigns. My word brings the flood into the Nile to water the land of Egypt. I make the hours, the days, and the yearly festivals. I am he who was, and is, and ever shall be.'

'Verily thou hast told me who thou art,' said Isis, 'but not yet hast thou spoken thy secret name. Wouldst thou be healed, thou must divulge it to me, that by its power and my lore I may overcome the evil wrought unto thee.'

Meanwhile the poison was coursing through the body of Ra, and making him very ill indeed; for you must remember that the serpent was a magic serpent, and also that it had not been created by Ra himself; for which reasons, though he was the greatest of the gods, he could not destroy the effects of its venom. One moment his body burnt as with fire, and the next it was icy cold, as the fever raged through and through him.

Finally he could no longer stand, and he sank down in the boat.

Then he called Isis to him. 'I consent,' he said to the company around him, 'I consent to be searched out by Isis, and that my name be yielded up unto her.' So Ra and Isis went apart, lest the assembled gods should also overhear the secret name, and Ra confessed that which the woman so greatly longed to know.

As soon as she had obtained her wish, Isis began to utter her magic spells, and here her ancient wisdom stood her in good stead. Then she cried aloud, 'Come out, poison, depart from the body of Ra. Let Ra live! May Ra live! Poison, depart from the body of Ra.' At the words a change came over the mighty god. No longer did he seem about to die. Quickly his strength returned, and ere long he was whole again, ready to continue his journey in the Boat of Millions of Years. And Isis, who by her wit had learnt what neither man nor god ever knew, was granted her desire, and henceforth was known as the mistress of the gods.

What was the secret name, do you ask? Ah! that I cannot tell you. It is what wise men have been seeking for thousands of years. Some few have found it, but the strange thing is that no one can tell it to anyone else. He can help others on the way to discover it for themselves, but that is all; and very often people neglect to hear it when it is whispered to them.

They let it pass, borne away on the wings of the wind, and the opportunity comes not again. But to those who do find out the secret name, it is all-sufficient. They need nothing more, for it is the greatest gift that heaven or earth can bestow.

THE STORY OF ISIS AND OSIRIS

THE KINGDOM OF OSIRIS

The Birth of the God

Far up the river Nile, on a fertile strip of land that borders the stream, once stood the mighty city of Thebes. Its ruins still cover a large area, and in the days of its greatest splendour it was the most magnificent city in the world. But at the time when this story opens, it was still young, and its gorgeous temples were not yet built. Its people worshipped, it is true, but not the God of Heaven. Amen they knew not, and the majesty of Ra they could not have understood. Their gods were images of wood and stone and the sun and the river Nile.

To these false gods a temple had been built, on a site destined to become the centre of a grand and noble worship. It stood amid a grove of shady trees, and from under its portals bubbled forth a spring of purest water, so sweet and sparkling that the people said it was blessed by the gods they honoured there.

To this spring a water-carrier was trudging one hot summer morning. He was young, but already his back was bowed with constant stooping under the weight of his goatskin bag.

'Why work at this hour?' asked a brother carrier, who, with goatskin slung over his shoulder, was wending homeward.

'Why work at all, I might ask,' replied the other sourly.

'True, but 'needs must,' you know,' said the first. 'Otherwise, methinks neither of us would be here now. Yet today is different. With this fierce heat blowing off the desert one cannot be blamed for resting early. It might do thee good,' he went on, seeing the other did not speak. 'Thou dost not seem in merry mood.'

'Nor do I feel so,' was the curt reply. 'But one must eat; and such as I cannot eat unless he works. There are many to feed now, for my father lies ill, and I must needs provide for all.'

'Well, I shall wait until evening; 'twill be cooler then,' said his companion as he walked away.

Pamyles, for such was the water carrier's name, watched his friend depart, and felt bitter in his heart against the fate that had made his lot so hard. Then, remembering the hungry mouths in the little hut of reeds by the river, he turned to the spring.

Just as he had filled the skin, he thought he heard his name called. He looked round, but saw no one. 'Pamyles,' came the voice again. There could be no doubt about it this time, and he paused in lifting the water bag to stare at the steps leading up to the temple. 'Pamyles,' came the voice a third time; and the poor man, knowing not what might befall him, dropped the goatskin to the ground, where the water gushed out unheeded, making a pool about his feet.

'Fear not,' said the voice, which to Pamyles's astonished senses seemed to come from the statue before the temple-door. 'Fear not; but go down into the town and say to the people, "Osiris, lord of all the earth, is born." Afterwards proclaim the message throughout the length and breadth of the land.'

The voice ceased, and, on the instant, Pamyles, forgetting all about the water-skin, took to his heels and never stopped until he reached his house. There he told

the story to his wife, who said the heat had muddled his wits, and bade him go back for the goatskin before someone came and stole it. But the old man, his sire, who lay with eyes closed on a bed of straw at the farther end of the room, called his son to him and asked him to repeat his tale.

'It was the voice of heaven,' said the old man, as Pamyles concluded. 'Go proclaim thy message as thou hast been bidden. For myself, I rejoice that I have lived to hear the gladsome tidings. May the blessing of the gods be upon thee, my son.' And the sufferer turned his face to the wall, and died.

Then Pamyles hastened to do as he had been commanded; and thus it was that the news of Osiris's birth came to the world.

The Coming of the God and Goddess

One evening in early summer, as the westering sun hung over the hills in a sea of crimson and purple and gold, a man halted under a sycamore tree near a rude temple that overlooked the Nile at Thebes. He was of enormous stature, yet so properly formed withal that one would scarce have heeded it until another man stood beside him. Then he seemed more than mortal.

By his side stood a woman, surely the most beautiful and most graceful on whom the sun had ever risen. The sweet and gentle face, fair of skin and tinted rosy-red, the comely figure clad in a robe of clinging white, and the wealth of chestnut hair that, when it fell down to her feet, covered her as with a garment and shone in the dying sunlight like burnished copper, told of a traveller from other lands than the burning plains of Egypt. As the sun's disk dipped behind the peak, changing the dull grey and brown of the hills to deepest purple, and painting the waters of the river in flaming red, she turned to the man and then toward the setting orb. Lifting their hands in adoration, they called on the name of Ra, bowed thrice to the ground, and sang a short hymn in the Sun-god's praise.

'Let us tarry here and rest,' said the man, and, spreading his mantle on a slab of stone, they sat down; when he took from his cloak a reed and began to blow upon it. Was it possible that this music was born of earth? Now soft as the cooing of the doves in the trees, now plaintive as a sea-bird's call; anon rippling like a stream over the pebbles in its bed, then loud and fast even as the rushing of a mountain torrent, it ended at last with such a burst of swelling sound as comes from a mighty choir that sings in unison. Then he played a simple song to the chant of the woman's voice. Wonderful had been the playing; marvellous beyond all words was the singing! Soft and low, yet thrilling in its richness and fulness, it seemed to tell of joy and sorrow, of brightness and shadow, of storm and sunshine, and of an infinity of love.

As the last sweet strains died away, a venerable old man, clad in a white robe encircled by a belt of gold, came slowly toward the two wayfarers.

'A pleasant evening to you both,' he said, a mixture of awe and wonder plainly written on his face.

'And to thee, O my father,' said the man. 'Canst tell us,' he asked, 'where in this city we may find lodging for a time? We are travellers, and would fain stay here to rest awhile.'

For some moments the newcomer said not a word, but continued to gaze with eyes that would read them through and through. At length he bowed his head to the ground, and kissed the sandal, first of the man then of the woman. Thereon, looking up, he spoke.

'The makers of music such as I have heard,' he said, 'should have the best the city can give. I am the priest of this temple, and in my study of the stars I have learned somewhat of the mysteries of the heavens. Long have I known of your coming, but never did I think that I should be the first to greet you here on earth.' And with worshipping eyes again the holy man gazed on the wondrous pair. 'Will my lord and lady deign to accept such hospitality as my poor house can offer?' he asked.

'It is because thou hast been so faithful in thy service that we came to thee first,' replied the man. 'We thank thee, and accept thy kindness. But I charge thee straitly to tell no man what thou knowest, whence we came or why. That shall be known as the gods will.'

'Your servant hears, and obeys,' said the priest, and he bowed his head to the dust.

'Now lead us to thy house,' continued the stranger. 'Come, Isis,' he said, turning to the woman, 'we will go with him, for the hour groweth late.'

'The blessing of Ra be with thee alway,' said the woman to the priest in her rich low voice; and, placing her arm within the other's, they went forward.

And in this way did Osiris and Isis his consort come to the land of Egypt.

The Power of Osiris

Every day Osiris and Isis went into the town that lay in the shadow of the temple. The wealthy palaces, the sacred buildings, the sphinx-lined avenues, and all the marks of grandeur and power for which Thebes became famous, were then unknown. The king's palace and the residences of some few of his great nobles were built of stone; but for the most part the houses were built of wood and reeds, or of bricks of mud baked in the sun, such as may be seen in any village of Egypt today.

As the two passed through the streets, the people stopped their work to look on them in amazement. Never had such majesty, such dignity, such power been seen in any man; never such sweetness, grace, and loveliness in any woman. Even their king and queen seemed insignificant compared with these godlike creatures. Instinctively they felt that the strangers were not of earth, and every mark of respect was shown them by the simple folk.

As you may guess, there were numerous inquiries at the house of the priest concerning the guests that abode there. But the high priest kept his own counsel; and for the rest of his household, they knew no more than did the people themselves.

'They are travellers,' was their reply to every inquirer, 'whom Ani the priest met in the temple grove and prayed to abide with him awhile. That is all we know.' Which way had they come? Did they travel by boat or on asses? What had they come for? But to these and all other questions no answer was forthcoming. The mystery of their arrival only added to the awe in which the people held them.

As time passed by, this awe deepened into a worshipping fear. Day by day Osiris and Isis went among the people, advising, helping, cheering. Wherever they were most needed there they always seemed to be. No hand was so cooling to the fevered brow as that of Isis, no voice so soothing to the fretful child; and, what was most remarkable, the sickness of those whom she touched and nursed quickly left them. Once when a distracted mother sought to ease the pain of her little boy, crushed and broken by the falling of a log, she felt the mysterious lady beside her. Gently Isis took the sufferer in her arms, and, as if by magic, the contorted face grew straight, the writhing limbs were stilled. Then she placed the tips of her fingers on his brow, and, after a moment, over his heart. The eyes slowly opened, the lips smiled. The child's look wandered from the nurse to his mother, and back again. 'Mother, mother,' he cried suddenly, 'I'm going with the beautiful lady. She says so, mother. I'm going to a beautiful house and I shall feel the pain no more.' He died that night, but he did not suffer again, and the stricken mother understood.

Osiris, too, was ever busy, but it was in the fields rather than in the houses of the city. He showed them how to make a plough, and then a water-raiser to lift the water from the river for the thirsty soil instead of carrying it all on their backs. Much else after the same manner did he teach them, to lighten their labour and to use more fruitfully the land they tilled. In the cool of the evening he would sit, surrounded by a crowd of rustics, young and old, all open-mouthed with admiration as he played to them upon his reed. Gradually he taught them how to play, too, and

oftentimes would be found a choir of churls pouring forth harmonious music in the liquid moonlight. And his little court would never let him depart until he had played to them one favourite hymn, that breathed of earth and sky, of life and death, and of a multitude of things beyond their knowing.

It was not long before the king heard of the strangers in their midst, and he sent for Osiris to come before him.

'Who art thou?' he asked; 'and whence comest thou?'

'I am a traveller,' said Osiris, 'who has heard much of the land of Egypt and desired to see it and its people. I came from the land of Aalu, and tarry here but a little while ere I return thither.'

'Where is this land thou speakest of?' asked the king. 'My armies have marched far and wide, but never have I heard of it before.'

'It lieth far away to the West,' replied Osiris, 'beyond the utmost limits that man can travel, unless he have a guide.'

'Then how didst thou come?' said the king. 'If thou couldst come hither, I can go thither. Tell me the road, for I would see this distant land.'

'That thou canst not do,' said Osiris. 'I have said that no man can reach it, so far away doth it lie.'

'Then thou wilt never return to thy own land?' said the monarch.

'Not while I live,' was the reply. 'I shall set out on the journey, but I do not look to reach it while life lasteth.'

'I have heard much of thy skill and cunning,' continued the king. 'I wish thee to come to my palace and teach my courtiers and magicians something of it.'

'Willingly,' answered Osiris. 'Yet I cannot forgo my work amongst thy poor people, also the right to help them as I have done hitherto.'

Thus it came to pass that Osiris went daily to the court, sitting with the wise men, who always learned something new from him. To all their entreaties,

however, to take up his abode in the palace, he remained obdurate. He had every comfort in the house of the priest, he said, and would stay with the man who had first befriended him.

Often in his discourse with the people he would speak with them of the temple wherein they worshipped, telling them that the stone image before which they uttered their prayers was powerless to aid them; but watching over them was a Divine Being who shielded them from harm and furnished all their needs. The golden sun that brought light and heat was a visible manifestation of this Being's power and majesty; the river Nile that watered the land, giving nourishment to their crops, was sent by Him from out of heaven.

By living noble and unselfish lives it was possible even for men to attain to the country where the great God lived in splendour and glory. In this way Osiris slowly inspired in the people a sense of worship of the Supreme Being; the more easily because his own deeds were so miraculous that his hearers were more than half disposed to look upon him as the God of whom he spoke.

Among the courtiers assembled in the open courtyard of the king on a certain day of audience, Osiris noted, as he entered, a young man standing, silent and apart, and withal a look of settled gloom upon his face. He was a warrior who had won the heart of Osiris, because of his fearless bearing, his chivalrous conduct, and his cheerful frankness. Clearly something was amiss, and Osiris crossed to where he stood.

'What aileth thee, Hotep?' he asked. 'Why dost thou brood here apart, instead of making merry with thy friends?'

'There is none will speak to me, or none who dares to,' said the young man, somewhat bitterly. 'Dost thou not know the king will visit thee with his displeasure doth he see thee with me now?'

Osiris then observed that the courtiers were talking chiefly in whispers and oftentimes glancing significantly toward the youth. 'What is thy fault?' he said.

'That I have not flattered those in high places, nor held my peace in face of wrong,' replied Hotep. Thus have I made many enemies, who have accused me of plotting against the king's life, and he has bid me attend here to answer the charge.'

'Ah!' exclaimed Osiris. 'So there are those who envy thy fearlessness and truth!' And he slowly moved away to speak to the temple priest, his head bowed in thought.

At that moment the king entered, and the attention of the courtiers was taken up with the audiences given by him. At last all were over; but, instead of rising to leave the hall as was his wont, the monarch sat on in his chair of state.

'Is our servant Hotep here?' he asked at length.

'Here, O King,' said the young man, stepping forward and making deep obeisance.

'We have received accusations against thy fidelity, that thou hast plotted against the royal throne,' said the king. 'Hast thou aught to say in answer to the charge?'

'I beg my lord to let me hear the charges more particularly,' replied Hotep.

The monarch frowned. It was not usual for a subject to imply doubt of the king's word; but after a moment he called the chamberlain to him. 'Read what the charges are,' he said.

'Hotep thy servant, captain in the king's army, is accused of plotting against the life of the king and his royal house,' recited the minister from the scroll in his hand, 'and of inciting others to aid him in his villainous work. Further, in his capacity of captain of the army of the South, he hath sought to create disaffection in the ranks of the king's troops, purposing to use them to carry out his evil designs.'

'What sayest thou to these accusations?' said the king, when the chamberlain had finished.

'Who are my accusers?' asked Hotep quietly.

Again the king's brow clouded. 'It matters not,' he said angrily. 'Thou hast heard the charge. Hast thou aught to reply?'

'Nothing, O King, save that it is a base lie, fabricated by my enemies,' said the fearless youth.

'O King, thou knowest the faithfulness of my service, and I abide thy decision, trusting to the king's honour.'

For a brief space the king was discomfited. Then his anger returned.

'The penalty for thy sin is death,' he answered, 'and thy guilt hath been proved. Take him away,' he said, turning to the guards behind him.

The warrior darted a swift look round the hall. He was young, and life was sweet. But no answering glance met his in the crowd of faces about him. Whatever it was that passed through his mind he recognized the hopelessness of it, and, with a bitter smile, turned to the men who had come to lead him away.

'Doth the king condemn a man unheard?' said Osiris, who, unmarked, had advanced to the throne. 'Is it to his honour or to his weal thus to send a well-tried servant to his death.'

A gasp of deep amaze sounded like a sudden wind through the hall. Never had anyone been known to question in this wise the will of the king. The monarch himself was for the moment too astounded to speak.

'Thou presumest too much on the favour I have shown thee,' he said, when at length words came to him. 'I have spoken. Were it not that thou art a stranger within our gates, thy rashness might have brought on thee the same punishment as his for whom thou speakest. Stand aside, and meddle no further, or it will be worse for thee.'

'Nevertheless, I ask thee to give the man justice,' said Osiris quietly. 'Wouldst thou – '

'Barest thou speak thus to me?' roared the king in a fury. 'Take this fool away too,' he cried to the guards, 'lest I kill him where he stands.' And the long lance quivered in his hand.

'I move not until thou hast dealt justice to thy servant Hotep,' answered Osiris, calm and unmoved as heretofore.

'Madman,' shouted the king, 'suffer for thy folly;' and he sprang forward, the lance poised to strike.

'Stand,' said Osiris. And now his voice rolled through the hall like thunder amid far-echoing hills.

Paralysed at the word the monarch halted, and the lance clattered upon the granite floor. The courtiers stared in utter dread, marvelling what would next betide. A very god seemed Osiris, towering above them all as a man might over a crowd of little children, his arm outstretched, his eyes gleaming like the lightning.

Slowly he lowered his arm to his side; slowly the king recovered consciousness, and, shaking with terror, sank back into his seat.

'Hadst thou come one step more,' said Osiris, 'thou wouldst now be wending to the shades below. Know that I have power to destroy thee and all these assembled round thee. Now wilt thou set free thy servant Hotep, falsely accused, and mete out punishment to those who would accomplish his death. Rouse not my wrath again, but remember, and fear.' And ere speech or movement had returned to the affrighted throng the god had gone.

The Coming of Evil

It came to pass that soon after these things the king fell ill and died and was gathered to his fathers; and, because he left no one to succeed him, it behoved the nobles and counsellors of the realm to choose one to reign in his stead. With one accord they prayed Osiris to accept the crown, but he would not; until at length, seeing they would make no other ruler over them, and that without a king they were fast becoming like unto sheep without a shepherd, he yielded to their entreaties.

For many years did he and his consort Isis rule the land, and he continued to instruct the people in those arts that had so greatly helped them when first he came

among them. Gradually he extended his rule far beyond the confines of Egypt, subduing the people not by force of arms, but by gentle words and a knowledge of the arts of agriculture and other peaceful pursuits that hitherto had been unknown. Ofttimes on such travels he was absent many months, and Isis ruled in his stead. To the love and honour which her gentleness and kindness had inspired was added a reverence second only to that shown Osiris, by reason of her ability and wisdom in government when she was left alone.

One day there came to the gates of the palace at Thebes a stranger, accompanied by a train of armed men. Tall was he and strong, but the most ill-favoured man that the guard of the gate had ever seen. With long arms swinging loosely by his side, a huge head set on a short, thick neck, beetling brows, nose thick and squat, upper lip cut, imparting an evil sneer at all times to his face, he was a man to terrify even the brave keeper of the gate.

'Who art thou, and what seekest thou here?' asked the soldier, when he had clanged-to the massive gates.

'Is this the palace of Osiris?' inquired the stranger.

'It is,' answered the man. 'What wouldst thou have of it?'

'Go thou and tell him that his brother Typhon hath come, and would fain yield him a kinsman's greeting,' replied the giant.

'Thou his brother!' exclaimed the guard; and he laughed aloud. Impossible that such a monster could be brother to their godlike king!

The stranger grew angry. 'Yea, his brother,' he bellowed. 'Hasten with my message, or I will pull these gates about thy ears, and then spit thee on my pike.' And, stretching forth a great hairy hand, he seized a bar of the gate and shook it as though to tear it from its socket.

The guard deemed it best to humour him. 'I will send one with thy message,' said he; and, turning, bade a comrade carry the news to the palace. To his surprise

the man returned commanding that the strangers should be admitted and escorted to the presence of the king.

Osiris stood on the topmost of the entrance steps awaiting his brother. He welcomed him to the city and begged him to abide with him in the palace, where apartments were already being prepared for his use. But many a man who stood around noticed that the king's greeting lacked somewhat of its wonted cordiality; while the evil leer on Typhon's face was remarked by all.

From this time forth the peace and happiness that had marked Osiris's reign seemed to depart. In field and city smouldered a spirit of restlessness. How it came or whence no man could tell. Men were more prone to quarrel and to grumble against their lot; yet none could say wherein lay the cause of his discontent. But insensibly they often found themselves wishing for the days before the king's brother came into their midst.

Typhon took no part in the government. In truth, Osiris knew him too well to entrust any share of it to him. When not carousing with his fellows in his apartments he would set out on long hunting expeditions, from which he sometimes did not return for many months. In his absence the Thebans again dwelt in content; yet most guessed that the giant was plotting against his brother, and that his seeming love of the chase was but a cloak to hide his evil plans.

When Osiris was away Isis was so vigilant that Typhon had no opportunity to work any harm. More cautious even than the king, she never allowed the knave to leave the city without sending some trusty servant to watch and to report to her all his doings.

So the years passed by, Isis and Osiris always striving to improve the lot of their subjects and to increase their happiness; Typhon waiting and watching for a chance to seize this fair land for his own, and his hatred against his brother growing ever fiercer in his heart.

The Murder of Osiris

For many days the king's brother had remained shut up in his rooms. To all inquirers he surlily replied that he wished only to be left alone; even his boon companions were excluded. These spent the time in riotous living and stirring up brawls, until the captain of the guard seized a dozen of them and kept them in close confinement; whereon, though their shameless revelries were no wise checked, they were more heedful to practise them secretly.

Typhon, however, kept to himself. Sometimes he would not touch the food served up to him, and on such days the menials learnt to flee his cruel wrath. Of a sudden he sprang from his couch. 'I can do it, and I will,' he said.

Crossing over to a heavy wooden chest he took therefrom a long roll of cloth. This cloth was different from that worn by the Egyptians. It was softer, smoother, and in the sun shone rainbow-hued. Taking this with him the knave went forth to seek Osiris.

As chance would have it, the king was alone. 'How fare you, brother?': he said kindly. 'I hope your sickness has left you.'

''Tis quite gone,' replied Typhon; and you would not have known him for the Typhon of old, so gentle and bland were air and voice. 'Quite gone, and I thank you for your brotherly solicitude; in token whereof I wish to make you a small gift. What think you of this?' and he proffered the roll of cloth to the king.

'It is indeed beautiful,' replied Osiris. 'There is not its like in this land.'

'Therefore it should clothe a king,' said Typhon. 'If my brother will accept it, it shall be made into a robe for him, worthy of his kingly form.'

'I thank you for your generosity,' answered Osiris, with no suspicion of evil. 'Do you desire it, I will accept the cloth, but it shall not cause you further trouble. Leave it to the robemakers of my court. I will bid them see to it.'

'That would be to deprive the robe of half its beauty,' said Typhon. 'I know a cunning craftsman, whose work is as superior to that of your court-followers as is this cloth to that of your weavers. Let me but take what measurements are needful, and my pleasure shall be to see it finished for you.'

'So be it then, if you will,' agreed the monarch; and he stood up while Typhon measured off on the cloth his length from head to heel.

'But sooth, the robe is not to cover my head also, is it?' said the king laughing.

'Ah! to be sure not,' cried the rogue, in pretended confusion; and he marked off on the cloth the length from shoulder to the ground. In like manner he took other measurements, until at length he announced that they were complete.

'Ere long it shall be ready,' he said. 'I will take it to my craftsman at once.'

When he had gained his own apartments, he summoned his followers, and in an hour they were hurrying away to the south. Toward evening they came to a marsh, on the shores of which stood a small hut.

'Wait here,' said Typhon, and he strode off toward the hut, the roll of cloth under his arm. The business took long to settle, and, had anyone been near, he would have wondered both at the constant repetition of directions and yet more at the directions themselves. Carving, gilding, inlaying, are not words applied to the making of robes; yet these were the burden of the talk. Moreover, when Typhon emerged from the hut, the roll of cloth was still in his possession.

Again the party set out, riding most of the night. In two days they came to another lonely hut, and here the cloth was left with full instructions as to its

disposal. Once more they took to the road, and after seventeen days came to the capital of Ethiopia.

On his arrival Typhon went straight to the royal palace and demanded admittance. Without delay he was ushered in, and forthwith conducted to the dusky queen.

'Well, hast thou been successful?' she asked.

'Not yet,' replied Typhon. 'They are ever on the watch. I fear the queen suspects, yea, mayhap knows somewhat of my plans.'

'Not yet,' repeated the other, ignoring his last remark. 'Always the same story thou bringest. I thought thou wert sure of victory last time.'

'Dear Aso,' answered Typhon, 'no one could do more than I have done. But the first step rests on guile, not on force. Afterward the more strength I can show the better.'

'Well?' questioned the other briefly, as he ceased.

'I have a plan,' said Typhon. ''Tis for that I am come hither. It is sure to succeed if I can lure Osiris from his watchful wife. Thou hast the troops ready to aid me?'

'My promise still holds good,' replied Aso.

'Then we start back tomorrow,' said Typhon, 'and this time shall see me victorious.'

On the following day the return journey was begun. Besides his seventy-two companions he had now a large body of soldiers in his train. On the seventh day he, with a score of his followers, rode ahead, bidding the remainder come after with all speed.

Day and night they rode, resting only for a few hours at noon and midnight. When they reached the hut where the cloth had been left, Typhon stopped, and called the man to the door.

'Hast thou finished?' he demanded.

'All is ready,' replied the man. 'Will my lord see the robe?'

'No, I know 'twill be well,' replied the giant. 'Give it, and let me be gone.'

Again they hurried onward, and twice had the Sun-god made the circuit of heaven when they arrived at the hut by the marsh. As before Typhon entered alone and remained closeted with the hermit workman. Then he came to the door and called up his company.

'We will finish our journey by way of the river,' he said. 'Take this and put it on the boat ye will find hidden at the entrance to the marsh.'

The object to which he pointed was something concealed beneath a skilfully plaited cover of papyrus. In appearance it was like a long box – a coffin, as one remarked to his companion. But their master did not explain, and they knew better than to ask; so without more ado they carried it down to the boat. Then they pushed out of the narrow channel into mid-river, and were carried swiftly down the stream.

The following night the boat reached Thebes, and was drawn up at the steps leading to that part of the palace where Typhon dwelt. The mysterious object was lifted out, and quietly carried within.

Next morning Typhon waited upon the king, taking with him the robe he had promised. When the brothers had saluted, Typhon presented the garment.

'Will my lord be pleased to wear it?' he asked.

'Certainly, my brother,' replied Osiris. 'Let me put it on now.'

The robe fitted perfectly, and as it hung from his shoulders, shimmering in the morning sunlight, it added dignity even to his regal figure.

'It is indeed a royal gift,' he said, 'and I thank thee for it. What can I give thee in return?'

'The pleasure of thy company in this robe at a banquet in my hall this night,' said the crafty rogue, smiling. 'So seldom is my table graced with thy presence that a visit will more than repay me for the little trouble the robe hath cost.'

Now Osiris had no liking for the banquets of his brother, for he knew they were wont to develop into wild and drunken orgies, for which he felt an utter loathing. But

he could not well seem churlish now; and perhaps it was not altogether his brother's fault that his instincts led him into such shameless courses, he thought generously.

When Typhon had departed Osiris sought the queen and showed her the beautiful present he had received. He told her, too, of his promise to eat with his brother that evening.

Isis looked up in alarm. 'But thou saidst thou wouldst never go there again,' she answered.

'After such a kindly deed, how could I refuse so small a favour?' said Osiris.

''Tis Typhon's treachery,' cried the queen in great fear. 'There is some evil behind this that thou wottest not of.'

'Art thou not a little unjust toward him?' asked the king gently. 'He hath not been favoured in many ways as we have.'

'I am sorry for him, but I am not unjust,' replied the queen, her eyes full of tears. 'His misshapen body is the image of a misshapen mind. He designeth evil against thee, and I pray thee go not tonight.'

Now, though Osiris and Isis were in truth god and goddess, they had lived so long among men and women and had entered so completely into their thoughts, their joys and sorrows, hopes and fears, that they had become more than half human themselves, stirred by the same feelings and passions. And that day her human heart spoke loudly of impending sorrow, and urged Isis to plead yet again with her husband, as she clung passionately to him.

'What ill could he do me?' said Osiris. 'Moreover, in my own palace he would not dare attempt anything against my person. Yet, to calm thy fears, I promise to return ere midnight,' he concluded, as he embraced her fondly.

All that evening the heart of the queen troubled her. Strange and horrid shapes danced and grimaced before her, and once the air was suffused with red. She retired to her chamber and lay down on the couch, but sleep refused to kiss

her eyes. Away on the other side of the great courtyard she could see the bright lights of the banqueting hall, whence came the sounds of wild laughter and high revelry.

Meanwhile the banquet was served, a feast worthy of a king. At one end of the table sat Osiris, and at the other his brother. Dish after dish of rare meats and choicest dainties was brought, and the winecups were kept full by the watchful servitors. When at length the meal was over, Typhon, who had apparently succumbed more and more to the influence of the wine, jumped up.

'A pledge!' he shouted. 'Pledge me, O king, and ye, my friends, drink to his Majesty, the mighty King of Egypt.'

A shout of glee rent the air. The pledge was drunk, and Typhon spoke again.

'Much have I heard,' he said, 'of the cunning of the workmen of Egypt. But, my brother, when of late I was absent travelling in distant lands, I chanced upon a wondrous box, so marvellously wrought that I declare its equal does not anywhere exist. Let me show it to you, O King.'

Thereupon Typhon commanded his servants to undo the wrappings of the mysterious box that lay at the end of the hall, and to bring it forward into the light. As the papyrus rolled away, cries of amazement and delight burst from all present. There it lay, a long box of wondrously wrought metal, with strange symbols and devices worked into the lotus-lily patterns. Upon the inner surface of the lid the double crown of Egypt was picked out in precious stones.

Everyone expressed his admiration for the beautiful object, and Osiris admitted that no workman known to him could have made it. The excitement increased, the babel grew louder, when suddenly Typhon, who seemed to have grown ever more reckless, shouted, 'I will give the box to whomsoever it fits perfectly.'

The menials had retired from the hall, and on the word the roisterers rushed toward the box. One after another climbed in, and, amid shouts of boisterous

merriment, was dragged out by the rest, who each sought to claim the treasure for his own. But it was far too big for any of them.

'O King, will you not try?' cried Typhon. ''Twould make a fitting coffer for your robe.'

The king protested, laughing at the conceit; but, to humour the company, now frenzied with excitement, he rose from his seat and stepped to the box. He failed to see the baleful light that gleamed in the monster's eyes and the fingers trembling with eagerness as they stretched involuntarily toward the lid. As he lay down another cry of utter astonishment burst from all around. For the box fitted him as perfectly as if it had been made for him: as, in fact, it had.

Then, before he could move to get out, Typhon, with a fierce shout, crashed down the cover and slid home the bolts. Those in the plot brought nails and fastened down the lid. To make it doubly sure, molten lead was poured round the edges and the box absolutely sealed.

'Into the river with it,' shouted Typhon; 'and then hie ye to the frontier where our friends await us. Egypt is ours.'

Stilling the tumult they passed out of the hall and down the steps to the river, into which the box was plunged. The swift-flowing waters whirled it round and round, sucking it ever toward the middle of the stream, and, as the current caught it, launched it forward. At the same instant from out the turbid depths there rushed a lurid ame that lighted up the palace and the town like day.

Typhon stood alone on the shore, his companions having already taken to the boats; and, as the light fell athwart the stream, he cried aloud in fear. Then, seizing a boat, he rowed for life in the wake of his eeing men.

Meantime, exhausted with her anxious vigil, the queen had fallen into a fitful slumber, only to be haunted by such hideous dreams that she sought to keep awake. Again the red mist clouded her sight, and, as the last fierce shout from Typhon's hall

awoke her, she saw Osiris, his face streaming with blood, his hand pointing upward. With a heart-rending cry she sprang from the couch to where the vision stood, but her arms clasped empty air. In utmost terror she waited for the coming of her lord, listening to the noises below. At length the shouts grew still, and soon there followed the sound of oars beating rapidly on the water. 'Now will Osiris come,' she said.

At that moment the flame leapt up from the river, and, her fears increased a thousandfold, Isis stared with tear-stained eyes upon the river scene. She caught a glimpse of Typhon springing into a boat and fleeing madly up the river before the flame died out. One by one the last faint sounds faded away in the distance, and the town was enwrapped in peace. Still Isis waited. But he for whom she waited would come no more. For Osiris, King of Egypt, was dead, the victim of a brother's hatred.

THE QUEST OF ISIS

The Beginning of the Quest

It was almost dawn before Isis awoke from the swoon into which she had fallen. At first she looked about her dazed and bewildered, wondering what had happened; then with a rush the events of the previous night crowded into her memory, and she fell back, overwhelmed with horror. Rousing herself with an effort, she began to make arrangements for the future. Well she knew that her lord was dead, and the hand that had sent him to his doom would quickly return to seize the crown. She feared, too, that Typhon had still more terrible designs, and soon her fears proved true.

Ten days after the murder of the king a mighty army encamped on the plain before Thebes. As evening drew in a herald approached the gates and asked to see the queen. This request Isis refused, and bade him send by the captain of the guard any message he had to deliver. Soon the soldier returned, and, making a deep obeisance, spoke.

'Typhon, King of Egypt, sendeth humble greetings to his sister Isis. If Isis will consent to marry him, she still shall share the throne and government as heretofore. But if Isis refuse then will Typhon wage war against court and city till not one stone be left upon another, nor man nor woman live to tell the tale.

'What sayest thou, Hotep?' said Isis, when the captain ceased; for this officer was the same whom Osiris had saved from the tyranny of the king who ruled before him.

'That I would I had the vain boaster before me, O Queen,' answered Hotep, 'free to work my will upon him for as long as a man may count a hundred. Egypt would then be rid of its evil.'

'And the other officers, what will they say? 'she asked.

'What I have said, your Majesty,' he answered. 'Our forces are small, for the base wretch hath taken advantage of the absence of those troops that went to the land of the north; but we shall not yield the city while one man remaineth alive to defend it.'

'I know thou wilt do thy best,' replied the queen; 'but I fear our power is too weak to withstand him. Go now, and make such arrangements as thou deemest best. For me I spurn the offer as worse than death. Whatever betide I shall soon leave Thebes. I must go and search for Osiris, my lord and thine.'

'I pray you may find him, O Queen,' said Hotep reverently.

For six days the defence held out, but on the seventh a breach was made in the walls, and Typhon's black horde poured in. Men, women, and children were slaughtered until the streets ran blood, and the dead lay in heaps. Then the enemy came to the palace, where the remnant of the faithful army had gathered.

Typhon again sent in his offer to Isis, but she would not deign to reply. To wed the murderer of her husband, to accept him as king and lord! The very thought made her burn with shame. Next day his soldiers succeeded in scaling the outer wall, and Isis knew that the end was near.

She retired to her room, and, after distributing gifts to her hand-maidens and bidding them escape by the river gate while yet there was time, commanded that

she should be left alone. Taking off her outer robe, she arrayed herself in white samite. Over this she let fall her long bright hair, that shone in the sun like a radiant flame.

Stretching herself on the couch, with arms outspread, she began to chant a hymn, strange and mystical. As she sang, all around her slowly changed. The walls of the room faded away into the distance, the furniture, the very couch on which she lay, became impalpable; everything grew formless, unreal, seeming but 'the baseless fabric of a dream.' The clash of arms without drew nearer, but Isis heeded it not. To things of earth she was bound no more. Not for naught had she studied enchantments; not in vain had she wrested the words of power from Ra.

Dashing aside the faithful girl who sought to guard the sanctity of her queen, Typhon burst into the room. But no beautiful woman stood before him. As his foot crossed the threshold, a bird resembling a large swallow, with a crest of feathers that gleamed like burnished copper, rose from the couch, and, with a mournful cry, floated through the window and out over the river.

The quest of Isis for Osiris had begun.

The Story of a Satyr

Isis knew not which way to turn to find the body of her husband, but as she flew along she sometimes descended to earth in human form and inquired of those she thought might help her. For some days she learned nothing; then one day hope was born within her.

A woman of the people knelt beside the river, drawing water, and Isis approached her to ask if she had seen aught of the chest floating down the stream. The woman replied that she had not, but her husband, who was a shepherd, had heard of some such thing. Early one morning he surprised a number of strange creatures in the valley below. They had faces and bodies like men, she said, but the legs and feet of goats, and from the sides of their heads goats' horns grew. They

were called Satyrs, and their ruler was named Pan, and the shepherds looked on them as the guardians of their flocks.

'One of the Satyrs came up to my husband,' said the woman. 'At first he was frightened and would have run away, for it is unlucky to meet a Satyr after sunrise. Then he noticed the sun had not yet risen, for he was in a narrow valley; so he stood still until the god came to him.'

'What did the Satyr say?' queried Isis eagerly.

'He bade my husband attend carefully to his words. The night before while the Satyrs were sporting in the reeds hard by the river, a pale light came floating down the stream, and in the midst of the light a box. 'That box,' he said, 'contains the body of your king. It is going straight downstream. Remember.' Before my man could speak the Satyr had run back to his companions, and the next instant they had all vanished. But surely,' added the woman, 'the king could not have been in that box. He is in Thebes.' And her eyes looked for support to the face of the beautiful woman beside her.

'The Satyr spoke truth,' said Isis. 'Your king hath been cruelly done to death, and his body cast away. One who loved him seeketh him.'

The sorrowful eyes filled with tears. The peasant woman fell on her face in the sand, and kissed the hem of Isis' robe. 'My gracious queen,' she murmured; 'we who live so far away knew nothing of it. May heaven guide you in your search!'

Away went Isis, following the course of the river. She had news now, true and clear, and swiftly she sped above the water. Near the head of the delta she came to another pause. Here the river divided into two wide channels, and she knew not which to follow. To take the wrong branch would mean much loss of time, perhaps the loss of her husband's body.

In this perplexity she came upon a number of little children playing beside the

river. She loved all children, and, thinking they might distract her from her sorrow for a while, she came down to earth, and, assuming her human form, drew near to them.

One of the little ones was weeping bitterly, and in another moment Isis had him in her arms. To all her questions he would answer nothing; only he gazed across the river as if seeking something. She thereupon began to question the others, when straightway the weeper began to speak.

'I want the pretty box,' he said. 'Which box?' asked Isis. 'The pretty shining box that was in the river,' he replied. 'In the river? Where?' she asked quickly. There could not be two chests in the river, she thought.

'There, in the reeds,' answered the boy.

'What kind of box was it?' asked the queen.

'Long and bright and shining,' he answered, 'with pretty flowers on it; and I touched it, but I could not lift it.'

'When was it there?' she said.

'Yesterday morning,' replied the child. 'I went home to fetch my father to get it out of the reeds, and when we came back, it was floating away down the river.'

'Poor little boy,' she said. 'Never mind, I will give you another box. Come here tomorrow morning, and you shall find a pretty box that you can take away yourself.'

'A bright box?' asked the child eagerly, his former sorrow already forgotten in the anticipation of a new treasure. 'Will it be shining, and have flowers on it?'

'Bright and beautiful as the other,' answered Isis; 'but smaller that you may carry it yourself. Now tell me which way this box in the river went.'

'Down that stream,' said the boy, pointing to one of the two big channels.

'Thank you,' she said. 'Now I am going to find it.'

'Will you bring it back for me?' cried the boy.

'Not that one,' said Isis. 'I may not find it. But whether I do or not, your little box shall be waiting for you here tomorrow.'

And, when the little fellow ran early next morning to the place by the river where he had met the goddess, there on the sand, shining in the rays of the rising sun like silver, lay a curiously wrought box; and in the joy of its possession the lost one was quickly forgotten.

The search was renewed, Isis expecting every hour to come up with the chest. But in the delta the river widened out and in many parts was little more than a vast marsh with papyrus growing thickly out of the water. Thus it behoved her to take the utmost care, lest she should pass it by; and many days sped away without any trace of the chest being seen.

One evening about sunset a large swallow alighted on the crosstree of a ruined hut that stood on the shore of a marsh. The bird seemed weary, for its head drooped, and it swayed as though blown by the breeze. After some moments it looked around and spoke, as to itself.

You will have guessed that the bird was Isis, tired with the long and fruitless search. She had followed the windings of the river, exploring each papyrus clump, scanning every overhanging bush, but not a sign of the chest could she discover. She had now approached the mouth of the river, and was wondering if the box could have escaped her vigilance, or if it had been carried straight on and was now out upon the broad bosom of the sea. Many months had elapsed since the search began, and sometimes she was filled with despair.

'I will rest here in this hut for the night,' she said to herself. 'Perhaps tomorrow will see the end.' Often had she comforted herself with the same hope, but the morrow went and the end came not.

She was about to descend from the roof of the hut, when from a grove of sycamore trees she heard the sound of shrill music, followed by peals of laughter.

In a moment she was flying above the trees, in the direction of the voices, and came to a sudden stop as her eyes fell on the peculiar scene below.

At one side of a glade fringed with wild rose and jasmine, honeysuckle and trumpet-flower, a man was seated on a fallen tree, and round him were gathered a number of tiny people, chattering and laughing and clapping their hands with delight. In his hand the man held a musical instrument, made of a set of reeds of various lengths skilfully fastened together. When he put it to his lips it gave forth the most enchanting music, and the little folk at once spread out and began a stately dance. Then Isis could see that the man was not really a man at all, for he had goat's legs and on his head were two horns.

It was Pan, the most famous of all musicians, playing for his little friends the elves and fairies. As his music rang out, they advanced and retired, at first gravely and in measured step, then wheeling and turning, and finally spinning round and round in wild abandon. Faster went the music, and faster flew the tiny feet, until the dancers were an indistinct, whirling mass of colour. With a high clear note the music ceased, the blurred mass resolved itself into fairy shapes, and with shouts of happy laughter they gathered round the music-god.

'Dear Pan! Kind Pan!' they cried. 'Another dance, Pan. Just one more! They are never the same as when you pipe for us.'

'Not tonight,' said Pan. 'Tomorrow if ye will; but now I must away to the Satyrs who await my coming. To your homes, friends all, and I will pipe a measure as ye go.' He took up his reed and played again as the merry throng tripped away, singing a lilting song the while.

The half-man was about to move from the tree whereon he sat, when he became aware of another figure before him, no elf this time, but of human shape.

'Thou art Pan?' queried the newcomer.

'I am, Beautiful One,' he replied.

'Thou hast seen a wonderful chest floating down the river. Canst tell me whither it is gone?'

'The chest wherein lay the body of Osiris,' said Pan. 'Yes, I saw it. You will not find it here. It is gone.'

'Gone!' cried Isis. 'Gone! Shall I never see my lord again?' And all the weariness and grief and heartache of the world welled up in her cry of despair.

'Be not disheartened,' said the half-man. 'Though the chest is gone, mayhap it is not irrecoverable. The power of Isis is great. But hark! The fairies sing to you, and their knowledge is wide as the sea.'

As he spoke, there came borne on the soft night air a low throbbing note, gentle and sweet and full of compassion. It rose and fell, as the breeze wafted the strains of the invisible choir through the glade, and Isis listened with rapt attention, her heart drinking in every word of this song.

Beautiful lady, lo! him whom thou seekest
Not here on Nilus' dark waters thou'lt see;
If thou wouldst find him, go, leave these sad marshes,
Search in the heart of the tamarisk tree.
There close enwrapped by its wide-spreading branches
Typhon's fell work lies concealed from the sight;
Cruelty shameless, dark deed of the monster,
Soon by thy love to be brought to the light.
Faint not, nor weary; thy task is nigh ended;
Love great as thine must prevail by its might.
Then shall the lord of the world rule in glory,
Wrong vanquished, Truth 'stablished, Darkness made Light.

The music ceased, yet still Isis listened. It had soothed her, and she thought she might learn yet more of her lost lord. Then, leaning forward to the Satyr, she said, 'What is this I hear about a tamarisk tree and Typhon's cruelty, the defeat of wrong and the triumph of right? Knowest thou further of these things?'

'Listen, O Goddess,' said Pan, 'and I will tell you what I know. Many days past, the chest you seek floated downstream and was carried far out to sea, to be tossed about by the waves until it was cast up at Byblos into the branches of a tamarisk tree.'

'And shall I find it there now?' cried Isis eagerly.

'Not so,' answered Pan. 'The tamarisk tree grew so quickly that soon it had enfolded the box in its midst and it could not be seen. The King of Byblos, riding by when hunting, remarked the huge size of the tree-trunk, and resolved to remove it.'

'Well?' said the queen impatiently, as he paused.

'Next day,' continued Pan, 'an army of men came with axes and ropes and cut down the tree, placed it on a waggon, and carried it off to the king's palace, where it was set up as a pillar to support the roof.'

'With the chest still inside it?' asked Isis.

'Yes,' replied Pan. 'No one save my brothers and myself knew of its existence, and we would not speak. So there it remains, upholding the roof of the king's house.'

'The thanks of Isis are thine,' said the queen. 'Is there anything I can do to show my gratitude?'

'The power of Isis is great,' replied Pan. 'I am ugly, having neither the dignity of man nor the grace of an animal. Both laugh at me and make a mock of my deformity. I pray you grant me some gift that shall make them hereafter think kindly of me.'

'Thy prayer is granted,' answered Isis. 'Henceforth when men speak the name of Pan, it shall be in admiration of his music.'

So today there are thousands of people who could not tell you what Pan was like, but they know that he was a god of olden times who played divinest music on a pipe of reeds.

The Secret of the Tree

The walls of the palace of King Melecander gleamed white in the morning sun. Not a breath stirred the air. Even the water that plashed in the marble fountain seemed to rise and fall lazily. The acacia grove looked very inviting, and a woman, tired and travel-stained, halted to rest in its welcoming shade.

Many paused to question the beautiful sad-eyed woman, but to one and all she answered nothing; only when the Queen's waiting-girls came tripping through the grove did she show any sign of interest in her surroundings. They started to see the stranger, for, save those whose business took them to the palace, no one was allowed here, nor dare they linger, however attractive the shade might be. One, a pretty maid of fourteen summers, went up to her.

'Seek you anyone here, lady?' she asked.

'Yes,' answered the traveller. 'The lord of all the world is here, and I come to find him.'

'The king is away hunting,' said the girl, for she thought the stranger spoke of her royal master.

'I said not your king,' was the reply. 'The stranger seeketh another stranger, long in your midst, unknown to you all, his name on every tongue.' Seeing the mystified look on the girl's face, 'Come here,' she said, 'and tell me of this place.'

Like every girl the maid was willing enough to talk on that which interested her, and soon was chattering away as if she had known the lady all her life. As she knelt before her, Isis, for it was she, toyed with the girl's hair, plaiting it into a long coil that fell to the ground.

'Who are you?' asked the girl.

'The nurse of my people,' was the reply.

Again the child looked puzzled. But a nurse, that at least she understood. 'Can you heal anyone who is ill?' she asked.

'If I will,' replied the other.

The girl remained thoughtful. Of a sudden a great bell clanged out, and she started up. 'I must go now,' she said. 'Do you live here, or are you going away again?'

'When the tree yieldeth up the god who lieth at its heart, I go,' said the woman. The girl looked wistfully at her, but could make nothing of her words and the bell clanging out once more, she hurriedly said goodbye.

The other maidens had disappeared, and, by the time she reached the royal apartments, two of them were already returning in search of her. 'The Queen would speak with you,' they said.

'Thou art late, Melita,' said the Queen, when she entered. 'Dost thou play alone that thou comest not with thy sisters? Or is it,' she added, as her eye fell on the coil in which Isis had bound the girl's hair, 'is it thy vanity that taketh so long to satisfy? Who did this, child?' she continued, without waiting for a reply, 'thou couldst not alone have braided thy hair like this.'

'A lady in the acacia grove did it,' said the frightened Melita. 'While I spoke to her she tied my hair. She saith she is a nurse, and I wondered if she could cure the prince, O Queen.'

'A nurse forsooth!' cried the Queen contemptuously.

'Think'st thou that where the court physicians fail, a wandering nurse-woman can succeed! But with what hath she anointed thy hair? It smelleth of primroses and violets and other fragrant flowers that love not the burning sun of Byblos. Who is this woman?'

'She said she was the nurse of her people,' replied the girl. 'When I asked her if she dwelt here she said, "When the tree yieldeth up the god at its heart, I go." What she meant I know not, O Queen. Perhaps you understand, lady.'

Now Astarte, the queen, knew no more of what was meant than did the maid, but she would not say so. She stood thoughtful for a few moments; then, turning to the child, 'Fetch the stranger here,' she said.

Melita gladly ran back to the grove, where she found the lady gazing out over the lake as absently as when she first saw her. 'The Queen desires to see you,' she said. 'Will you come?' She did not say the queen had commanded her presence, for in some unknown way she felt it would be an indignity to her, and, moreover, this woman might refuse to obey even the Queen herself.

'I will come,' she said, after a moment's pause. 'Lead on.' And together they crossed the greensward to the massive pylon fronting the palace. As Isis stepped across the threshold a great trembling came upon her. She knew the treasure was at hand.

In the hall her eyes fell upon a magnificent pillar supporting the roof. It was the trunk of a single tree, straight and firm, but most wondrous were the markings on the bark. Figures of men and animals wrought amid a tracery of lotus flowers seemed to have been graven upon it ; and, high above all, on the side facing the door, was represented the crown of the kings of the North and South. On closer approach it was revealed, however, that the devices had not been carved into the bark, but were a natural growth; and this peculiarity and the beauty of the pattern had led King Melecander to cut down the tamarisk tree and bring it to his palace.

For a moment Isis stood motionless. Her face paled, and her limbs shook beneath her. At last her wanderings were o'er. Here she had found the burial-place of her lord, and soon would come reward and rest. Then, even as Melita turned round to see wherefore she lingered, she recovered herself and moved on, following the tiring-maid through the maze of rooms.

As she passed, the chatter of the waiting-women and girls ceased or fell to whispers. Was this regal figure only a nurse? Could she be a wanderer on the face of the earth? But Isis heeded none of them, and with eyes fixed on the vision of future happiness that now rose bright before her, she proceeded to the Queen's chamber.

Astarte eyed her with wonder and somewhat of awe. This was not the sort of woman she had expected. The haughty words with which she would have greeted her died on her tongue. Suddenly a shaft of sunlight fell athwart the ruddy hair, turning it to a crown of flame. Perchance some long-forgotten memory was awakened at the sight; mayhap she guessed something of the truth. So, when she spoke, her voice was gentle and kind.

'This maid telleth me thou art a nurse,' said Astarte. 'Couldst nurse my child and cure him?'

'Nurse him, yes,' answered Isis. 'Whether I cure him or not will depend on thee.'

'Bring the prince hither,' commanded the Queen, turning to Melita. 'Who art thou, and whence comest thou?' she asked. 'Thou bringest with thee the fragrance and perfume of the spring flowers on my native mountains. Art of this land? No?'

'I came from a land far, far to the west,' replied Isis. 'Long I lived happily with my husband among our people. Then was he cruelly done to death, and I was driven away.'

'Poor woman,' said the Queen. 'Thou, too, hast tasted the bitterness of sorrow.'

Melita entered with a nurse bearing the prince on a cushion. 'Knowest thou what aileth him?' asked Astarte anxiously, taking the babe to Isis. 'He wasteth away, and our most skilled physicians can do naught. Make him well and strong, and the King will refuse thee nothing. And the prayers of a grateful mother will alway go with thee,' she added, the tears springing to her eyes.

Without a word Isis laid the babe on her arm. He moaned as in pain, and the pinched wan face was marked with suffering. Placing her fingertips on his brow, she gazed intently at the closed eyes. They opened, and a faint smile flickered on the white lips. Next she pulled back his silken robe, drew her cool hand down the thin body, and finally put her finger in his mouth, at which for some minutes he sucked vigorously. Then she handed him back to his mother.

'Your child will be well,' she said simply.

In three more days the little boy was running about in all the wanton joy of childhood; and Isis had been installed as mistress of the royal nursery.

The Revelation of the Goddess

Day by day the royal boy grew stronger and handsomer, and his quickness and intelligence were remarked by all. He had been healed when doctors had failed; and seemingly the mysterious nurse had power also to improve his mind as well as his body. By day he was with other nurses of the palace; but at night, at Isis' request, he slept in her room, where none other was allowed to attend him.

So for many days all went well. Then began rumours of strange doings in the newcomer's room during the dark watches of the night. Unwonted sounds were heard behind the heavy doors, sounds of baby laughter mingled with the crackling of flames; bright lights were burning when all should have been asleep; and the music of a woman's beautiful voice, clear and soft as a distant evening bell, floated on the still night air. Yet when the ancient dame, aforetime charged with the prince's safety, knocked at the chamber door, the lights went out, the music ceased;

and, on entering the room, child and nurse were both found fast asleep.

Twice had fate thus cheated her, and she resolved that the Queen must learn of these proceedings. A long tale she poured out, in fear and anger. 'I am not the only one, O Queen, to hear and see things,' she said. 'All your waiting women have witnessed that I have seen. Nay, more; the guard in the hall says that, ever since the strange woman arrived, a swallow comes from her room every night about the middle watch and flies round the big carved pillar in the hall, uttering mournful cries. Once he started to drive the bird away, when he found he could not move, whilst it looked at him with eyes full of sorrow, the eyes, he says, of the stranger.'

'Idle tales,' said the Queen. 'I will prove for myself the folly of your words.'

That night she concealed herself in the sleeping-room of Isis. She felt it ill accorded with her queenly dignity thus to spy upon the woman who was at once her guest and her benefactor; but the story of the nurse had disquieted her, and her mother-love sought to shield her child against all harm. She watched Isis come into the room, bend over and kiss the sleeping child, and then retire to her own couch.

Hour after hour passed by, and nothing happened. The Queen began to think she was more foolish than her attendants in that she had given credence to their stories. It was very uncomfortable, too, cramped up in the narrow closet, with no chance of escape before morning. The wind sighed and moaned, sometimes rising to an angry scream, and distant mutterings foretold a coming storm. Verily it would have been much wiser, thought the Queen, to have gone quietly to bed, instead of listening to old women's tales of witchcraft, and demeaning herself in the eyes of her own household, as well as risking offence to the woman to whom she was so deeply beholden.

Suddenly every nerve in her body tingled with amaze and expectation. All the torches in the room had burst into flame, and, peering out from her hiding-place,

Astarte perceived Isis standing in the middle of the room, the babe cradled on her arm. Her long hair was loose, shrouding herself and child. But what was this? From her fingertips, from every strand of hair, trickled streams of fire; her face was lighted up like the sun at noonday, and her eyes gleamed like stars. The child laughed and cooed and screamed with delight, the flames blazed and crackled while she bathed the naked child in their livid glow; and mingling with the sounds came the rich low voice of Isis, chanting mysterious words in a tongue she did not understand.

For an interval while one might count a hundred, mayhap, the Queen remained spellbound; then with a shriek of utmost fear she sprang forth from her place of concealment. But ere she could take three paces forward the chamber was in darkness, save for the tiny torch that remained alight throughout the night, and Isis stood calmly in the centre of the room, the babe sleeping in her arms.

Aghast at the miraculous change, Astarte could only stare at the stranger woman, whose eyes rested on her, piercing her through and through.

'Who art thou?' she said at length, her voice hoarse with fear.

A flash of lightning illuminated the room, playing for some moments about the nurse's head before passing away and leaving them in a denser gloom.

'Unhappy woman!' said Isis. 'Womanlike, thou didst fear for thy child, and thy love hath lost him immortality. This night I would have purged him from all that is mortal and endowed him as one of the gods. Thy rash interference hath broken the spell, and never now can I make him other than he is. Take him. Immortality cannot be his: old age and death must come to him as to others.'

'Who art thou?' whispered Astarte again.

Flash after flash of brilliant light made the room brighter than day, the long tongues of flame flickering and dancing round the mysterious figure, and adding to the Queen's terrors a thousandfold. But that was not all. As she gazed, head forward, face white, and eyes starting from their sockets in the extremity of fear and dread, a

transformation came over the woman before her. The coruscations of vivid light gathering together descended upon her head in a ball of golden fire, from which issued bright-eyed serpents with darting heads and quivering tongues, like those adorning the Egyptian crown while Isis' flowing hair changed to wings of glistening red and blue and gold. Her face was kindly and gentle as ever, but wrapped now in the calm dignity that belongs to the gods in Aalu.

Chained to the spot, Astarte stared at the awful sight. Next moment, with a terrific crash that shook the palace to its foundations, the storm broke; and, with a shuddering wail of unutterable misery, she clasped the infant to her heart and fled from the room.

The Moving of the Chest

Isis sat in the low window, gazing out over the row of acacias to the line of sand that bordered the sea. The storm of the previous night had long ago spent itself, but away to north and west the clouds were still banked up in dark and threatening masses; in the east the sun gleamed fitfully through the cloud-belt. The grove was strewn with wreckage and drift of the storm, and the bright-hued flowers lay whipped and torn and bedrabbled in mud. But Isis saw none of these. Her thoughts were fixed on greater things, for was not her search to end today? She knew the King would send a messenger to her, and she waited patiently, thinking of the happy days to come.

Melecander was not in good humour. He had returned from his hunting to be annoyed by foolish tales about the new nurse, and in the middle of the night his rest had been disturbed by an urgent message that the Queen was beside herself with fear and called for his presence. When he reached her bedside she could at first only babble incoherently of nurse and lightning, golden wings and shining serpents, goddesses and crowns of fire, and much more that he could in no wise understand;

and only after long questioning did he gather that the nurse who had so successfully tended the young Prince was in the Queen's opinion a goddess, and must be propitiated and then sent on her way.

Now had Melecander been asked to entertain some neighbouring prince he would have done it nobly and enjoyed it too. Crocodile and hippopotamus hunting would provide sport enough during the day, and the richness of his feasts and banquets was known to all. But to get rid of a goddess-guest was a problem with which he had heretofore not met.

But it had to be faced, and, after pacing the chamber for some time, he beat sharply upon the brazen gong. 'Fetch the girl Melita,' he said to the attendant who answered the summons. 'I will see this stranger lady if she will admit me,' he said to himself. 'Haply something will transpire to show me how I should act.' So when Melita came from the Queen's chamber, where she had been through this eventful night, he bade her ask Isis if she would receive him.

Wondering what these unwonted happenings might portend, the maid knocked timidly at the door of Isis' room. In answer to the command from within she entered and, curtseying humbly, advanced to the window-seat.

'The King would know if he can see you,' she said, when at length words came to her.

'Yes,' said Isis quietly. 'Tell the King I will receive him here.'

When the King entered he crossed the room and, taking the outstretched hand, knelt and kissed it. Thus did he pay homage to the goddess who was his guest.

'The Queen is not well,' he began slowly; 'the happenings of the night have tried her sorely. But she begs me thank you for the care you have bestowed upon the Prince our son; and no words can express my own gratitude for the favour you have shown in coming to us. Who you are I know not, but before you depart I pray you say if there be aught in which I can serve you.'

'Melecander,' answered she, touched by the gentle tone and quiet dignity of the King's simple words, 'Melecander, thou knowest much that thou wilt not say. For thine ease I will tell thee that the Queen will soon be well. As for thy son, his name and prowess shall in days to come be noised abroad through all the land of Byblos. For me the hour of my departure is nigh, and, ere I go, I ask a boon of thee.'

'Thy wishes even now are granted,' said the King.

'The pillar that stands in the great hall,' said Isis, 'I ask it of thee.'

Melecander was not prepared for this demand. The pillar had cost him dear, in labour and treasure, to set in place, but not for that did he hesitate. The column was unique, and from far and near men came to admire the curious device that had grown in the bark. His hesitation, however, was but momentary. He had pledged his word, and, had Isis asked for the palace and all within, he would not have refused her.

'It shall be removed at once,' he answered.

'You value it for that which is without,' said Isis. 'I seek it for that which is within. Thus may we both be satisfied.'

All that day artificers were busy taking down the pillar of the tree, and next morning Isis, in the presence of the King and Queen, came into the hall to take possession. But when they would have carried it to the boat which she had asked should be in readiness for her, she bade them stay; and, taking a long knife, she drew it four times down the trunk where it lay. The outer part fell away, and there, in the heart of the tree, lay the most wondrous piece of workmanship that eye had ever beheld. It was the chest of Typhon.

For a moment her emotion overcame her, and the scene swam before her eyes. Conquering her weakness, she took a great length of pure white linen, spread it out, and laid thereon the fragments of bark. Having poured perfumed oil upon them, uttering as she did so strange and mystic words, she turned to the King.

'These sacred relics have enshrined the body of a god,' she said. 'Keep them with all reverence. Thus shall thy treasure be preserved to thee, and whilst thou and thy people do honour to them your land shall have the favour of the gods. Hear and remember.'

Later in the day a solemn procession was formed, and the sacred tree was brought to the great temple of the city. By the King's orders, it was carefully pieced together as it had been in life, and set up above the altar of their god, where it abode for many hundreds of years, an object of reverence and awe for the miracles that it wrought.

Meantime twelve stalwart bearers had raised the metal chest and borne it to the boat. The King and Queen and all the Court had followed to the waterside to attend on the goddess as she bade the land farewell, and a great multitude of the humbler folk had gathered on the shore. The boat was draped in cloth of purple and gold, and the great sail was of black silk. Gently and with utmost reverence the chest was lowered to its place, and when all was ready Isis turned to the Queen, who led the Prince by the hand. Taking him in her arms, she passed her hand over his brow, and then kissed him long and passionately. 'I loved him too,' she said simply, as she gave him back to his mother.

Then she stepped into the boat and stood at the foot of the chest. The sail was run out, the chains were cast off, and, guided by invisible hands, the royal vessel dropped down the stream. The quest of Isis had ended.

THE PERSECUTION BY TYPHON

The Awakening of Osiris

Up the dark stream went the boat, amid the rustling reeds and under overhanging sycamore and lebbek trees, whose arms stretched gaunt and grim above the waters,

Isis standing meantime in the stern, with eyes fixed on the chest before her. The sail's black shadow fell athwart the stream, and the dark pall gleamed dull beneath the heavy clouds. Not a living thing was to be seen; man and beast and bird had left these dreary wastes, and loneliness and death reigned there.

At about the going down of the sun the royal barge came to a reach of the river where the bank sloped away in a long sandy beach. Here for the first time Isis looked up, and, with a touch of her hand, guided the ship into a little creek thickly fringed with high-grown reeds. She stepped out and looked around; nothing here but sand and reeds and water and sky, and a few tall palms looming up a hundred yards away.

Returning to the boat, she examined the chest carefully. The long immersion in the water had rotted the wood and rusted the fastenings. With a sharp tool she quickly dug out some of the wood round the lid, and inserted in the hole the handle of an oar. As she pressed upon it, one after another the fastenings snapped, and the heavy lid swung back.

What had she expected to find within the chest? Did she know the truth? Doubtless she did. But as her eyes fell on the well-loved form and features of Osiris, as perfect and unchanged as when she last parted from him, she could not withhold a deep sigh nor check the tears that coursed down her cheeks: it was the triumph of the woman over the goddess.

For long she gazed upon him, thoughts of the happy days of old filling her mind. Never again could she listen to his loved voice nor walk with him in the cool of the evening when work was done and they were for a while alone together. Never? Perhaps not in the courts of Thebes: but, never! Not yet should that word be said.

Quickly stooping, she raised him tenderly in her arms and bore him to the strand. Next she removed her outer robe, and loosed her flowing hair that covered her with a garment of bright red gold as the rays of the westering sun

fell upon it. Three times she bowed in adoration to the sun-god Ra, and then lay down, with arms outstretched and face toward the west, beside the body of the dead King.

A low song of mourning stirred the evening air. Gently it rose and fell, now swelling out into wildest passion, now dying away in infinite sorrow. There followed utter silence; then the voice of Isis chanting the fateful words of magic that she had learnt in the days of long ago.

As she sang her eyes slowly closed, and once again did peace steal o'er the scene. Not a breath stirred her body, not a feature moved. The whispering in the reeds died away, and the rustling leaves were still. To outward seeming Isis was dead like the King by her side, and nature had died in sympathy.

But what is this? From her side there rises another figure, borne on gossamer wings, that flits above the prostrate forms, and finally comes to rest beside Osiris. Is it the Queen? Surely those are the lineaments of Isis, that her graceful form! But no! The face is that of Isis, transformed with a grandeur and majesty that the earthly form never knew; the body is that of the Queen, etherealized and pure. It is the triumph of the goddess over the woman.

Her eyes bent upon the form on the sand. Such pity, such love filled them as human eyes could never show. A look of power and great resolve crossed the face, and the goddess, rising on her wings, hung above Osiris. The soft hum of her voice, as she uttered the words of enchantment, sounded like the murmur of a far distant sea, the gentle beat of her wings as the sighing of the spirits of night.

Suddenly she looks up. The Sun-god in his boat rests atop of yonder hill, a glorious disc of gold. The supreme moment has come. Now must she put to the test the secret knowledge aforetime gained from Ra. Others has she cured by enchantment, but never has she brought one back to earth from beyond the grave. One mistake now, one error of speech, one fault in sound or tone as the awful enchant-

ment is uttered, and all the pain, the heartache, and the weariness of the past months shall have availed her naught.

But not for an instant does the goddess hesitate. No quiver in the voice, no pallor of the cheek marks the immensity of the issue of the next moment. With hands uplifted, and eyes reflecting in their depths the flaming orb in the west, at the very instant he sinks behind the hill-top to enter the valley of Amentet, she cries aloud the hidden name of Ra, the name that Isis alone of gods and men has learned, the potent name that rules the universe.

And now a miracle happens. The Boat of Millions of Years that has sunk behind the hill appears again on the summit, and in it can be seen the Sun-god Ra himself, standing, his face turned toward the group upon the sand. A livid flame overspreads the heavens and bathes the earth in blood. Then, with a crash like the crash of doom, the Boat and its dread occupant have vanished, and blackness, utter and profound, enwraps the world.

When the stars came out, and the crescent moon cast her silvery beams across the river, the goddess had gone; but two figures gently breathing, side by side upon the strand, told of the victory that love had won over evil.

The Second Murder of Osiris

The next two years were years of great joy to the exiled King and Queen. A little hut of branches and reeds made their home; the river provided wealth of fish and wildfowl for food; and a plot of ground beyond the trees, on which were still a few stalks of corn, was tilled by Osiris to yield a prolific harvest. And when the baby Horus was born, their cup of happiness was full to overflowing.

In the evening they would sit without the hut, Osiris playing on his reed pipe while Isis crooned a lullaby over the babe in her lap; or, again, they would go for long sails on the river, wafted by the evening breeze that breathed of peace. At other

times they talked softly of the future, of the wisdom of making an attack upon Typhon to wrest from him their own, watching the while the boy Horus kicking and rolling on the sand.

Verily it was a happy life, a life of joyful rest. The stress and storm of the years in Thebes was past; yet they sometimes longed to be there again. Not for themselves, oh no! But because they loved the land and its people, who were now groaning under the sway of the usurping tyrant. For by the aid of his Ethiopian allies Typhon had made himself master of the country, and ruled his subjects with a rod of iron, yea, chastised them with whips and scorpions. Hated of all was he, but his grip upon the land was too tight to permit an attempt to throw off his yoke.

Ofttimes did Isis and Osiris speak of these things, their hearts bleeding for the wrongs of their people, and many were the plans they formed for their deliverance. But seldom were these projects to be executed by their own hand; almost invariably they centred round the merry boy playing by the stream. When he had come to man's estate, then would be the hour of vengeance.

So the days slipped on into months and the months into years, and the child grew up lusty and strong and beauteous of form. Sometimes he would take one of the spears that his father had wrought for him, and catch the fish that swam in the river; or he would craftily set up a net to trap the quail and wild duck that frequented the marge. His father taught him, too, young though he was, the use of club and spear; and it was his delight to show his mother how skilfully he could wield them, whirling the club around his head till it seemed a flashing wheel of light, and hurling the spear straight and true to its mark.

But one drop of bitterness lingered in the woman's cup of happiness. Sometimes Osiris would go off on long hunting expeditions, saying it behoved him to find fresh diet. At these times he would be absent for two or three days, and Isis lived in a fever of anxiety until she heard his cheery call across the marsh. Then she would snatch

up the boy in her arms and hurry forth to welcome the wanderer, tears of relief and gladness filling her eyes.

Once he failed to return on the third evening, the longest time he had ever been away. The full moon rose, and Isis walked down to the river and along the bank, but no sign of Osiris could she see. Visions of his dead form rose before her eyes, of an iron-bound chest in which it was sealed, of that terrible night long ago when ruin and desolation stood before her. Distractedly she paced back and forth, praying the livelong night that Osiris might not be taken from her again. Just as day dawned a shout from the trees sent her flying across the waste, to be enfolded next moment in her husband's arms. He had been hunting a gazelle, and had followed it farther than he purposed; yet, knowing how anxious Isis would be, he had hurried back, travelling all night in the bright moonlight. Hereafter Osiris was careful not to be absent for more than one day at a time, and the heart of Isis was gladdened thereby.

But some months later it came to pass that he was away for two days and did not return. The third day likewise passed without him. The long, long night wore away, but no welcome shout greeted the sorrow-stricken wife. Four days, five days, six days dragged by, and no Osiris came. Then Isis knew that never would she see him more. His enemies had taken him again; and for her the sun had ceased to shine.

She sat down in the hut, gazing with unseeing eyes across the waste of sand and water. Hour after hour passed by, and no movement betrayed that the lonely figure was alive. The little Horus came to her, and, after vainly trying to attract her attention, cried himself to sleep in her lap. To worldly things Isis was dead; and she lived only in the past.

The Boat of Millions of Years had almost completed its daily journey when, with a shuddering sigh, Isis awoke. She went down to the creek where the boat in which she had come from Byblos was kept, thinking to see if it was all in good

condition, and with some vague idea of starting out in it to find the lost one. It lay close-hidden amid the reeds, and almost had she stepped into it when she saw that it had an occupant. She moved back with a little cry, that rose next moment to a shriek of terror.

'I startled thee, fair sister,' said the one in the boat; and, as he looked up, he revealed the repulsive features and misshapen body of Typhon.

'I startled thee,' he repeated. 'Believe me, 'twas not my wish to do so, for I was coming to see thee as soon as the boat was ready. I would take thee on a journey.'

Isis stared aghast at him, answering never a word. The deceit and cruelty of this monster rushed to her memory, and now she knew what had befallen her husband.

'Methinks thou art not overjoyed to see me,' said the evil one, when she did not speak. 'In sooth, it is not friendly to greet me thus.'

His mocking words brought Isis to herself. Calmly she walked up to him, looking him straight in the face. 'Thou hast killed him?' she said.

Typhon quailed before that proud glance, but, despite himself, he felt compelled to answer.

'Yea, I killed him,' he replied defiantly, yet full of fear withal.

'Wicked and cruel monster,' said Isis then, 'couldst thou not leave us alone here? When all the country was thine, didst thou begrudge us our happiness in this solitude? Was there still more for which thy malignant heart craved?'

'Yea,' said Typhon, 'it craved for thee. I would marry thee and make thee Queen again. Wilt thou accept the crown I offer?'

'Where is Osiris?' asked Isis, ignoring his words.

'Where thou shalt never find him,' replied the archfiend savagely. 'Not again shalt thou restore the dead to life by spells and enchantments. I surprised him as he hunted, and I slew him; and, to make sure that my end should not again be frustrated, I dismembered him and scattered the parts throughout the length of Egypt. Doth that suffice thee?'

Isis shrank not at the brutal recital, though her soul felt sick within her. Casting upon him a look of contempt, she spoke. 'Coward and traitor,' she said, 'soon shall come the day of reckoning, and in that day shall thy measure be pressed down and running over.' Then turning away, she moved toward the hut.

'Stay,' roared Typhon, laying a detaining hand on her arm. 'Thou shalt not go from me thus. I have offered thee a throne, and thou shalt answer me.'

The eyes of the goddess blazed upon him so furiously that his hand fell to his side. 'Touch me again,' she said, and her voice quivered with anger, 'and thou shalt learn somewhat of the power of Isis. As for thee and thy thrones, I spurn them as the vermin beneath my feet.'

Typhon gnashed his teeth in fury. 'I, too, am a god,' he cried. 'Thy magic arts will not avail with me. Tomorrow, whether it like thee or not, thou shalt go with me, and I will place thee where thou wilt be in safe ward. Mayhap thy proud heart will soften in time,' and he laughed meaningly.

The next day, escorted by half a hundred of his choice companions, they set off up the stream, rowing hard all day until at eventide they came to a grim fortress. Here they disembarked, and Typhon led Isis and her son within the gates, that clanged to after them with a hollow sound. 'The emptiness of the tomb,' thought Isis.

In the hall they were met by an ancient servitor and his wife, to whose charge they were confided. Typhon gave precise commands that they were to be treated with all honour and respect, but on no account to be allowed out of sight, night or day. Then, with a mocking smile to Isis, but never a word, he returned to his friends.

The Escape of Isis

Many days had Isis and Horus been shut up in the prison, and no deliverance came nigh. At first they had been visited daily by Typhon, who sought to obtain his ends by fair promises of freedom and future power; but Isis being deaf to promises and

threats alike, even these visits ceased. Albeit she was thus relieved of this source of annoyance, her heart greatly misgave her; for she knew her persecutor had not abandoned his designs; his absence but betokened that he was plotting more wickedness against her.

Many a time and oft did she call on Ra to send her help, but her prayers remained unanswered. Her only visitor was the janitor who brought her food, or his wife who occasionally would come to see whether her services were needed. Her gentle disposition and kindness won their hearts, and, had it lain in their power, her keepers would readily have connived at her escape. But, had they dared, they could do nothing; for Typhon, or Set, as he was called here, had magic power too, and had enchanted them and the prison so that they knew not the way in or out.

One evening as Isis was playing with her child before the hour of sleep, a tall, grave-faced stranger suddenly appeared before her. Thinking it was one of her enemy's minions, she caught the boy and, pushing him behind her, confronted the intruder.

'Who art thou,' she said haughtily, 'and what seekest thou here?'

'Be not alarmed, Isis,' said the stranger; 'I come to aid thee, not to harm. Had I come as I am wont to appear in heaven, thou wouldst have known me. I am Thoth, sent hither by Ra to help thee escape from the hand of the tyrant and to aid in the restoration of Osiris.'

Now Thoth was the wisest of all the gods; he held the keys of knowledge, and against him none might prevail. So Isis was content.

At the mention of her husband's name she would have poured out a flood of questions, but the god held up a protesting hand.

'This is no time for speech,' he said. 'If thou wouldst save thy life and the life of Osiris's son, prepare to follow me. Yet for thy soul's peace I will add that the day shall come when thou shalt find the body of Osiris, who, restored to life, shall rule over a kingdom greater than thou hast ever dreamed of.'

This, as you already know, came to pass, for Osiris became judge of the realms of the dead; but Isis, understanding not the hidden meaning of the words, heard the god with amaze, not thinking of what kingdom greater than Egypt he spoke. Yet she was gladdened and comforted at the knowledge vouchsafed her, for would she not one day meet her lord and husband and with him be happy? She picked up her babe, therefore, and followed Thoth.

Along many a winding way they went, past doors and gates that opened at the god's potent touch, down darksome passages that shone with a mystic light as they threaded them, until at last they emerged on the open plain.

'Here I leave you,' said Thoth. 'I commit you both to the care of my servants and the servants of the mighty Ra. Follow them until thou comest to a certain city far away to the south that they will tell thee of, and there abide. Fare ye well.' And before Isis could thank him Thoth had vanished, and the two were alone.

Where were the servants he had spoken of? She looked around, but none was in sight. Perhaps they would be long in coming, and meantime Typhon's menials

might discover her escape. Should she stay where she was or hide in the papyrus until the men of Ra arrived?

'When the lady Isis is ready we will set forth,' said a voice which seemed to come from under her feet.

Isis looked down, and there perceived an enormous scorpion, then another, and another, and another, until she had counted seven. Were these the servants of Thoth? Another woman would have sprung away in terror from the deadly creatures, but Isis knew that God uses the most unlikely means as his instruments.

'Why are ye gathered here?' she said.

'I am Tefen,' said the biggest of the scorpions.

'I come to follow the lady Isis and her son Horus, and to protect them from harm.'

'I am Befen,' said the one next him, 'and go with my brother Tefen to watch from behind.'

'I am Mestet,' said a third, 'and will walk on the right hand of the lady Isis.'

'I am Mestetef,' said the fourth, 'and will keep watch and ward on her left.'

'We are Petet, Thetet, and Maatet,' cried the other three, 'and are sent by Ra to lead the lady Isis to the city of the south.'

'It is well,' said Isis, when they had all spoken. 'Let your faces be turned to the ground that ye may show me the way.'

Thus did they fare forth. For many days Isis journeyed, the sun beating fiercely down upon her, and the sand glaring until her eyes ached. Always she was oppressed, too, with the thought that Typhon would discover her flight and set out in pursuit. She would have urged her guides to hasten, impatient at the delays occasioned by the needful stops for rest; but they, directed by the divine power, never varied their pace. They knew that all was under Ra's direction and must be well.

At length they reached a city called Teb, and the scorpions informed Isis that here for the present she must abide.

The Restoration of the Fen-Woman's Child

On arriving at Teb, Isis went to the house of the women of the overlord of that district, and asked for shelter. The chief woman, however, was angry with her because of the scorpions that were her companions, and not only refused her admittance, but forbade any of the other women to take her in. Isis was thus compelled to seek other refuge, and returned to the road that led past the marsh, where she sat down to rest.

As she leaned wearily against the trunk of a tree, a woman of the fens came by.

'You look tired, lady,' said she; for, like everyone else, she easily recognised the superiority of the exiled Queen. 'My house is poor, and I have little to offer; but such as it is I freely give it to you. Come with me. I will carry the boy.' And without waiting for a reply she picked up the child and walked toward a reed-made hut on the edge of the marsh.

There she quickly set before Isis a bowl of milk, some bread, and fruit, and while the goddess ate, the fen-woman fed Horus from another dish of milk.

By skilful questioning she discovered the treatment that Isis had received at the hands of the overlord's wife. 'Verily she is a hard woman,' said she, 'cold and selfish. She thinks only of her own, and will help none if she can avoid it. May Ra be more merciful to her!'

When it came to the ears of the overlord's wife that this woman had befriended the traveller whom she had driven out, she came down in great wrath to the hut by the marsh.

'How darest thou show favour to one whom I have frowned upon?' she cried. 'Were my lord here I would have thee whipped for thy temerity.'

'The lady was weary,' said the poor woman humbly. 'I did but give her to eat and drink and offer her my house wherein to rest a space. Could I do less?'

'Couldst thou do less!' cried the other in a fury. 'Thou darest ask me if thou couldst do less! Did not I refuse her admittance because of her evil companions, and

wouldst thou censure me by showing her kindness? Leave this house at once. If thou art here when my lord the governor returns on the morrow, thou shalt be flogged and put in irons.'

As soon as she had gone the fen-woman burst into tears. 'All I have ever loved is bound up with this house,' she sobbed; 'and now must I leave it. Ah, she is a cruel, cruel woman!'

'Is her husband also cruel?' asked Isis.

'No,' replied the woman, 'but he fears her bitter tongue and does what she commands him to do; and, would he listen to my prayers, she will not let him.'

'Weep no more,' said Isis. 'Thou knowest not who I am, but I can help thee, and thou shalt not leave thy home.'

Meanwhile the scorpions, which had marked the insult offered to their charge, held converse together as to how they might best avenge it. At length they all came to Tefen, and emptied the poison of their tails upon his tail, and thus, charged with a sevenfold measure of poison, he entered under the door of the overlord's house. Once inside, he crawled along beneath the matting that covered the floor until he came to the cot wherein lay the woman's infant son, and stung him.

The child's cries speedily brought his mother and a host of servants to see what was amiss, but he was beyond all human help. The poison, sevenfold strong, was too deadly for any remedies they knew, and in a brief space he was no more. To add to the disaster, one of the women in her excitement overturned a live brazier, and, the dry rushes catching fire, the house was soon ablaze.

While the men-servants were labouring to overcome the flames, the distraught mother went about the city uttering cries of lamentation. But none came to her call; her selfishness and hardness of heart had estranged the people from her, and in her grief she was alone. Yet there was one who felt for her. The stranger whom she had turned from her door had a son, and her mother's heart was filled with compassion

for the stricken woman and for the child that had suffered through no fault of his own. As the woman passed by she called to her.

'Come to me,' she said, 'for my speech hath in it the power to protect, and it possesseth life. I can drive out the evil from thy son by one of my utterances which my father taught me. If thou wilt, bring him hither and I will heal the boy.'

At first the woman was loth to accept a favour from one whom she had so shamefully treated, and went on her way. But as none other could help her, she was at length fain to test the power of the despised stranger. So she brought the child and laid him down before her.

Then Isis placed her hands upon the dead child and spoke. 'O poison of Tefen,' she cried, 'come forth, and appear on the ground; come not in, approach not! O poison of Befen, come forth! For I am Isis the goddess, and I am she of words of power, and I know how to work with words of power, and most mighty are my words. O all ye reptiles which sting, hearken unto me, and fall down on the ground! O poison of Mestet, come not hither! O poison of Mestetef, rise not up! O poison of Petet and Thetet, enter not here! O poison of Maatet, fall down!'

Then followed the magical words that she had learned from Thoth, and that no one knew save her alone. And the shadows lengthened, and the wind fell to a gentle whisper in the reeds, and yet the child stirred not. As the sun-disk touched the distant hilltops Isis arose, and stretching out her arms she cried, 'The child liveth and the poison dieth! The sun liveth and all evil dieth!'

The waiting women looked down, and, true enough, the boy was gently breathing. 'Take him,' said Isis, as she turned into the hut. At the selfsame hour the men at the house overcame the flames and saved it from utter destruction, the gods having accepted the prayers of Isis on the woman's behalf.

In the dark of the night there came a gentle knock at the door of the hut, and, when the fen-woman opened it, the overlord's wife walked in. Going straight up to

Isis she sat down at her feet. 'This morn I closed my door upon you,' she said, very humbly. 'I feared your scorpions, and I was angered that you brought them where my child was, so I turned you away. I have been punished, and I come to crave your pardon for my harshness. Will you forgive me?'

'I have naught to forgive thee,' was the reply. 'Thou didst act as thou deemedst best, and 'twas love for thy boy and not ill-will that prompted thee. Strive to be more thoughtful and generous hereafter, and know that love and gentleness avail more than bitterness and malice.'

'Is there aught in which I can help you now,' asked the other; 'aught to atone for my unkindness?'

'There is one thing,' said Isis. 'This woman who liveth here thou hast threatened to drive from her home, the home to which her heart is given. Take back thy hasty words, and, further, as a token of thy sincerity, give the house to her as a possession so long as she shall live. Tomorrow proclaim abroad the gift that all may know of thy goodness and bounty.'

At first the overlord's wife was taken aback with the boldness of the request. She had been willing and even anxious to make amends to one so powerful as the stranger who had restored her son to life; but to show favour to the fen-woman, to eat her words of the morning, was more than she had counted upon. Yet, she reflected, none but themselves would be the wiser; they had been alone when she had uttered her menaces earlier in the day, and she thought she saw a way to keep the woman's tongue silent.

'If she will forget what happened this morning,' she said, 'and keep silence on what I spoke in my haste, I on my part will think no ill of her, but feel grateful to her for having befriended you. And tomorrow what you ask shall be done, and this house given to her and hers for ever.'

'So be it,' replied Isis. 'The fen-woman shall remember thy words no more, but shall always speak well of thee.'

With this assurance the ruler's wife returned to her house, while the woman of the fens fell on her knees and poured out a flood of thanks to the lady of mysteries.

The Death of Horus

After these things it came to pass that Isis resolved to depart from Teb; the tale of her doings was noised abroad in the land, and mayhap she thought that news of her presence among them would come to the ears of Set. So she called the scorpions, and when they were all assembled she said, 'Turn your faces down to the ground, and find me straightway a road to the swamps and to the hidden places in Khebet.' Whereupon the scorpions turned their faces to the north and the Delta, and again the procession set out.

The land of Khebet of which Isis spoke was an enchanted isle that floated on the Nile's broad bosom, near to the town of Busiris. He who knew the secret could make this island move away from its foundations and float about the stream at will. But the secret was known to few, only Isis and her sister Nephthys, and another their friend who lived on the island, being aware of its magic properties and how to use them.

Thither, then, Isis went. The way was long and arduous, but, guided by her faithful allies, she pressed on till she came to the land of Am. There the people hailed her as a goddess, and, yielding to their entreaties, she promised to dwell awhile among them. Being near to Khebet, and needing no longer the friendly services of the scorpions, she thanked them and gave them leave to depart.

Now followed a life of restful happiness. No cruel enemy to harass her, no haunting fear that her baby boy might be snatched away by her grim foe; for him she had protected by spells and magic words culled from ancient lore, and now he was safe from Set and all his minions. The roses of life again began to bloom, and in watching her son grow up toward manhood she somewhat forgot the sorrows of the past.

Daily she went out to win food and raiment for herself and child, whom she left meanwhile with kind friends. They would fain have supplied all her needs from their own store, and felt honoured in the acceptance of their gifts; but Isis would have none of such.

She would not be a burden to them; and, moreover, by going about among the people she could better glean news of her enemy.

What joy it was to come home in the cool of the day and find Horus running down the dusty path to meet her! How she laughed to see his childish efforts to use the spear and club and bow, and called him her new Osiris, her avenger! And with what a wealth of mother-love she hugged him to her heart when alone at night, and crooned her lullabies over his slumbering form! He was her all. For him and the work he had to do she lived and moved and had her being.

But with all her care she had neglected one thing, and suddenly the roses withered beneath the icy touch of death, and earth was bare and void. One evening when she came home Horus failed to run to meet her as was his wont, and, struck with a sudden chill foreboding, she hurried forward to the house. There, stretched out on the floor, his body swollen and shapeless, his face livid, and his limbs all tense and rigid, the curly-headed boy lay – dead. She had protected him against Set and all men, but she had overlooked the most dangerous reptile in the land; and in her absence he had been stung by a scorpion, and was now no more.

Resenting the silent reproof she had expressed at their conduct by healing the child of the woman of Teb, one of the scorpions lent her by Thoth had gone to Typhon and told him where the fugitives lay hid. But the evil one could not touch them now; the charms of Isis proved too strong for him. Wherefore he took the scorpion and by sorcery fortified its poison against the power of Isis, and bade it then return to Am and sting the boy, knowing that by his death he would hurt the mother most.

The dwellers in the swamps came round about her, and the fen-men drew near, and they seated themselves on the ground and wept at the greatness of her misery. Yet no one opened his mouth to speak to her; words would have seemed sacrilege at such a time, and they sat around in silent sorrow. The women, too, assembled and mourned with her; and one of them, the wife of a great ruler of the district, and a wise woman withal, sought to heal Horus of his wound; but he remained motionless and stirred not. Loudly Isis lamented, bitter tears she shed. But all was unavailing; tears and lamentations could not restore life to her boy.

As she sat on the ground, rocking to and fro in the bitterness of grief, her sister Nephthys passed by. With her was the scorpion goddess, Serqet.

'What aileth thee?' asked Nephthys. 'Wherefore this show of grief?'

'Alas!' cried Isis. 'My boy is dead. My beautiful Horus is taken from me.' And her tears broke forth afresh.

'Dead!' exclaimed Nephthys. 'Dead! Of what hath he died?' Her voice shook with distress and tears sprang to her eyes, for the merry boy had endeared himself to her.

'This evening,' said Isis brokenly, 'when I came home, lo! he lay on the floor, dead, stung by a scorpion under the spell of Set; and now mine only treasure is taken from me.'

Nephthys turned to Serqet. 'Here is work for thee,' she said briefly.

'Nay, 'tis too late for my power to avail aught,' answered the goddess. 'Had Isis invoked my aid before, I could have stayed the scorpion from touching her son. But 'tis not mine to rule o'er life and death. That power belongs to Ra the Mighty.'

''Tis even so,' replied Nephthys. Then, turning to her sister, she said, 'Isis, call on almighty Ra, our father. Beseech him to hear thee, and to restore life to thy son.'

So at dawn, as Ra came forth from the vale of Amentet and entered the Boat of Millions of Years, the prayer of Isis rose up through the morning mists to heaven.

With words broken by tears and sobs she begged the Maker of all Things to listen to her cry of woe. By Typhon's cruelty her beloved Osiris had been foully slain; she had been driven out of home, a wanderer on the earth; and now she had been robbed of her only child. 'Give him back to me, O Ra,' she cried. 'Thou who holdest the keys of death and life, hearken to my prayer, and let not my son, mine only son, be reft from me.'

Thus did she give words to her grief; and as the sorrowing company gazed with awestruck faces up to heaven, a miracle was revealed to them. The prayer of Isis reached the ears of Ra, and the boat was stopped. Thoth, the god of knowledge, descended to earth, and once again he stood before the exiled Queen.

'Ra, the Mighty One, life, strength, and health to him! hath heard thy prayer, O Isis,' he said. 'Hearken to his words. Thou goddess, thou who hast knowledge how to use thy mouth, behold, no evil shall come upon the child Horus, for his protection cometh from the boat of Ra. I have come this day in the Boat of the Disk from the place where it was yesterday. When the night cometh the light shall drive it away in the healing of Horus for the sake of his mother Isis."'

At first Isis had been too astonished to speak, and now, without a word, she led the god to the couch whereon lay the body of her son. Pointing silently to the huddled form, the tears coursing down her cheeks the while, she whispered, 'Is it not too late? Yet no, thou hast power over all things and thy word is the word of life. Heal him, I beseech thee.'

'Fear not, Isis,' said Thoth, 'and weep not, O Nephthys; for I have come from heaven to save the child for his mother.'

The god bent over the body of Horus, and quickly spoke the magical words of power; when lo, what a transformation! The rigid limbs relaxed, the formless body waxed round and firm, a ruddy tint spread over cheek and face, and there – yea, it could not be mistaken – a smile played on the dimpling lips.

'Thy boy is thine again,' said Thoth, turning to Isis. 'Take him, and give thanks to Ra, the Mighty One, that he hath heard thy prayer; and know that he is ever mindful of the righteous.'

With a cry of rapture Isis sprang to the couch and clasped the boy to her heart. For the moment the world was forgotten in her intense joy; then, remembering, she turned to thank him who had brought the answer to her prayer. But Thoth had gone, and even now the Boat of Millions of Years was speeding on its way.

The Second Resurrection of Osiris

The time had come when Isis must begin anew the search for the body of Osiris, but ere she started out it behoved her to find some safe refuge for her son. He was proof against all hurt from man or beast or creeping thing; but any of Typhon's creatures, should they find him, might seize and carry him off, bringing further sorrow upon her. She went therefore to her sister Nephthys, and asked counsel of her.

'In sooth,' said Nephthys, 'what better home couldst thou find than with Ahura on the floating isle? Besides ourselves, she is the only one who knoweth its secret. 'Tis unlikely that Horus's life will be endangered again, but, should such a mischance occur, he will be safer there than elsewhere, for at a word he can be borne far away from it.'

'True,' replied Isis. 'Set is so wickedly cunning that I know not whether he may one day find out some countercharm to my enchantments. On the island my boy will be safe.'

So next morning the two sisters sailed down the river to Busiris. Against the farther bank they saw the enchanted isle, and bespoke the boatman to cross over thither, but this he stoutly refused to do.

'That island is not of earth,' he said in answer to their remonstrances. 'There live the spirits of the dead. No man can touch its shores and return alive. Anything else ye ask of me will I gladly do, but that I cannot, dare not do.'

'As thou wilt. Put us ashore here,' said Nephthys; and, having rewarded the man for his labour, she dismissed him.

''Tis so much the better,' she said, when he had departed. 'If that be the tale told in this neighbourhood, it is unlikely that the whereabouts of Horus will ever become known to Set.'

'Even so,' Isis answered. 'Call, I prithee, on the woman of the isle.'

Nephthys rounded her hand, and through it her clear voice rang out across the water. 'Ahura! Ahura!' she called.

'Who calleth for Ahura?' cried a woman, descending to the water's edge.

'One born of heaven and earth, whom thou knowest. Come quickly,' was the reply.

Soon the island could be seen approaching the shore whereon they stood, and in a brief space the two women and the child could step upon it. The woman who had spoken to them was very old, but her face was pleasant to look upon, for it was ever wreathed in smiles.

She fell down in silent adoration before her visitors, but Isis, stepping forward, raised her. 'I see thou knowest me,' she said. 'But I am not come for worship. Hearken carefully to my words, for on thy scrupulous obedience hangeth more than thou wottest of.'

Briefly she explained the purpose of her visit, giving many injunctions for the safe keeping of Horus; and then, bidding her son a tearful farewell, she moved away to the shore.

'Remember,' she said, looking across the pretty wooded island, with its grove of trees and bubbling spring. 'Remember, and guard him well from all scathe and ill.'

'I will remember,' replied the woman. 'No harm can touch him here. Behold!' And the island quickly receded from the bank until it stood in mid-stream.

One last look and Isis turned her back upon the island; and so began her second search.

First she made a boat of reeds, light and strong, which she covered well within and without with pitch. The reeds were of papyrus, and that is why the Egyptians said that a crocodile would not touch anyone in a boat made of this plant, for, in honour of the goddess, all papyrus things were sacred. When the boat was quite finished, she launched it and sailed downstream.

Difficult as the other quest had been, it was nothing compared to this. The baleful Typhon had dismembered the body of his brother, and had buried the fourteen pieces into which he had cut it up in different parts of Egypt. By this he hoped that it would be impossible to find them all and so to restore the body of Osiris a second time to life. What wonder if Isis felt nigh to despair, knowing neither where nor how to begin!

At every town she passed through she inquired of the people for any sign or token that might lead to the discovery of some limb or member, and wherever such was found, she erected a beautiful temple over the spot and placed therein a golden image of the god. The limb was carefully wrapped in linen cloth woven by herself and Nephthys, and Nephthys' son, Anubis, embalmed it so skilfully that it never decayed nor changed. Often, however, long weeks and endless months dragged slowly by with no success, and at such times the heart of Isis grew heavy within her.

One eventide the boat drew in to shore near a large town called Abydos. The sun was setting in a sea of crimson and gold; the sandy hills, brown and bare by day, were bathed in its warm glow, that swiftly changed to blue and purple; the grey river gave back the vivid colours of the sky in red and scarlet, yellow and orange, blue and purple, and a score of delicate tints; the glaring white of the houses and temples on the bank was toned down to a quiet grey; even the ugly outline of the mud huts was softened, sharing in the witchery of the hour. For as the Sun-god sinks to rest he leaves his blessing on the land, transforming the monotony that pains the eye and crushes the mind into a picture of most gorgeous hues.

The calm of the scene stole in on Isis' troubled soul, and lulled it to rest. Her eyes lost the far-away look that was wont to dwell in them, and began to wander idly along the strip of sand beside the river. A shaft of light struck full upon a gilded dome and was reflected, a radiant bar of purple flame, across the palm trees to the beach. There it ended in a ball of living fire, from which shot out rays of such dazzling brightness that the two women had to shade their eyes to look.

Suddenly Isis stood up in the prow, staring hard at the fiery ball; then she sprang to the helm and ran the boat on the beach. Leaping out, she hurried forward, and a moment later threw herself upon the sand.

Quickly the sunset light faded away, and darkness stole over the earth; but the wonderful thing on the sand glowed on. It seemed alive, and, now the sun had gone, to be the fount of light itself. But these things Isis heeded not, for there had she found the head of her lord Osiris.

In gratitude for its recovery, Isis built a magnificent temple in Abydos, on the site of the building whence had been reflected the ray of light that had guided her to the treasure. To this temple, which became one of the most famous throughout Egypt, she presented two granite statues of Osiris and herself; and on the highest pinnacle, so situate that it should catch the first rays of the rising sun and his last rays as he sank to rest, was placed an image of the god in purest gold.

What need to follow the goddess in all her wanderings? Day followed day, and one week succeeded another, as failure and disappointment became more frequent. But never again did despair loom dark and frowning. The finding of Osiris's head had filled her with a faith in her ultimate success that could not die, and resolutely she pursued her quest.

At last the long and trying search was ended, the separate limbs had been assembled, and the dismembered body of her husband lay in the boat. With her faithful sister in attendance, Isis returned to the Delta and the papyrus swamps,

where she reverently laid the body on the sands beside the river, and repeated over it the magical words taught her by Thoth. The wondrous scene that once before had hallowed the dreary reaches of the Nile was re-enacted in all its awful solemnity; and, in virtue of her power as a goddess, to which was added a woman's love, Osiris was again made whole.

THE WORK OF HORUS

THE PREPARATION OF HORUS

It was many years later. The little boy who had been left on the floating island had grown a tall man, of mighty frame and giant strength. None could hurl the spear so true to the mark as he, none draw the bow with such unerring aim; in wrestling-bouts he was more than a match for acknowledged champions, and at quarterstaff he beat all adversaries from the field; his skill in swimming and diving was beyond compare, and his fleetness of foot had become a proverb. Fearless, manly, and just was he withal, and gifted with his father's power of winning all men's hearts to him. Such was the youth Horus, son of Isis and Osiris.

As yet the Prince knew nothing of his high destiny. He had been brought up a humble peasant, and it was chiefly among the peasants that his days at first were passed. But he soon attracted the notice of the elders of the town, and the wise ones were not slow to recognize that in the noble and kingly-looking youth, who had come so mysteriously into their midst, was someone higher than of peasant blood, one superior to themselves; and ere long Horus became a welcome guest to each and all, were he governor or peasant. Every door was open to him; every house cried forth a greeting.

Now when all these things had been accomplished, Osiris deemed it wise to tell his son of the mission that lay before him; so one evening, after the day's work was done, he called the lad to him.

'Didst see the soldiers that passed this way today?' asked Osiris.

'Yea, my father,' replied Horus. ''Tis said there is war in the lands of the south, and they are going to help the King's troops.'

'It will be many days before they reach the capital,' said his father, 'for they must walk all the way. If thou wert a soldier, what animal wouldst thou think most serviceable to thee?'

'A horse,' promptly answered the boy.

'Why?' queried Osiris. 'Why dost thou consider a horse more serviceable than, say, a trained lion?'

'Because,' answered Horus, 'though a lion is more useful to a man that needs help, the horse is better for overtaking and cutting off an enemy. And that is what the true soldier should be doing rather than seeking help,' he concluded.

The father smiled, and looked with pride at his noble and fearless son. 'And what is the most glorious deed a man can do?' he asked, after a pause.

'To avenge the injuries done to his father and mother,' straightway replied the youth.

For a while the elder spoke not, and his eyes, full of fond affection, seemed to read his son's heart. 'Sit down beside me,' he said at length. 'I have somewhat to say to thee.'

Then Osiris told his son the story of his life in Thebes, and his work among the people, whereby he had gained their love and reverence; of the coming of Typhon and the shameless monster's deceit and treachery; of his cruel murder and the usurpation of his throne. As he went on to describe the wanderings and sufferings of Isis, her first success and his second murder and mutilation by Typhon, and the

tyrant's indignities and cruelty to her afterwards, the face of Horus grew black with anger; his eyes blazed, his hands clenched, and his whole frame trembled with the wrath that seethed within him. But never a word did he speak. In silence he listened to his father's story, drinking in every word until he had grasped the full measure of the usurping tyrant's crimes.

'And now,' said Osiris in conclusion, 'the time draweth nigh when the reckoning must be paid. I cannot stay with thee. The gods call me home. To thee, my son, mine only son, is entrusted the work of avenging the wrongs of thy father and the indignities of thy mother. But I know that our honour will be restored. From my new home I shall watch over thee and thy coming struggle, well aware that I do not watch in vain. Thou wilt go forth to war, in the knowledge that thou art fighting for right and truth, and, keeping that aim always before thee, thou must win.'

The two men stood up and looked each other in the eyes. Then the younger dropped on his knee, and, taking his father's hand, he bowed his head and kissed it

'I will win, my father,' he said.

THE DAY OF RECKONING

The barge of silken sails sped swiftly up the stream, this time not draped in black as when it bore the body of Osiris, but in dazzling white; and the three who sat silent beneath the thick canopy at the helm watched the passing banks with unseeing eyes. What thoughts were theirs on this last voyage together! Sweet memories of happy hours spent in this quiet solitude, darkened ever and anon as the sinister figure of their arch-enemy crossed the mind; but that grim spectre was quickly put aside, and when they spoke 'twas only to recall some glad remembrance of the days now past.

Quickly the boat sailed on. There lies Buto, a great city even in those early days; now over in the east can be espied the temple pinnacles of that which grew to be the mighty city On; then on the opposite bank a few mud huts, the site of future Memphis,

unaware of its high destiny. At none of these do they pause; and not until the golden statue of Osiris, that crowns the temple at Abydos and casts back the rays of Ra in streams of living fire, comes into view, does Horus, at a word from his father, turn the helm to the western bank. Here, before a deep cleft in the hills, the boat is made fast, the little party step ashore, and Osiris breaks the stillness with these words.

'The hour hath come to bid you both farewell,' he said. 'Would I might have tarried to complete the work I began, and purge this land of evil. But it hath been willed otherwise and I must go. To thee, my son, I bequeath all godly power, and here invest thee with the title 'Son of Ra,' in whose might shalt thou prevail over all thine enemies. Go forth, then, and do that thou hast to do, strong in the knowledge that Ra will always be with thee. And I, too, shall watch to protect thee from peril. Fare thee well, my son. My noble boy, farewell.'

His eyes dimmed with tears, Horus looked up into his father's face. 'Farewell, O my father,' he said. 'Verily I will live worthy of the name and honour thou hast given me.'

Then Osiris and Isis moved toward the hills. 'And to thee, O my wife,' he said, 'to thee who hast been so brave and unselfish and true must I also bid farewell. But never for a moment do I forget thee, and I await the hour when thou shalt join me again.'

'Must it be so, my beloved?' said Isis brokenly. 'Have I always to find thee only to suffer the pangs of parting? Can I not come with thee whither thou art going?'

'Not yet,' replied Osiris. 'It may not be. The gods have ordained that I join them now; but for thee there is still work to do here. Yet 'tis only for a season, and then shall I return for thee, and there shall be no more partings and no more tears.'

''Tis hard,' moaned the woman. ''Tis hard to lose thee again, my husband. But the will of heaven be done.'

'Farewell, my loved one,' said Osiris softly. ''Tis not for long. But lo! The Sun-god waiteth for me, and I must go. Again, farewell.' And with a last embrace they parted.

As he neared the cleft in the hills the Boat of Millions of Years sank lower and lower until it filled the gap, and when Osiris reached it a figure stood up and raised him into the boat. A moment later the watchers by the river saw him near the helm, and beside him stood the Sun-god himself. Stretching forth his hand Osiris spoke. 'My blessing is with you,' he said, 'and my care shall be to watch over you always. And Ra biddeth me send his blessing too.'

Then a deep, rich voice spoke through the evening air, the words swelling like the music of a mighty organ into endless waves of mellow sound. 'To those who have been faithful unto the end, even unto death, shall be given a crown of everlasting life and happiness. Ye weep now, but joy cometh in the morning, and glad shall be the awakening. Trust ye and fear not.' And as the Sun-god ceased, the Boat of Millions of Years glided on into the night.

After Osiris had left them, Isis and Horus sailed on for many days, pausing not until they came to a land far to the south.

Now it happened that Ra, in virtue of his omnipresence, had taken upon himself the shape of man, and had come to rule this land on behalf of his son. At that time Typhon was in the Delta, the papyrus swamps of which formed a home more to his taste than the drier plains of the south. Moreover, the inhabitants of that part, groaning under his yoke, and longing for the restoration of Osiris's rule, were only awaiting an opportunity to break out into open revolt; so for the nonce the monster had to leave the southern lands to their own devices.

But in the country yet beyond, called Nubia, there lived a race of savage barbarians who preferred the lawless rule of Typhon to the orderly government of Ra, and these set his authority at naught. Thereupon Ra entered their territories, quelled the uprising, and captured and slew the rebel chiefs. Then he returned to Edfu, whither Horus had come, and requested him to go and complete the work of conquest.

Horus had not forgotten the heavenly powers bestowed upon him by his father, and forthwith flew up to heaven in the form of a winged disk of the sun. From his lofty station he espied his father's enemies again massing together, wherefore he descended and fell upon them with such fury as to rob them of their senses; and they, panic-stricken, attacked and slew one another. Horus then returned to the boat of Ra, who proposed that they should journey on the water to the scene of battle.

It must be remembered that in those days there were giants in the land, who often possessed miraculous powers. When Ra and Horus went down to the river, certain of their enemies, noting their movements, changed themselves into crocodiles and hippopotami and entered the water. Crocodiles, as you know, are more at home in water than on land, and hippopotami nearly so. In this guise, therefore, they hoped to take the two gods at a disadvantage.

The weapons of the dwellers in the Nile valley, like those of most primitive people, were at first sharp flints, such as can be seen in any museum today; but Horus had discovered the use of iron, and had armed his followers with spears and arrows tipped with this metal. Nor was it long ere the weapons proved their superiority and worth.

When the army of Horus perceived the enemy in the water, they went eagerly forward to the attack. In addition to his spear each man had a long iron chain. The spears they hurled at the beasts, and those they hit and maimed were afterwards bound with the chains and brought to shore, where they were slain. But some of the enemy had escaped and fled to the north, and Horus followed in hot pursuit. Several minor conflicts took place, in which the rebels were routed with much loss, but it was not till they had reached the town of Dendera that another pitched battle was fought. Here, after waiting a whole day and night, Horus perceived his foes approaching, and, falling upon them, routed them with great slaughter.

Then followed a long chase, the foe ever fleeing toward the north before the

relentless god. When they reached the Delta, they hurried to the palace of Typhon and offered to fight under his banner. The tyrant, angered by the open flouting of his authority in the south, had already prepared to march thither, and to crush these troublesome people once for all. But the advent of the fugitives from Horus changed his plans. Here was his old enemy, reborn in the son, come into the very heart of his own dominion. First, therefore, would he meet the usurper and blot out his race from off the face of the earth.

Now the spies of Horus had brought him word of the mighty force awaiting him, and he sent swift messengers throughout the land, bidding those who adhered to the house of Osiris to gather round his standard without delay. Meanwhile he went to see his mother Isis, who was at that time on the floating island near Busiris.

'The hour is come,' said Horus, after they had warmly greeted each other. 'Typhon awaiteth me, and the trial must anon be made. Of the success of our cause I have no fear; but, lest I fall in the fight, I come to say farewell.'

The mother took her son in her arms. How tall he was, how strong, how fearless! And how noble in all his thoughts! He was truly his father born again, and her mind flew back to the days when she and Osiris were young together.

'I will come with thee, child,' she said suddenly. 'Fear not for me. I shall be safe; and I would see the end of mine enemy.'

So the two set out for the field where the issue was to be decided. Loud shouts of welcome greeted the return of the leader; then the warriors, seeing who was with him, bowed to the ground in silent adoration. Nor would they rise until Isis had given them her blessing for the coming fight.

Early next morning the forces of Typhon came in sight, and without delay Horus began the attack. So sudden and terrific was the shock that many of the tyrant's forces fled in dismay; but he, by dint of words and blows, urged the rest into the press of battle, which now raged furiously on all sides.

Fierce and terrible was the conflict. Now victory inclined to this side, now to that; at one moment it seemed that Horus had won the day, then the towering figure of the evil one rushed forward with tenfold fury, and, by the wondrous might of his arm, drove the enemy before him. For two long days the fight was waged, and yet the issue lay in doubt. The third day dawned, and as the sky blushed rosy red beneath the Sun-god's gaze, the opposing forces were locked together in a last deadly struggle.

All day long the battle lasted and the sunset flame had already begun to tip the distant hills, when Horus came face to face with Typhon.

'At last, thou murderer,' he said. 'Now is come the day of reckoning, and the score shall be paid in full.'

'At last, thou son of my hate,' roared Typhon. 'Now will I slay thee, and utterly destroy thee and thine.'

Their spears met. Fiercer and fiercer the weapons clashed, and gradually the two armies ceased their strife to watch the terrible duel. Breathless they stood, with eyes only for the giant forms fighting in their midst. This way and that the rivals reeled under the shower of blows they rained on each other. Now Horus is down, and mingled cries of exultation and dismay burst from the watching hosts. But instantly he springs to his feet, with resolution undiminished. Back and forth they sway, to right and to left, the vantage with neither. But his lusty youth and greater nimbleness are beginning to tell in Horus's favour, and Typhon is showing signs of weariness.

The Sun-god in his boat is fast nearing Manu, and soon will have entered the dark vale of the Tuat. His rays are flashed back from the glinting spear-points, his crimson sea dyes all the field in blood. Now he rests on the mountain-peak, and looks down on the close of that Titanic struggle. At this moment the long spear of Horus is hurled forward. Swifter than the lightning flash it goes, and catches Typhon off his guard. Through shield and corselet it cleaves its way, piercing him to the heart; and with a groan that shakes the earth the giant falls, as a cry of frenzied joy bursts from the followers of Horus. Calmly the youth steps forward, and, drawing forth his spear, looks down on the evil face at his feet. But the lips speak not, nor the features change; for Typhon is dead, and will trouble the land no more.

THE RIDDLE OF THE SPHINX

Rising out of the sand in front of the Pyramids is a great human head carved in stone. The features have been much damaged, chiefly by the Mameluke rulers of Egypt, who wantonly used it as a target for their weapons; but, in spite of this and the ravages of time, the face still gazes forward across the rolling flood and sandy wastes as it has gazed for untold centuries. Calm and impassive it is, a smile that seems sometimes of scorn, sometimes of pity, playing round the lips, a look of infinite wisdom in the never-closing eyes. To countless thousands in ages long gone by it was an object of devotion and worship; to one and all of the innumerable multitudes that have since looked upon it, it has been an object of admiration and wonder, to most, of awe.

What is this figure, and when and how came it there? It is the Sphinx, an image representing the god Horus, of whom you have already read something; but when it was carved no man can certainly tell. Some say that when the Pyramids were young, the Sphinx was old; that long, long before those mighty tombs were built, the mysterious smile and the human eyes had inspired reverent homage in the hearts of beholders: nor has it to-day lost aught of its mystical witchery.

But what it is and why it was made, wise men have learnt something. What is seen on approaching is a colossal head standing seemingly on the sand, but careful search

has shown that this is not so. The whole figure is in the likeness of a man-headed lion, lying down with paws outstretched before it, and all hewn from the solid rock. The body of this monstrous creature is 150 feet in length, the paws 50 feet, the head 30 feet, and the height from the paws to the crown of the head about 70 feet. The face was erstwhile painted red, and on the head reposed a crown embellished with the sacred uraeus, the symbol of divinity and immortality. Only traces of these now remain, but sufficient to prove that they added to the majesty of the god.

Often the Sphinx has been covered over by the ever-shifting sands of the desert on the edge of which it stands. Even in the days of the building of the third pyramid it had become almost entirely buried. In later times yet less care was taken to keep it clear, and gradually it was overwhelmed in the sea of sand.

A curious story is told of a king of Egypt and the Sphinx which you may like to hear.

Thothmes was a prince of the royal house, but not the direct heir to the throne. He was thus not concerned with affairs of state, and often went out on long expeditions for hunting and pleasure. In his chariot he drove two horses that were fleeter than the wind, and he was wont to set out with but two attendants, no man knowing whither he had gone.

On one of these hunting-trips he was separated from his friends, and, growing weary from his wanderings and the heat of the day, he lay down in the shadow of the Sphinx and fell asleep. In his sleep the god Horus-Ra appeared to him.

'Thothmes,' called the god.

The Prince looked up in some surprise, and at first did not recognize his visitor; but as soon as he did so he hastened to make obeisance to him.

'Thothmes,' said Horus again. 'The throne of Egypt is not thine inheritance, yet, because thou hast faithfully observed the laws of Ra and ever been duteous to the gods, thou hast found favour in their eyes and shalt be raised to kingly power.'

Thothmes bowed to the ground. 'One thing thou hast not done,' continued Horus. 'My image lieth buried in the sand, and none of all thy royal house hath thought fit to free it, though in the time of thy fathers it was reverenced by king and people alike. Now the sand whereon it hath its being hath closed it in on every side, and none honoureth me enough to make it clear as of yore. Say unto me that thou wilt do this thing, and I shall know that thou art verily my son and he that worshippeth me.'

'The wishes of my lord are the commands of his servant Thothmes,' said the Prince.

'Be it so,' answered the god. 'Draw nigh unto me, and I will be with thee, and I will guide thee.' With these words Thothmes woke up.

As the god had spoken, so it came to pass; Thothmes succeeded to the throne and ruled wisely and justly over Egypt. He was as good as his word, too, and had the image of Horus cleared of the sand that submerged it, and commanded that homage should be paid to it as in the days of old. Moreover, between the mighty paws he built a small temple, in which were recorded the circumstances that had led to its construction.

Another temple, much larger and considerably earlier than this, lies a few yards to the south-east of the image. For this reason it is usually called the Temple of the Sphinx, although it is of later date than that figure, and is probably connected with the building of the Pyramids. Its walls and columns are of alabaster and red granite, much of which is beautifully polished and most carefully wrought. This was also covered with sand, and only in the last century was it found again and the sand removed.

But beautiful as is the temple, stupendous as are the Pyramids, wonderful in their magnitude and perfection as are all the monuments of ancient Egypt, there is none that possesses the strange fascination, the mysterious enchantment of the quiet face that for unnumbered centuries has watched the eastern horizon to greet the first faint rays of the rising sun, and whose inscrutable smile has given birth to the expression, 'The Riddle of the Sphinx.'

THE LADY OF THE OBELISKS

Behind the Hall of Columns at Karnak is another part of the same vast temple, the part that formed a centre round which the rest of the numerous courts and temples were built. This small hall holds little of attraction in itself; but at the farther end stand two giant pillars, in a way more wondrous than the columns in the great Hall of Rameses.

These two pillars are called Obelisks. They were not the first, nor are they the only ones of their kind, but they are the grandest and the most famous that ever were set up. One of them has fallen, shaken by an earthquake, but the other still tapers skyward as proudly as when it was first erected. Its height is almost one hundred feet, and, like its companion, it is a monolith, that is, a single stone, 'and has in it,' says the ruler who put it there, 'neither join nor division.' The tops of both were once covered with gold, but that was stolen long ago.

Just think of it. A single stone of solid granite, one hundred feet in height, polished smooth and crowned with gold, 'towering up among the pillars of this venerable hall,' as the ancient record says, so that 'they should pierce the sky.' Where did they come from and how were they put up? This story will tell you.

In the days of old, long even before Rameses was King, a Princess was born in the royal house of Thebes. There was nothing very remarkable in that; many

princesses had been born before, but this one was different from all the rest. Indeed, it was said that her birth was miraculous, and that when it took place, Amen, the chief of the gods, called all the other gods around him and asked each one to give her a blessing. 'In her,' he said, 'I will unite in peace the two lands of Egypt, and I will give her all lands for her dominion. Bless her, therefore, and make her rich and prosperous.'

The gods, of course, did what Amen desired, and when the Princess was born she was gifted with all the virtues that woman could possess.

When she was about twelve years old, Hatshepset—for that was the Princess's name—was taken into the temple to undergo a ceremony of purification at the hands of the gods; and, the rites having been duly performed, they each renewed the promises they had made at her birth, and added others too. 'We bestow life and peace upon Hatshepset,' they said to Amen. 'She is thy daughter, and she is adorned with all thy qualities. Thou hast given unto her thy soul and thy words of power and thy great crown. Whatsoever is covered by the sky and surrounded by the sea thou makest to be her possessions.'

With these and many other blessings did Hatshepset start out in life, and it was not long before she began to show her power. Her father took her on a journey in which they traversed Egypt from one end to the other, receiving homage and admiration from all the people. Nor were they unmindful of the temples, and in many cities they carried out long-needed repairs and made additions to the places of worship. In several of the shrines they thus visited the promises of great glory to come to the Princess were repeated by the gods, who also foretold what she would do when she came to reign.

On their return to Thebes the King resolved to make his daughter co-regent with him, that is, she should rule with him and be in all matters of government even as the King's majesty. This was not to the liking of the people, for they had never

had a woman to rule over them, and they were fearful lest she should prove too weak to maintain the glory and prowess of their country. But the King turned a deaf ear to all objections, pointed out her divine origin, and commanded a large tent to be prepared where the coronation of his daughter should take place.

On the appointed day there were forgathered all the nobles and chief men of the empire, and ambassadors from many foreign countries, to do honour to the Princess; while the common people were like to swarms of bees for multitude. Loud cheers, mingled with deep-throated shouts of welcome, burst from them as the chariots of the bidden guests dashed by, cries that grew to a mighty roar when the royal coach drove past. For, though they resented the idea of a woman ruling over them, they truly loved and revered the Princess.

When the monarch and his daughter had passed through the lines of assembled nobles and princes, they mounted the dais at the end of the tent and sat down in the chairs of ivory and gold. First were read the wonted speeches of welcome to the foreign envoys and their replies, and as soon as these were finished the King arose and ascended to the royal throne. Seating himself, he spoke.

'Hereby,' he said, 'I set my daughter Hatshepset in my place and seat her upon my throne, and from this time henceforward she shall sit on the holy throne with steps. She shall give her commands unto all the dwellers in the palace, and she shall be your leader, and ye shall hearken unto her words and obey her commands.' Then, standing up and looking defiantly around, he continued, 'Whosoever shall ascribe praise unto her shall live, but he who speaketh evil against her Majesty shall surely die.'

At the words the trumpets blared, and the heralds made the proclamation to the people without. Within the tent the nobles, on hearing the sovereign's words, cast themselves on the ground and swore fealty and homage to the King and his daughter, acknowledging her as their ruler, and then rose up and danced for joy, whereat the heart of the King was exceeding glad.

After the death of the King, Hatshepset during some years ruled alone, and although she married a prince who was looked upon as the sovereign, and who took to himself the credit of whatsoever was done, Hatshepset was the real ruler of Egypt. She used her power and ability wisely and well, and the people her subjects had no cause to complain that a woman and not a man held sway.

It was at this time that Hatshepset conceived the idea of setting up the two great obelisks in the temple, for a memorial to her father and to the glory of Amen. Her architect, Sen-mut, one of the cleverest men of his craft, was called, and, having received directions from the Queen upon the nature of the modal, he sent armies of workmen to the quarries near Assuan to prepare it.

The huge stones were cut and shaped in the quarries, then moved on rollers to the river, where they were embarked on rafts and floated down to Thebes. Albeit they are so large and must have involved enormous labour, only seven months elapsed from the beginning of the work to the erection of the monoliths in the temple. There they stood, as they stood throughout long centuries, a monument not only to the glory of Amen but also to the skill and craftsmanship of these early workers in stone.

'They shall be seen from untold distances,' said Hatshepset in her decree; 'and they shall flood the land with their rays of light, and the sun shall rise up between them in the morning, even as he riseth from the horizon of heaven. I, as I sat in my palace, remembered the god who made me, and my heart was moved to make for him two obelisks with copper and gold upon them, which should tower up among the pillars in this hall. This have I done that my name should abide permanently in this temple, and endure there for ever and ever.' And her wish was gratified.

To the glory of Hatshepset there is yet another memorial to be recorded. This is a temple, said to be the most artistic of all these relics of the past. When she had been Queen for many years, she resolved to construct a burial-place

worthy of her dignity and majesty, and bade Sen-mut prepare designs such as no king had ever known.

The result of his labours was the temple of Der-el-Bahari, a building about 800 feet in length, and consisting of three terraces, one above the other, built into the hillside itself. The upper one consisted of a series of burial-chambers; the middle one was a large hall extending deep into the hill, and formed the shrine of the god to whose glory the temple was built; while the third and lowest portion consisted of another series of rooms set apart for the service of the priests and for other duties connected with the temple worship.

The walls of this building are adorned with sculptures of the various journeys of Hatshepset through her kingdom, and of the expeditions made by her soldiers to distant lands. One of the most interesting of these was the voyage to a land called Punt, which is believed to have been the country whence came the gold and silver and precious stones that adorned the Temple of King Solomon in Jerusalem. The series of pictures tells very vividly the story of the Egyptian travellers, their reception by the King and Queen of Punt, the honours paid them, and the treasures of gold and silver, ivory and feathers and skins, precious woods and spices and incense that they brought back.

In this temple, after a long and happy reign, the great Hatshepset, 'Child of Amen,' was laid to rest; and if her temple was dishonoured by her successor, and in time became forgotten, this very forgetfulness preserved her remains from the desecration often shown to her more famous brethren, and left her undisturbed in her neglected tomb until long centuries had rolled away.

THE JOURNEY OF KHENSU TO BEKHTEN

In the days of long ago there was a king of Egypt so powerful that he conquered all the neighbouring countries and even extended his rule far into Asia. Every year he sent his ministers to bring home the taxes collected by the governors of each district, and these were used both to enrich his treasuries and to improve his army for further warfare. One year he resolved that, instead of sending the usual official, he would go himself to gather the tribute. Perhaps he thought he was being cheated; perhaps he wished to find out where next he could best pursue his conquests. Whatever his motive was, he had no sooner made up his mind than he sent for the Lord High Chamberlain, and bade him make preparations for the journey.

That worthy official put forward every objection he could think of against the proposal; for he was growing old, and it suited him much better to live at ease in the royal palace than to undertake a long and arduous journey. There were rumours of a rising among the people of the Delta, he said. 'We leave our army to keep order,' replied the King. One of the great religious festivals was at hand, said the Chamberlain. 'The priests will perform the necessary sacrifices,' answered the monarch. 'Thou will be away many months,' finally objected the official. 'Is it wise to leave the kingdom so long O King?' 'We shall be all the more appreciated

when we come back,' smiled his Majesty. A few days afterward the royal progress began.

As the Chamberlain had foretold, the journey took many months; but it was not quite so unpleasant as he had pictured. Everywhere the people flocked to the route they followed, to see the royal procession pass by. The gleaming armour of the soldiers and the gold and silver trappings of their steeds truly made a brave show, and the pomp and glitter of the Court attracted the humble rustics from far and wide.

At last they reached a large city, whither the chiefs of all the conquered tribes had been bidden to come, for there his Majesty, son of the Sun, would deign to meet them in person. To the brilliance which ever surrounded the personage of the King was added a note of quaint picturesqueness, as one chieftain after another took up his station about the royal tent. Fierce-looking warriors from the mountains of Armenia, clad in garments of fur; tall nomads from the deserts of Kheta, garbed in loose cloaks of red, blue, green, and yellow; grave and dignified elders from the east and from the west, with flowing robes of finest linen, mixed together in strange confusion. Men who at another time would gladly have flown at one another's throats shook hands in solemn friendship. For was not the King himself come in his might to see them!

On the day of audience the chieftains were assembled in the great tent of the King, and one by one came forward to lay their tribute at the foot of the throne. In addition to the annual sum demanded, they brought beautiful presents of gold and silver work, cunningly wrought carvings set with rubies, turquoise, and lapis-lazuli, and sweet-smelling incense, myrrh, and sandalwood.

When the King of Bekhten came to the throne, he had little to lay there except the usual tribute, and for a moment a cloud loomed on the great monarch's brow. But it speedily passed away, for this king was a faithful ally and had rendered him signal service in the past.

'We welcome thee to our presence, O Prince of Bekhten,' he said, 'and we would fain see thee at our Court. Why hast thou never come?'

'Your servant thanks you for your kindness,' said the chieftain, 'but he is old. Such a journey is not for him. Yet if you will accept a substitute, O King, there is one of your servant's house now here who is more fitting to accompany you.'

'Let us see him,' answered the King.

Thereupon the King of Bekhten made a sign to an attendant, who left the tent. In a few minutes he returned, leading by the hand a woman, closely veiled.

'If my lord will accept this representative,' said the chief, bringing the woman to the seat of the King, 'I pray you do me so much honour. She can wait upon the Queen, if my lord so wills. And she is considered somewhat beautiful,' he concluded naively, as he drew back the veil from her face.

The King of Egypt started from his seat. Never had he seen such loveliness before. Of regal carriage and bearing, fair-skinned, blue-eyed, rosy-cheeked, with long black hair, she was very different from the duskier beauties of his own land.

'By the might of Amen,' cried the monarch, 'she shall be no waiting-maid. She shall be my Queen, and, by token of my troth, I take her now beside me in the presence of you all.'

Descending to the woman he led her to the throne, seated her on it, and stood beside her. The simple grace of the action touched the imagination of the wild chieftains, and a great burst of cheering rent the air.

The festivities had now to be prolonged in honour of the King's marriage. When seven days had passed the procession set out for the land of Egypt, and in due time reached Thebes.

For many years affairs took their usual course, and the King and Queen were very happy together. One day the Chamberlain entered the royal presence and announced that an embassy from the lord of Bekhten craved audience of his Majesty.

'Let them enter,' said the King readily.

'Who art thou, and why comest thou to our Court?' he asked of the leader, not unkindly, when the embassy had been ushered in.

'Your slave is the son of your servant ruling in Bekhten,' answered the young man, 'and I come here to crave a boon of our father.'

'Say on,' replied the monarch.

'Long have we known of the might of Egypt, and of the wisdom of its learned men,' said the Prince. 'Since the day when my lord honoured our humble house by raising a daughter to sit by his side we have learned much more. Now another daughter, the sister of her who shareth my lord's throne, lieth grievously ill, and all

the skill of our land availeth not to cure her. Your servant, my father, therefore requesteth that a wise man of Egypt be sent that she may be made whole.'

'We grieve to hear of our sister's affliction,' answered the King. 'We will see what can be done.'

Straightway all the wisest men in Thebes, the doctors, physicians, and magicians, were assembled in the great hall of the palace. After much discussion they chose one of their number, named Tehuti, a man famed throughout the land for wisdom and learning, to accompany the Prince; and the embassy returned at once to Bekhten.

Three more years had sped their course, when one day the Chamberlain entered the King's presence to say that Tehuti had returned, and with him the Prince of the land. Without delay they were brought to the royal chamber.

'How fareth our sister of Bekhten?' inquired the monarch, after the usual salutations had passed. 'We hope you bring a good report of her.'

'It is because we are unable to speak well of her that we have hastened our return,' replied the Prince. 'The wise man whom you, O King, sent with us, saith that she is possessed of an evil spirit, against which the power of a god alone can prevail. Your servant, my father, craveth that you will send, therefore, one of the gods of the land of Egypt, of whose might he hath heard much; and perhaps the deity will have mercy on the daughter of your servant.'

The King of Egypt was discomfited to hear of the continued illness of the Princess, for he knew that his Queen grieved exceedingly for her sister, and he was anxious to make her happy. At this season he was celebrating a great religious festival; so he went into the temple, and, standing before the image of the Moon-god, prayed to him. This god not only ruled the month, but had power over all evil spirits in earth and air and sea ; and as it was these which attacked man and brought upon him disease, sickness, madness, and even death itself, the King invoked the aid of the god on behalf of the Princess of Bekhten.

'O my fair lord,' he said, 'once again do I come into thy presence to ask thy aid. Our sister of Bekhten lieth ill, and none can cure her. Allow therefore, I beseech thee, the god Khensu to go to Bekhten that he may heal her. Grant that thy saving grace may go with his divine Majesty, and deliver the Princess from the power of the demon.'

As the King ceased his prayer the image of the god nodded twice, and he knew that the god gave his approval to the request. Indeed, the Moon-god later bade the image of Khensu to be brought before him, and, laying his hands upon it, he bestowed upon the statue a fourfold portion of his power and spirit.

The return journey to Bekhten was a far more magnificent progress than it had been before. A great escort of soldiers and many priests and followers accompanied the Prince, for it behoved them to show due honour to the god. At last, after seventeen months, they arrived at the capital. The whole army of Bekhten was drawn up on the plain outside the city, and the King himself, with all his nobles and chiefs, came forward to do homage to the god. Khensu requested that he might be brought without delay into the presence of the Princess, and the statue was placed within the sick chamber. Then the priests went out from before him, and the handmaidens of the Princess likewise left the room.

When they went back after two or three hours they found the Princess sleeping peacefully. A faint colour tinged her cheeks, and her lips curved in a gentle smile; so they knew that the evil spirit had departed from her. So speedy was her recovery that in a few days she was restored to perfect health.

'If this god is so powerful,' said the lord of Bekhten to his chief counsellors, 'he could help us against our mortal enemies too. Let us keep him here instead of sending him back to Egypt.'

At this proposal there was great dissension among the courtiers. Some were in favour of it, others strongly against it. 'You have received a great blessing from the Majesty of Egypt,' said they to the King, 'and now you would rob him of that which

is his. Would you bring down upon us not only the wrath of the god himself, but also the might of the land of Egypt?'

Nevertheless the King's wishes triumphed, and the god Khensu actually tarried in Bekhten three years, four months, and five days. One morning, however, when the priests went into his shrine they found him not, and forthwith they reported his disappearance to the King.

The monarch was now greatly afraid, and messengers were dispatched in every direction to trace the statue. But it soon became evident that no mortal hand had been guilty of its removal. Several men told how in the early morning, just as the sun rose, they had seen a great hawk of gold fly up from the top of the temple, and, after rising high in the air and hovering for a few minutes above the city, its mighty wings gleaming so that they could scarce bear to look on it, the bird had turned away toward the south.

'It was the god Khensu,' said his priests. 'He wearied of staying in Bekhten and would return to his own temple in Thebes.'

Then the King called before him the priests who had accompanied the god when he came from Egypt, and declared to them that he had always been desirous to return the statue, but no fitting occasion had presented itself. 'Moreover,' he added, 'we sought to send with him such gifts as would show our gratitude for the favour he hath done us, and these have not yet been gathered. But bring the chariot of the god,' he commanded, turning to his chief minister; 'we will at least send those offerings that it lieth in our power to make.'

So the chariot was brought and loaded with gifts and offerings of gold and silver and precious stones. Nor did the wise old King forget to reward with great riches all the priests and nobles who had come in the train of the god.

When they reached Thebes they found that Khensu had already taken up his abode in the temple, so the treasures were carried from the chariot and laid before him. But the god, knowing that his recent power was only a gift of the Moon-god, caused the offerings to be removed to his shrine, where they long remained.

IN THE DAYS OF FAMINE

The life of Egypt depends on the great river that flows through its midst. Every year it brings down with it a mighty flood of water that formerly spread over the land, changing the low-lying districts into broad lakes. As the flood diminished the waters receded until again they were confined within the channel of the river, and, through the rich deposit of mud that covered the earth upon which the flood waters had lain, there sprang up wheat and maize and plants of every kind. But should the flood fail or be small in amount, want and suffering were the lot of the people.

The Nile flood issued from the island of Elephantine, in the far south, whereon stood the first city that ever was built. Thence, too, rose the Sun-god when he went forth to give life to man and beast and plant. In the centre of the island was a large, gloomy cavern, and here the tumultuous waters were held back by the god Khnemu. At the proper moment Khnemu drew back the bolts and threw open the doors, and the pent-up waters surged forth to fill the country with their bounty.

Now it chanced that once Khnemu was wroth with the people of Egypt, and refused to allow the Nile flood to perform its beneficent work. For seven years the waters failed, and the Egyptians were reduced to terrible plight. In his extremity the king, Zosiri by name, wrote to his viceroy Mater, who ruled the island and all the lands adjoining thereto, asking for information and help.

'By reason of the reports which are daily brought to us as we sit upon our throne in the royal palace,' wrote Zosiri, 'we are filled with sorrow, and our heart is stricken with grief for the calamities of our people. For seven years the god of Nile hath hidden his face from us; for seven years his waters have brought no life to the land. The corn from the storehouses is nigh exhausted, fruit and vegetables cannot be found, no green thing liveth on the earth, and the people starve for lack of food. So great is their need that men are robbing one another, and violence and outrage are rife. Children cry of hunger in the streets, the young men can scarce walk because of their weakness, and the old men, crushed to the earth, lay themselves down to die.

'Now we have remembered that on a like occasion in the days of our fathers, the son of Ptah, god of the South Wall, delivered the land from the enemy. But the son of Ptah is no more, and cannot come to our aid. Tell us therefore, O Mater, whence come the Nile and his waters, and who are the gods that watch over them.'

'Methinks,' said Mater to himself, on reading the letter, 'that I shall do best to go to the King. Thus can I tell him what he desireth to know, and peradventure find some profit to myself in the event.' And without more ado the governor of Elephantine and all the territories of the south set about his journey, and in due course arrived at Thebes.

The King was overjoyed to see him, and, in his anxiety to learn all about the Nile-god, almost forgot to wait until Mater had performed the customary obeisance. He gave him a seat beside the royal throne, bade him put himself at ease, and anon plunged into the subject he had so much at heart.

'Who is the god, Mater,' he asked, 'that ruleth the Nile, and why hath the flood failed us for so long?'

'The god of the flood,' replied the governor, 'is Klmumu, and he holdeth the water in check in the island of Elephantine.'

'Where and how lieth this island?' asked Zosiri; for, although he ruled over it, he knew no more of it than its name.

'Elephantine is a beautiful isle in the midst of the stream,' said Mater. 'Above it lie the lofty rocks that form the outer breastwork of the great South Wall, and from the midst of which come the waters of the Nile; but the flood is concealed in a cavern in the island. The lands round about are not so rich as those of Thebes, yet they bring forth corn and wine and oil sufficient for the people's needs. On a knoll in the middle of the isle is a temple to Khnemu, but it hath fallen into disrepair; for it hath pleased the kings thy fathers to take away from him the lands that yielded him a revenue.' Here the viceroy made a significant pause.

'What then dost thou counsel?' asked the King.

'The Ruler of the North and South knoweth what is best,' answered Mater uncompromisingly; 'but it might be well if my lord the King appealed to the god Khnemu in his own temple within this city.'

'Thy words are the words of wisdom,' said Zosiri; and that self-same day he went into the temple and, after offering sacrifices to the god, knelt before him in his shrine. As he prayed Khnemu appeared unto him, and, raising his hand aloft, he spoke.

'I am Khnemu the Creator,' he said, 'My hands rest upon thee to protect thee. I gave thee life. I am the guide and protector of all men. I am the god of the Nile who riseth in his flood to give health and life to those who toil. Behold, I am the father of all men, and the possessor of all the earth. Yet do men neglect me, and in their foolish pride do harden their hearts and call not upon my name, nor hold my holy fane in worship anymore. Now inasmuch as thou hast come to me and besought my help, the waters shall rise as of old, and riches and wealth shall come upon the land of Egypt.'

It was even as the god had said, and that year the Nile rose as it was wont to do in the days of yore. King Zosiri remembered that the god had complained that his shrine had been left to fall into ruin, though stone lay nigh in abundance; and, in his gratitude, he gave command that it should be repaired without delay.

'To the great god Khnemu,' he decreed, 'we yield the sovereignty of all the land for two days' journey round about Elephantine. Henceforth tithes of all the produce of the earth, of corn, wine, oil, animals, birds, and fish, shall be delivered to the temple of the god. All precious stones, metals, and woods sent thence to other lands shall likewise pay dues for the maintenance of his shrine.'

'And what reward hath my lord for his faithful servant?' asked Mater on the morn of his departure, as he slipped the roll of papyrus containing the decree into the folds of his gown.

'To our beloved servant Mater,' said the King, 'we entrust the collection and application of those tithes and dues; and we give him our assurance that, so long as Khnemu withholdeth his anger from us, so long shall he be free from our royal displeasure, whatsoever his enemies may urge against him.'

THE TREASURE-CHAMBER OF RHAMPSINITUS

Usually the kings of Egypt were as lavish in their bounties and as reckless in their extravagance as they were eager to gather treasure, be it in peace or war. They accumulated great riches, and distributed and spent them freely, a practice that contributed in no small degree to their popularity with their subjects. More than one king, on the complaint of some injustice from a poor subject, bade his ministers recompense the man from his own private treasury. But now and again a Pharaoh came to the throne who loved money above all other things, and played the part of miser in a position where every opportunity was offered for the amassing of wealth.

Rhampsinitus was a king of early Egypt. He had waged several wars against neighbouring tribes, and returned on each occasion rich in captives and treasure. His captives he put to ransom or sold as slaves, thereby increasing the wealth the wars had given him. This instead of spending he carefully put away. The spirit of greed was upon him, and his one ambition was to add to the pile of riches that was already greater than any king had hitherto possessed. But with the spirit of greed there always comes close on its heels another evil spirit, named Fear, which never allows the one possessed a moment's rest: he lives in hourly dread lest his heart's delight should be taken from him.

Now, albeit Rhampsinitus was a king, this evil spirit spared him not, and he grew afraid that the treasure he had so diligently amassed might be stolen and lost. Thereupon he sent for his architect and told him to construct a chamber such that it would be impossible for anyone to enter therein without his knowledge. A room was built adjoining one of the walls of the palace, and the stones were so cleverly hewn and so well cemented together that the most crafty robber would never have been able to effect an entrance. The architect, you see, was a very skilful man, so skilful, indeed, that the King himself knew not how cunning a brain he had. For he had guessed the purpose of this chamber, and had arranged one of the stones in such wise that it could easily be moved. By pressing upon a secret spot the stone swung noiselessly back as on a hinge, disclosing a cavity large enough to admit a man's body. But when the stone was closed, so well-wrought was it and so truly laid withal, that had a man looked never so closely he would not have remarked any difference in that part of the wall from the rest.

In this chamber, then, the wealth of the King was stored. Chests filled with gold and silver, urns stocked with gems, and richly wrought baskets of wondrous workmanship were heaped one upon another; and hither came Rhampsinitus almost every day to gloat upon their beauty and abundance.

It is easy to understand that the architect who built the room had designs upon the treasure; but, either from fear of being found out or from more honourable motives, he never made use of the secret entrance. Suddenly he was taken ill, and calling his two sons, Hophra and Sen-nu, to his bedside, he told them of what he had done, saying that it was for their sakes he had made this entrance, that they might never want. He then told them exactly the position and dimensions of the revolving stone, bidding them at the same time tell no man what they knew. Having thus made provision for his children, he soon afterward died.

King Rhampsinitus sat with head bowed in thought. Three mornings before he had gone to the treasure-chamber and found one of the boxes almost emptied of its coin; yet the seals upon the door were intact. That morning he had paid another visit, to find that an urn, containing great store of gems, had been de-spoiled of its treasure; yet were the seals unbroken, and the guard placed at the door swore that no one had come thither during the night. Clearly there was treachery at work, and Rhampsinitus knew not how to cope with it.

Sorely perplexed, he struck sharply on the gong by his side. 'Tell the Lord Chamberlain to come hither,' he said to the Ethiopian who answered the summons.

The Chamberlain had barely roused him from his slumbers, for he was not wont to receive a royal summons at this hour without due notice. Fearing that it boded no good for him, he hurried into his robes, revolving in his mind all his doings of the past week in the effort to find a cause for such unusual proceedings. But the suddenness of the order, coupled with the effects of the previous evening's festivities, only confused his mind the more; and, with a sigh of resignation, he ceased to think about it, and entered the royal presence with as dignified and virtuous an air as he could assume.

'Ha, Ra-men-ka,' said the King, 'thou seemest somewhat ruffled this morning. Methinks thou keepest too late hours while the Prince of Nubia honoureth us with his visit.'

'The cares of state, O King,' said the Chamberlain, 'are very exacting, and ofttimes detain me far into the night. There are many arrangements to be made for the pleasure and comfort of my lord's guests.'

'Yea, indeed,' replied the King drily. 'Howbeit, 'twas not for that I sent for thee. Dost thou know that thieves have twice been into my treasure-chamber?'

The question came so abruptly that Ra-men-ka was more discomfited than before, and for the moment was rendered speechless with surprise. 'Impossible, my lord,' he faltered at last.

'Ra-men-ka,' said the King gravely, 'presume not to say I speak that which is untrue. I have said that thieves have entered my treasure-chamber, and I add that they have stolen an urnful of most valuable jewels.'

'Imposs—' began the Chamberlain, when the glitter in the King's eye checked him. 'Certainly, my lord,' he corrected himself quickly.

'Certainly!' thundered Rhampsinitus. 'Certainly! What meanest thou, sirrah? What dost thou know about it to speak so certainly?'

'Nothing, my lord,' stammered the Chamberlain.

'I was merely approving of what you said, O King.'

'Approving, wert thou?' said the King shortly. 'Then approve no more of what I say.'

'O King, I will not,' said Ra-men-ka meekly.

'Wilt thou not, in sooth?' replied Rhampsinitus, glaring at him. But he did not pursue the subject.

'Now hearken to me,' said the King. 'These thieves are no common robbers, for they have extracted the jewels and left no trace behind of their presence. The seals I put upon the door are untouched, and the guard hath seen no one. We must set a trap for them.'

'Yes, sire,' answered the Chamberlain. 'I will have a small trap made such that it may not be noticed, and when the thief putteth his hand within the jar it will seize and hold him fast.'

'Didst ever hear of the fox that was caught in a trap by the tail?' said the King.

'No, sire,' replied the other.

'Once a fox was caught in a trap by the tail. He knew that unless he could get loose he would be killed when the hunter made his rounds next morning, so, although he sorely regretted the loss of his beautiful brush, he deliberately bit off his own tail and set himself free. The rest of the story is of no moment here, but dost not think thy thief would be like the fox?'

'But I propose to catch him by the hand,' replied the astonished Chamberlain.

'Ra-men-ka,' said the King, 'henceforth must I insist that thou keep better hours, or the cares of state will prove too much for thy health. Dost thou know if the dungeon under the west court of the palace is in as unwholesome state as ever?'

'Seeing that no one hath been in it for several years, it is probably much worse,' answered the Chamberlain.

'Ha!' said the monarch. 'Well, thou must devise a trap such that when the thief cometh and toucheth an urn, it will catch him forthwith and hold him fast – arms, legs, and body. And hearken! Whether thou succeed or not, I am thinking of giving that dungeon an occupant.' And, musing over this dark saying, the Chamberlain was dismissed.

The two brothers, Hophra and Sen-nu, were planning a third excursion to the royal palace. Riches easily obtained soon disappear, and they were not long in squandering their stolen wealth.

''Twill be dark tonight,' said Hophra; 'we will fetch a little more from the treasury.' And accordingly about midnight they set out.

Carefully they searched for the stone, pressed upon the secret spring, and, while Sen-nu remained on watch without, Hophra entered the treasure-chamber. But scarcely had he put his hand into one of the jars, when arms and legs and body were pinioned as in a vice, and he could not move a pace from where he stood.

'Brother,' he called softly.

'Here am I,' whispered Sen-nu. 'What wouldst thou?'

'Come hither quickly,' replied Hophra. When his brother had crawled in, pulling the stone almost to after him, 'Behold,' said Hophra, 'I am caught in a trap, and I cannot get free. Canst thou aid me?'

Sen-nu struggled stoutly with the bands of brass that gripped his brother fast, but all to no avail. He tugged and pulled and threw his weight on the fetters, but they never yielded, and at length he stared at Hophra in despair.

'Now in truth am I caught,' said Hophra. 'But 'tis not needful that both suffer. When the guards enter the room on the morrow, they will easily guess that two men were here, and if they find me they will know thou wert the other. Take then thy knife, and cut off my head and carry it home. Thus shall no one know who I am.'

Despite Sen-nu's remonstrances, Hophra insisted on this being done, pointing out that if they were both taken and put to death, their widowed mother would be deprived of her support, and this argument decided Sen-nu to carry out his brother's wish. Then he crept from the room, fitted the stone in its place, and went home, taking his brother's head with him.

When the King entered the chamber at dawn, the first thing that met his gaze was a headless man bound in the trap; yet, search as he would, he could find neither exit nor entrance to the chamber.

'This is passing strange,' he said to the Chamberlain, who accompanied him. 'But 'tis clear this robber had an ally whom we must catch. Let the body be taken and hung without the palace wall. Set a guard over it, with orders to seize anyone weeping or lamenting near it, and bring him to me.'

In giving this command the King made manifest his wisdom; for, as you have read, to attain a future life it was imperative that a corpse should be buried with all due rites and ceremonies, and the monarch expected some one either to claim the body or at least to come and mourn over it.

When the mother learnt of the shameful exposure of her firstborn, she wept bitterly and reproached her surviving son with cowardice. 'Bring me my son's body,' she cried, 'or, by the gods of my fathers, I will go to the King and tell him all that thou hast done.'

'How can I bring the body?' said Sen-nu. ''Tis guarded night and day, and anyone approaching it is closely watched. And didst thou tell the King, what would that avail? Thou wouldst lose two sons then instead of one.' But she refused to be comforted, and at length Sen-nu, yielding to her prayers, promised to fare forth to see what might be done.

Taking half a dozen asses, he loaded them with skins of wine and, as evening drew on, drove them along the streets toward the royal palace. When he came to the place where were the guards, he drew two or three of the skins toward him, and covertly untied the necks. The wine ran freely out, and he began to beat his head and breast, lamenting on the ill-luck that had befallen him; and the soldiers, seeing the mischance, picked up any vessel that was near, and, hurrying to the spot, caught as much of the wine as they could and eagerly drank it.

'Scoundrels, thieves, robbers,' cried Sen-nu in pretended rage, 'would ye seek to profit by my misfortune? May ye perish, all of you! Leave the wine alone, I say, leave it alone, or, by Amen, I will complain to the King of your knavery.'

'What!' cried the soldiers laughing. 'Wouldst thou have us let good wine run to waste? That would be folly. In sooth thou hast lost thy wit with the wine. We have taken nothing thou couldst have saved. Calm thy wrath and we will help thee to rearrange thy burdens better.'

So with fair words they pacified him, until Sen-nu, forgetting his anger, began to talk with them, and one of them made him laugh uproariously. Then he offered them one of the wineskins as a gift for their good fellowship, and sat down to drink with them. It was not long before the wine took effect, and one and all were chatting and laughing boisterously. Sen-nu presented the guards with a second skin of wine, and then a third; when, being drowsy from the heavy drinking, first one and then another fell asleep in the shade of the wall. Sen-nu, who had feigned to be as intoxicated as the worst, waited till it was quite dark, when he quietly took down his brother's body from the wall and bore it home to his mother.

As may be imagined, Rhampsinitus was sorely vexed at the second failure to catch the thief, and abused Ra-men-ka so roundly that that unhappy man would have resigned his office but he dared not. A third trick met with no better success; indeed, it brought public ridicule upon the King, and his Majesty was now weary of the task he had set himself. So he issued a proclamation which he commanded to be read in all the towns of his dominions, saying that he would pardon the offender and give him royal largess if he would but come forward and make himself known. He was not a little surprised when the self-same day a man presented himself at the palace and declared he was the culprit.

The King bade him be brought anon before him.

'Art thou not afraid,' he said, when Sen-nu was led into his presence, 'to come before me after all thou hast done?'

'The King hath promised me a free pardon, 'answered Sen-nu, 'and he will not dishonour his word.'

'Brave as thou art clever,' exclaimed the King. 'And in good sooth thou wert wise to trust to the word of the King. The pardon is thine, and more. I offered to reward the man who could prove to me that he was the culprit, and if thou dost this, truly thou shalt not regret it.' Then Sen-nu revealed to Rhampsinitus the secret entrance to his treasure-chamber, and proved that he was the brother of the dead man. So amazed was the King at the youth's sagacity and boldness that he gave him his daughter in marriage, and raised him to great honour in his house.

THE THEFT OF CUIRASS

In the reign of the Pharaoh Petoubastis the Delta and great part of Lower Egypt were divided into two rival factions, one part being headed by the chieftain Kamenophis, Prince of Mendes, and the other ruled by the king-priest of Heliopolis, Ierharerou, and his ally Pakrourou, the great chieftain of the east. Only four nomes in the middle of the Delta were subject to Kamenophis, whilst Ierharerou had succeeded in establishing either his children or relations in most of the other nomes. Ierharerou possessed a cuirass to which he attached great value and which was generally regarded as a talisman. At his death Kamenophis, taking advantage of the mourning and confusion in Heliopolis, seized the cuirass and placed it in one of his own strongholds. Prince Pimonî 'the little' – 'Pimonî of the strong fist,' as he is sometimes called in the narrative – the successor of Ierharerou, demanded its restoration. Kamenophis refused, and hence arose a quarrel in which all the provinces of Egypt were implicated.

Pimonî and Pakrourou both presented themselves before King Petoubastis, asking his permission to be revenged on Kamenophis; but Pharaoh, who knew that this would entail civil war, endeavoured to dissuade Pimonî from taking steps against Kamenophis and, indeed, forbade him to proceed with his intentions, promising as compensation a splendid funeral for Ierharerou. Unwillingly Pimonî

submitted, but after the funeral ceremonies were over resentment still burned within him, and he and Pakrourou, 'the great chieftain of the east,' returned again to Petoubastis at his court in Tanis. He received them rather impatiently, asking them why they troubled him again and declaring that he would not allow civil war during his reign. They, however, would not be satisfied and said they could not go on with the celebration of the feast that was to follow the religious rites of Ierharerou's funeral until the shield or cuirass was restored to its rightful owner.

Pharaoh then sent for Kamenophis, and requested him urgently to return the shield, but in vain. Kamenophis declined to do so.

Then said Pimonî, 'By Tem, the lord of Heliopolis, the great god, my god, were it not for Pharaoh's decree and that my respect for him protects you, I should kill you this very instant.'

Kamenophis replied, 'By the life of Mendes, the great god, the war which will break out in the nome, the battle which will break out in the city will stir up clan against clan, and man against man, before the cuirass shall be wrested from the stronghold where I have placed it.'

THE HORRORS OF WAR

Pakrourou then said before the king, 'Is it right what Kamenophis has done, and the words he has just spoken are they not said to provoke us to anger that we may measure our strength against his? I will make Kamenophis and the nome of Mendes feel the shame of these words uttered to provoke civil war which Pharaoh has forbidden; I will glut them with war. I said nothing because I knew the king did not want war; but if the king remains neutral I shall be silent no longer, and the king shall see all the horrors of civil war.'

Pharaoh said, 'Be neither boastful nor timid, Pakrourou, great chieftain of the east, but now go each one of you to your nomes and your towns in peace, and give

me but five days, and I swear by Amen-Ra that I shall cause the cuirass to be put back in the place from which it was taken.'

Pimonî then said that if the cuirass were replaced nothing more should be said about it, and there should be no war; but if it were withheld, he would fight for it, against the whole of Egypt if necessary.

Kamenophis at this respectfully asked and obtained permission from Pharaoh to order all his men to arm themselves, and to go with him to the Lake of the Gazelle and prepare to fight.

Then Pimonî, encouraged by Pakrourou, sent messages of a similar import to all his nomes and cities. Pakrourou further advised him to hasten to the Lake of the Gazelle and be there before Kamenophis had assembled all his men, and Pimonî, with only one band of men, took his advice and was first in the field, intending to wait there till his brothers, at the head of their respective clans, should join him.

News of this was taken to Kamenophis, and he hastily assembled his four nomes, Tanis, Mendes, Tahait, and Sebennytos. Arrived at the lake, he at once challenged Pimonî, and Pimonî, though his other forces had not yet arrived, accepted the challenge.

Pimonî put on a shirt of byssus embroidered with silver and gold, and over that a second shirt of gold tissue; he also donned his copper corselet and carried two golden swords; he put on his helmet and sallied forth to meet Kamenophis.

While they were fighting, Zinonfi, Pimonî's young servant, ran off to watch for the forces that were to come to Pimonî's aid, and he soon descried a flotilla so large that the river could hardly carry all the barges. They were the people of Heliopolis coming to help their chief. As soon as they came within earshot Zinonfi called out to them to hurry, because Pimonî was being hard pressed by Kamenophis, which, indeed, was true, for his horse was slain under him.

Kamenophis redoubled his efforts when he saw the fresh forces arriving, and Petekhousou, Pimonî's brother, challenged Anoukhoron, the king's son, to single combat. When Pharaoh heard this he was very angry. He went in person to the field of battle and forbade the combatants to proceed, and also commanded a truce until all the forces should be assembled.

Petoubastis and all the chieftains occupied prominent positions so that they could watch what was going on, and the men were as numerous as the sands of the seashore and their rage against each other uncontrollable. The bands of the four nomes were ranged behind Kamenophis, and the bands of the nome of Heliopolis behind Pimonî the Little.

Then Petoubastis gave Pakrourou a signal and he armed himself and went down among the forces, stirring them all to deeds of valour; he pitted man against man, and great was the ardour he aroused in them.

SUCCOUR FOR PAKROUROU

After Pakrourou had left the mêlée, he met a mighty man in armour leading forty galleys and eight thousand soldiers. This was Moutoubaal, a prince of Syria, who had been warned in a dream to repair to the Lake of the Gazelle to help to regain the stolen cuirass. Pakrourou gave him a place, though all the forces were now disposed; but he ordered him not to join in the fight until the opposite side – the men of Kamenophis – should attack their vessels. Moutoubaal, therefore, remained in his barque, and Pakrourou went back to his point of vantage to watch the progress of the battle. The two factions fought from four in the morning to nine in the evening. Finally Anoukhoron, the king's son, broke under the stress of the bands of Sebennytos and they rushed toward the boats. Then Moutoubaal took his opportunity and went against the bands of Sebennytos and overthrew them. He went on spreading destruction among the forces of Kamenophis till Pharaoh called a halt; then proceeded with Pakrourou to Moutoubaal and besought him to stay his hand, promising that he would see to it that the shield was restored. Moutoubaal accordingly quitted the lists after having wrought great havoc among the men of Kamenophis. Then Pharaoh and Pakrourou went with Moutoubaal to the place where Pimonî was found engaged in mortal combat with Kamenophis. Pimonî had got the upper hand and was about to slay his adversary, but they stopped him, and Pharaoh ordered Kamenophis to quit the lists.

After this Anoukhoron, the royal prince, was overthrown by Petekhousou, the brother of Pimonî, but Pharaoh interposed and persuaded Petekhousou to spare his son, so the young man was allowed to withdraw unhurt.

The king said, 'By Amen-Ra, the sceptre has fallen from the hands of Kamenophis, prince of Mendes. Petekhousou has vanquished my son, and the bands of the four strongest nomes in Egypt have been overthrown.'

THE SHIELD REGAINED

Then Minnemai, Prince of the Eupuantine, the son of Ierharerou, the priest-king, to whom the shield had belonged, advanced from Thebes with all his forces. They assigned him a place next the ship of Takhos, the chief soldier of the nome of Mendes, and it happened that in the galley of Takhos lay the cuirass itself. And Minnemai called upon his gods to let him behold his father's cuirass that he might be the instrument of its recapture. He armed himself, went to the galley of Takhos, and met there nine thousand soldiers guarding the cuirass of Ierharerou, son of Osiris. Minnemai placed thirty-four guards on the footbridge of the galley to prevent anyone from getting off, and he fell upon the soldiers guarding the cuirass. Takhos fought well and killed fifty-four men, but finally gave in and retired to his vessel, where Minnemai followed him with his Ethiopian warriors. The children of Ierharerou supported him and they seized the cuirass of Ierharerou.

Thus was the armour recaptured and brought back to its former place. There was great joy among the children of Ierharerou and the troops of Heliopolis. They went before Pharaoh and said to him, 'Great master, have the history of the war of the cuirass written, and the names of the warriors who waged it, that posterity may know what a war was made in Egypt on account of the cuirass, in the nomes and in the cities; then cause the history to be engraved on a stone stele in the temple of Heliopolis.' And King Petoubastis did as they asked.

THE STORY OF THE TWO BROTHERS

There were once two brothers, and they were sons of the same father and of the same mother. Anpu was the name of the elder, and the younger was called Bata. Now Anpu had a house of his own, and he had a wife. His brother lived with him as if he were his son, and made garments for him. It was Bata who drove the oxen to the field, it was he who ploughed the land, and it was he who harvested the grain. He laboured continually upon his brother's farm, and his equal was not to be found in the land of Egypt; he was imbued with the spirit of a god.

In this manner the brothers lived together, and many days went past. Each morning the younger brother went forth with the oxen, and when evening came on he drove them again to the byre, carrying upon his back a heavy burden of fodder which he gave to the animals to eat, and he brought with him also milk and herbs for Anpu and his wife. While these two ate and drank together in the house, Bata rested in the byre with the cattle and he slept beside them.

When day dawned, and the land grew bright again, the younger brother was first to rise up, and he baked bread for Anpu and carried his own portion to the field and ate it there. As he followed the oxen he heard and he understood their speech. They would say: 'Yonder is sweet herbage', and he would drive them to the place of

their choice, whereat they were well pleased. They were indeed noble animals, and they increased greatly.

The time of ploughing came on, and Anpu spoke unto Bata, saying: 'Now get ready the team of oxen, for the Nile flood is past and the land may be broken up. We shall begin to plough on the morrow; so carry seed to the field that we may sow it.'

As Anpu desired, so did Bata do. When the next day dawned, and the land grew bright, the two brothers laboured in the field together, and they were well pleased with the work which they accomplished. Several days went past in this manner, and it chanced that on an afternoon the seed was finished ere they had completed their day's task.

Anpu thereupon spoke to his younger brother saying: 'Hasten to the granary and procure more seed.'

Bata ran towards the house, and entered it. He beheld his brother's wife sitting upon a mat, languidly pleating her hair.

'Arise,' he said, 'and procure corn for me, so that I may hasten back to the field with it. Delay me not.'

The woman sat still and said: 'Go thou thyself and open the storeroom. Take whatsoever thou dost desire. If I were to rise for thee, my hair would fall in disorder.'

Bata opened the storeroom and went within. He took a large basket and poured into it a great quantity of seed. Then he came forth carrying the basket through the house.

The woman looked up and said: 'What is the weight of that great burden of thine?'

Bata answered: 'There are two measures of barley and three of wheat. I carry in all upon my shoulders five measures of seed.'

'Great indeed is thy strength,' sighed the woman. 'Ah, thee do I contemplate and admire each day!'

Her heart was moved towards him, and she stood up saying: 'Tarry here with me. I will clothe thee in fine raiment.'

The lad was made angry as the panther, and said: 'I regard thee as a mother, and my brother is like a father unto me. Thou hast spoken evil words and I desire not to hear them again, nor will I repeat unto any man what thou hast just spoken.'

He departed abruptly with his burden and hastened to the field, where he resumed his labour.

At eventide Anpu returned home and Bata prepared to follow after him. The elder brother entered his house and found his wife lying there, and it seemed as if she had suffered violence from an evildoer. She did not give him water to wash his hands, as was her custom. Nor did she light the lamp. The house was in darkness. She moaned where she lay, as if she were in sickness, and her garment was beside her.

'Who hath been here?' asked Anpu, her husband.

The woman answered him: 'No one came nigh me save thy younger brother. He spoke evil words unto me, and I said: 'Am I not as a mother, and is not thine elder brother as a father unto thee?' Then was he angry, and he struck me until I promised that I would not inform thee… Oh if thou wilt allow him to live now, I shall surely die.'

The elder brother became like an angry panther. He sharpened his dagger and went out and stood behind the door of the byre with purpose to slay young Bata when he came nigh.

The sun had gone down when the lad drove the oxen into the byre, carrying on his back fodder and herbs, and in one hand a vessel of milk, as was his custom each evening.

The first ox entered the byre, and then it spoke to Bata, saying: 'Beware, for thine elder brother is standing behind the door. In his hand is a dagger, and he desires to slay thee. Draw not nigh unto him.'

The lad heard with understanding what the animal had said. Then the second ox entered and went to its stall, and spoke likewise words of warning, saying: 'Take speedy flight.'

Bata peered below the byre door, and he saw the legs of his brother, who stood there with a dagger in his hand. He at once threw down his burden and made hurried escape. Anpu rushed after him furiously with the sharp dagger.

In his sore distress the younger brother cried unto the sun god Ra-Harmachis, saying: 'O blessed lord! thou art he who distinguisheth between falsehood and truth.'

The god heard his cry with compassion, and turned round. He caused a wide stream to flow between the two brothers, and, behold! It was full of crocodiles. Then it came that Anpu and Bata stood confronting one another, one upon the right bank and the other upon the left. The elder brother twice smote his hands with anguish because that he could not slay the youth.

Bata called out to Anpu, saying: 'Tarry where thou art until the earth is made bright once again. Lo! When Ra, the sun god, riseth up, I shall reveal in his presence all that I know, and he shall judge between us, discerning what is false and what is true… Know thou that I may not dwell with thee any longer, for I must depart unto the fair region of the flowering acacia.'

When day dawned, and the sun god Ra appeared in his glory, the two brothers stood gazing one upon the other across the stream of crocodiles. Then the lad spoke to his elder brother, saying: 'Why didst thou come against me, desiring to slay me with treachery ere yet I had spoken for myself? Am I not thy younger brother, and hast thou not been as a father and thy wife as a mother unto me? Hear and know now that when I hastened to procure seed thy wife spoke, saying: 'Tarry thou with me.' But this happening hath been related unto thee in another manner.'

So spoke Bata, and he told his brother what was true regarding the woman. Then he called to witness the sun god, and said: 'Great was thy wickedness in desiring

to murder me by treachery.' As he spoke he cut off a piece of his flesh and flung it into the stream, where it was devoured by a fish. He sank fainting upon the bank.

Anpu was stricken with anguish; tears ran from his eyes. He desired greatly to be beside his brother on the opposite bank of the stream of crocodiles.

Bata spoke again, saying: 'Verily, thou didst desire an evil thing, but if thy desire now is to do good, I shall instruct thee what thou shouldst do. Return unto thy home and tend thine oxen, for know now that I may not dwell with thee any longer, but must depart unto the fair region of the flowering acacia. What thou shalt do is to come to seek for me when I need thine aid, for my soul shall leave my body and have its dwelling in the highest blossom of the acacia. When the tree is cut down, my soul will fall upon the ground. There thou mayest seek it, even if thy quest be for seven years, for, verily, thou shalt find it if such is thy desire. Thou must then place it in a vessel of water, and I shall come to life again and reveal all that hath befallen and what shall happen thereafter. When the hour cometh to set forth on the quest, behold! the beer given to thee will bubble, and the wine will have a foul smell. These shall be as signs unto thee.'

Then Bata took his departure, and he went into the valley of the flowering acacia, which was across the ocean. His elder brother returned home. He lamented, throwing dust upon his head. He slew his wife and cast her to the dogs, and abandoned himself to mourning for his younger brother.

Many days went past, and Bata reached at length the valley of the flowering acacia. He dwelt there alone and hunted wild beasts. At eventide he lay down to rest below the acacia, in whose highest blossom his soul was concealed. In time he built a dwelling place and he filled it with everything that he desired.

Now it chanced that on a day when he went forth he met the nine gods, who were surveying the whole land. They spoke one to another and then asked of Bata why he had forsaken his home because of his brother's wife, for she had since been

slain. 'Return again,' they said, 'for thou didst reveal unto thine elder brother the truth of what happened unto thee.'

They took pity on the youth, and Ra spoke, saying: 'Fashion now a bride for Bata, so that he may not be alone.'

Then the god Khnemu fashioned a wife whose body was more beautiful than any other woman's in the land, because that she was imbued with divinity.

Then came the seven Hathors and gazed upon her. In one voice they spoke, saying: 'She shall surely die a speedy death.'

Bata loved her dearly. Each day she remained in his house while he hunted wild beasts, and he carried them home and laid them at her feet. He warned her each day, saying: 'Walk not outside, lest the sea may come up and carry thee away. I could not rescue thee from the sea spirit, against whom I am as weak as thou art, because my soul is concealed in the highest blossom of the flowering acacia. If another should find my soul I must needs fight for it.'

Thus he opened unto her his whole heart and revealed its secrets.

Many days went past. Then on a morning when Bata had gone forth to hunt, as was his custom, his girl wife went out to walk below the acacia which was nigh to the house.

Lo! The sea spirit beheld her in all her beauty and caused his billows to pursue her. Hastily she fled away and returned to the house, whereat the sea spirit sang to the acacia: 'Oh, would she were mine!'

The acacia heard and cast to the sea spirit a lock of the girl wife's hair. The sea bore it away towards the land of Egypt and unto the place where the washers of the king cleansed the royal garments.

Sweet was the fragrance of the lock of hair, and it perfumed the linen of the king. There were disputes among the washers because the royal garments smelt of ointment, nor could anyone discover the secret thereof. The king rebuked them.

Then was the heart of the chief washer in sore distress, because of the words

which were spoken daily to him regarding this matter. He went down to the seashore; he stood at the place which was opposite the floating lock of hair, and he beheld it at length and caused it to be carried unto him. Sweet was its fragrance, and he hastened with it to the king.

Then the king summoned before him his scribes, and they spoke, saying: 'Lo! This is a lock from the hair of the divine daughter of Ra, and it is gifted unto thee from a distant land. Command now that messengers be sent abroad to seek for her. Let many men go with the one who is sent to the valley of the flowering acacia so that they may bring the woman unto thee.'

The king answered and said: 'Wise are your words, and they are pleasant unto me.'

So messengers were sent abroad unto all lands. But those who journeyed to the valley of the flowering acacia returned not, because that Bata slew them all; the king had no knowledge of what befell them.

Then the king sent forth more messengers and many soldiers also, so that the girl might be brought unto him. He sent also a woman, and she was laden with rare ornaments . . . and the wife of Bata came back with her.

Then was there great rejoicing in the land of Egypt. Dearly did the king love the divine girl, and he exalted her because of her beauty. He prevailed upon her to reveal the secrets of her husband, and the king then said: 'Let the acacia be cut down and splintered in pieces.'

Workmen and warriors were sent abroad, and they reached the acacia. They severed from it the highest blossom, in which the soul of Bata was concealed. The petals were scattered, and Bata dropped down dead.

A new day dawned, and the land grew bright. The acacia was then cut down.

Meanwhile Anpu, the elder brother of Bata, went into his house, and he sat down and washed his hands. He was given beer to drink, and it bubbled, and the wine had a foul smell.

He seized his staff, put on his shoes and his garment, and armed himself for his journey, and departed unto the valley of the flowering acacia.

When he reached the house of Bata he found the young man lying dead upon a mat. Bitterly he wept because of that. But he went out to search for the soul of his brother at the place where, below the flowering acacia, Bata was wont to lie down to rest at eventide. For three years he continued his search, and when the fourth year came his heart yearned greatly to return to the land of Egypt. At length he said: 'I shall depart at dawn tomorrow.'

A new day came, and the land grew bright. He looked over the ground again at the place of the acacia for his brother's soul. The time was spent thus. In the evening he continued his quest also, and he found a seed, which he carried to the house, and, lo! The soul of his brother was in it. He dropped the seed into a vessel filled with cold water, and sat down as was his custom at evening.

Night came on, and then the soul absorbed the water. The limbs of Bata quivered and his eyes opened and gazed upon his elder brother, but his heart was without feeling. Then Anpu raised the vessel which contained the soul to the lips of Bata, and he drank the water. Thus did his soul return to its place, and Bata was as he had been before.

The brothers embraced and spoke one to the other. Bata said: 'Now I must become a mighty bull with every sacred mark. None will know my secret. Ride thou upon my back, and when the day breaks I shall be at the place where my wife is. Unto her must I speak. Lead me before the king, and thou shalt find favour in his eyes. The people will wonder when they behold me, and shout welcome. But thou must return unto thine own home.'

A new day dawned, and the land grew bright. Bata was a bull, and Anpu sat upon his back and they drew nigh to the royal dwelling. The king was made glad, and he said: 'This is indeed a miracle.' There was much rejoicing throughout the land. Silver and gold were given to the elder brother, and he went away to his own home and waited there.

In time the sacred bull stood in a holy place, and the beautiful girl wife was there. Bata spoke unto her, saying: 'Look thou upon me where I stand, for, lo! I am still alive.'

Then said the woman: 'And who art thou?'

The bull made answer: 'Verily, I am Bata. It was thou who didst cause the acacia to be cut down; it was thou who didst reveal unto Pharaoh that my soul had dwelling in the highest blossom, so that it might be destroyed and I might cease to be. But, lo! I live on, and I am become a sacred bull.'

The woman trembled; fear possessed her heart when Bata spoke unto her in this manner. She at once went out of the holy place.

It chanced that the king sat by her side at the feast, and made merry, for he loved her dearly. She spoke, saying: 'Promise before the god that thou wilt do what I ask of thee.'

His Majesty took a vow to grant her the wish of her heart, and she said: 'It is my desire to eat of the liver of the sacred bull, for he is naught to thee.'

Sorrowful was the king then, and his heart was troubled, because of the words which she spoke...

A new day dawned, and the land grew bright. Then the king commanded that the bull should be offered in sacrifice.

One of the king's chief servants went out, and when the bull was held high upon the shoulders of the people he smote its neck and it cast two drops of blood towards the gate of the palace, and one drop fell upon the right side and one upon the left. There grew up in the night two stately Persea trees from where the drops of blood fell down.

This great miracle was told unto the king, and the people rejoiced and made offerings of water and fruit to the sacred trees.

A day came when his majesty rode forth in his golden chariot. He wore his collar of lapis lazuli, and round his neck was a garland of flowers. The girl wife was with him, and he caused her to stand below one of the trees, and it whispered unto her:

'Thou false woman, I am still alive. Lo! I am even Bata, whom thou didst wrong. It was thou who didst cause the acacia to be cut down. It was thou who didst cause the sacred bull to be slain, so that I might cease to be.'

Many days went past, and the woman sat with the king at the feast, and he loved her dearly. She spoke, saying: 'Promise now before the god that thou wilt do what I ask of thee.'

His Majesty made a vow of promise, and she said: 'It is my desire that the Persea trees be cut down so that two fair seats may be made of them.'

As she desired, so was it done. The king commanded that the trees should be cut down by skilled workmen, and the fair woman went out to watch them. As she stood there, a small chip of wood entered her mouth, and she swallowed it.

After many days a son was born to her, and he was brought before the king, and one said: 'Unto thee a son is given.'

A nurse and servants were appointed to watch over the babe.

There was great rejoicing throughout the land when the time came to name the girl wife's son. The king made merry, and from that hour he loved the child, and he appointed him Prince of Ethiopia.

Many days went past, and then the king chose him to be heir to the kingdom.

In time His Majesty fulfilled his years, and he died, and his soul flew to the heavens.

The new king (Bata) then said: 'Summon before me the great men of my Court, so that I may now reveal unto them all that hath befallen me and the truth concerning the queen.'

His wife was then brought before him. He revealed himself unto her, and she was judged before the great men, and they confirmed the sentence.

Then Anpu was summoned before His Majesty, and he was chosen to be the royal heir.

When Bata had reigned for thirty years, he came to his death, and on the day of his burial his elder brother stood in his place.

THE DOOMED PRINCE

Now hear the tale of the doomed prince. Once upon a time there was a king in Egypt whose heart was heavy because that he had no son. He called upon the gods, and the gods heard, and they decreed that an heir should be born to him. In time came the day of the child's birth. The seven Hathors (Fates) greeted the prince and pronounced his destiny; they said he would meet with a sudden death, either by a crocodile, or a serpent, or a dog.

The nurses informed the king what the Hathors had said, and the heart of His Majesty was troubled. He commanded that a house should be erected in a lonely place, so that the child might be guarded well, and he provided servants, and all kinds of luxuries, and gave orders that the prince should not be taken outside his safe retreat.

It came to pass that the boy grew strong and big. One day he climbed to the flat roof of the house. Looking down, he saw a dog which followed a man, and wondered greatly thereat.

Then he spoke to one of the servants, saying: 'What is that which follows the man walking along the road?'

'That,' answered the servant, 'is a dog.'

The boy said: 'I should like to have one for myself. Bring a dog to me.'

When he spoke thus, the servant informed the king. His Majesty said: 'Let him have a young boar hunter, so that he may not fret.'

So the prince was given a dog as he had desired.

The boy grew into young manhood, and his limbs were stout; he was indeed a prince of the land. He grew restless in the lonely house, and sent a message to his royal father, saying: 'Hear me. Why am I kept a prisoner here? I am destined to die either by a crocodile, a serpent, or a dog; it is the will of the gods. Then let me go forth and follow my heart's desire while I live.'

His Majesty considered the matter, and said he would grant the lad's wish. So he caused him to be provided with all kinds of weapons, and consented that the dog should follow him.

A servant of the king conducted the young prince to the eastern frontier, and said: 'Now you may go wherever you desire.'

The lad called his dog, and set his face toward the north. He hunted on his way and fared well. In time he reached the country of Naharina (Mitanni), and went to the house of a chief.

Now the chief was without a son, and he had but one daughter and she was very fair. He had caused to be erected for her a stately tower with seventy windows, on the summit of a cliff 700 feet from the ground. The fame of the girl went abroad, and her father sent for all the sons of chiefs in the land and said to them: 'My daughter will be given in marriage to the youth who can climb up to her window.'

Day after day the lads endeavoured to scale the cliff, and one afternoon when they were so engaged the young prince arrived and saw them. He was given hearty welcome. They took him to their house, they cleansed him with water and gave him perfumes, and then they set food before him and gave fodder to his horse. They showed him great kindness, and brought sandals to him.

Then they said: 'Whence come ye, young man?'

The prince answered: 'I am the son of one of the Pharaoh's charioteers. My mother died, and my father then took another wife, who hates me. I have run away from home.'

He said no more. They kissed him as if he were a brother, and prevailed upon him to tarry with them a while.

'What can I do here?' asked the prince.

The young men said: 'Each day we try to scale the cliff and reach the window of the chief's daughter. She is very fair, and will be given in marriage to the fortunate one who can climb up to her.'

On the next day they resumed their wonted task, and the prince stood apart, watching them. Then day followed day, and they endeavoured in vain to reach the window, while he looked on.

It came to pass at length that the prince said to the others: 'If you consent, I will make endeavour also; I should like to climb among you.'

They gave him leave to join them in the daily task. Now it chanced that the beautiful daughter of the chief in Naharina looked down from her window in the high tower, gazing upon the youths. The prince saw her, and he began to climb with the sons of the chiefs, and he went up and up until he reached the window of the great chief's daughter, the fair one. She took him in her arms and she kissed him.

Then one who had looked on, sought to make glad the heart of the girl's father, and hastened to him and spoke, saying:

'At last one of the youths has reached the window of your daughter.'

The great chief asked: 'Whose son is he?'

He was told: 'The youth is the son of one of the Pharaoh's charioteers, who fled from Egypt because of his stepmother.'

Then was the great chief very angry, and he said: 'Am I to give my daughter in marriage to an Egyptian fugitive? Order him to return at once to his own land.'

Messengers were sent to the youth in the tower, and they said to him: 'Begone! You must return to the place whence you came.'

But the fair maid clung to him. She called upon the god, and swore an oath, saying: 'By the name of Ra Harmachis, if he is not to be mine, I will neither eat nor drink again.'

When she had spoken thus she grew faint, as if she were about to die.

A messenger hastened to her father and told him what the girl had vowed and how she thereupon sank fainting.

The great chief then sent men to put the stranger to death if he remained in the tower.

When they came nigh the girl, she cried: 'By the god, if you slay my chosen one, I will die also. I will not live a single hour if he is taken from me.'

The girl's words were repeated to her father, and he, the great chief, said: 'Let the young man, this stranger, be brought into my presence.'

Then was the prince taken before the great chief. He was stricken with fear, but the girl's father embraced him and kissed him, saying: 'You are indeed a noble youth. Tell me who you are. I love you as if you were mine own son.'

The prince made answer: 'My father is a charioteer in the army of the Pharaoh. My mother died, and my father then took another wife, who hates me. I have run away from home.'

The great chief gave his daughter to the prince for wife, and provided a goodly dwelling, with servants, a portion of land, and many cattle.

It came to pass some time after this that the prince spoke to his wife, saying:

'It is my destiny to die one of three deaths-either by a crocodile, or a serpent, or a dog.'

'Let the dog be slain at once,' urged the woman.

Said the prince: 'I will not permit that my dog be slain. Besides, he would never do me harm.'

His wife was much concerned for his safety. He would not let the dog go out unless he went with it.

It came to pass that the prince travelled with his wife to the land of Egypt, and visited the place in which he had formerly dwelt. A giant was with him there. The giant would not allow him to go out after dark, because a crocodile came up from the river each night. But the giant himself went forth, and the crocodile sought in vain to escape him. He bewitched it.

He continued to go out each night, and when dawn came the prince went abroad, and the giant lay down to sleep. This continued for the space of two months.

It came to pass on a certain day that the prince made merry in his house. There was a great feast. When darkness fell he lay down to rest, and he fell asleep. His wife busied herself cleansing and anointing her body. Suddenly she beheld a serpent which crept out of a hole to sting the prince. She was sitting beside him, and she called the servants to fill a bowl with milk and honeyed wine for the serpent, and it drank thereof and was intoxicated. Then it was rendered helpless, and rolled over. The woman seized her dagger and slew the serpent, which she ung into her bath.

When she had finished, she awoke the prince, who marvelled greatly that he had escaped, and his wife said: 'Behold the god has given me the chance to remove one of your dooms. He will let me strike another blow.'

The prince made offerings to the god, and prostrated himself, and he continued so to do every day.

It came to pass many days afterwards that the prince went out to walk some distance from his house. He did not go alone, for his dog followed him. It chanced that the dog seized an animal in ight, and the prince followed the chase, running. He reached a place near the bank of the river and went down after the dog. Now the dog was beside the crocodile, who led the prince to the place where the giant was. The crocodile said: 'I am your doom and I follow you . . . (I cannot contend) with the giant, but, remember, I will watch you... You may bewitch me (like) the giant, but if you see (me coming once again you will certainly perish).

Now it came to pass, after the space of two months, that the prince went . . .

Here the British Museum papyrus, which contains several doubtful sentences, is mutilated and ends abruptly. The conclusion of the story is left, therefore, to our imaginations.

One cannot help being struck with certain resemblances in the ancient narrative to a familiar type of Celtic story, which relates the adventures of a king's son who

goes forth disguised as 'a poor lad' to seek his fortunes and win a bride by performing some heroic deed in a foreign country. The lady in the lofty tower is familiar. In Irish mythology she is the daughter of Balor, King of Night, who had her secluded thus because it was prophesied that her son would slay him. But the Cyclopean smith, Mackinley, won her, and her son Lugh, the dawn god, killed Balor with the 'round stone', which was the sun. The mother of the Greek Hermes, who slew his grandson, Argus, with the 'round stone', was concealed in a secret underground chamber, from which her lover rescued her.

Apparently the Egyptian prince was safe so long as he resided in a foreign country, and that may be the reason why his father had him conducted to the frontier. It would appear also that he has nothing to fear during the day. The crocodile is bewitched so long as the giant ties in slumber. In certain European stories a man who works a spell must similarly go to sleep. When Sigurd (the Norse Siegfried) roasts the dragon's heart, Regin lies down to sleep, and when Finn-mac-

Coul (the, Scottish Finn) roasts the salmon, Black Arky, his father's murderer, lies asleep also. (See Teutonic Myth and Legend.) In a Sutherlandshire story a magician goes to sleep while snakes are being boiled to obtain a curative potion.

The Egyptian protecting giant (also translated 'mighty man') is likewise familiar in a certain class of Scottish folktales.

In our Northern legends which relate the wonderful feats of the disguised son of a king he invariably lies asleep with his head on the knees of the fair lady who 'combs his hair'. She sees 'the beast' (or dragon) coming against her and awakens him. In this Egyptian tale the woman, however, slays the serpent, which comes against the man instead.

Readers will naturally ask: 'Was the prince killed by the crocodile or by the dog? . . Or did he escape? Was his wife given the opportunity to strike a blow?'

In 'Celtic' stories the 'first blow' is allowed, and it is invariably successful. One relates that a woman saved a hero's life by striking, as was her privilege, the first blow, and, as she used a magic wand, she slew the sleeping giant who was to strike the next 'trial blow'.

Was the crocodile slain in the end, and did the dog kill his master by accident? This faithful animal is of familiar type. He is one of the dogs 'which has its day'. In Northern tales the dog is sometimes slain by its master after it has successfully overcome a monster of the night. The terrible combat renders it dangerous afterwards. Besides, 'it had its day'.

Did the Egyptian dog kill the crocodile? Or did the prince's wife slay the dog, thinking the crocodile was unable to injure her husband? And was the spell then broken, and the crocodile permitted to slay the prince?

The problem may be solved if, and when, another version of this ancient story is discovered.

THE STORY OF SENUHET

Senuhet, 'son of the sycamore', was a hereditary prince of Egypt. When war was waged against the Libyans he accompanied the royal army, which was commanded by Senusert, the chosen heir of the great Amenemhet. As it fell, the old king died suddenly on the seventh day of the second month of Shait. Like the Horus hawk he ew towards the sun. Then there was great mourning in the palace; the gates were shut and sealed and noblemen prostrated themselves outside; silence fell upon the city.

The campaign was being conducted with much success. Many prisoners were taken and large herds of cattle were captured. The enemy were scattered in ight.

Now the nobles who were in possession of the palace took counsel together, and they dispatched a trusted messenger to Prince Senusert, so that he might be secretly informed of the death of his royal father. All the king's sons were with the army, but none of them were called when the messenger arrived. The messenger spoke unto no man of what had befallen save Senusert alone.

Now it chanced that Senuhet was concealed nigh to the new king when the secret tidings were brought to him. He heard the words which the messenger spoke, and immediately he was stricken with fear; his heart shook and his limbs trembled. But he retained his presence of mind. His first thought was for his own safety; so he

crept softly away until he found a safe hiding place. He waited until the new king and the messenger walked on together, and they passed very close to him as he lay concealed in a thicket. No sooner had they gone out of hearing than Senuhet hastened to escape from the land of Egypt. He made his way southward, wondering greatly as he went if civil war had broken out. When night was far spent he lay down in an open field and slept there. In the morning he hastened along the highway and overtook a man who showed signs of fear. The day passed, and at eventide he crossed the river on a raft to a place where there were quarries. He was then in the region of the goddess Hirit of the Red Mountains, and he turned northward. On reaching a frontier fortress, which had been built to repel the raiding Bedouin archers, he concealed himself lest he should be observed by the sentinels.

As soon as it grew dark he continued his journey. He travelled all night long, and when dawn broke he reached the Qumor valley... His strength was well-nigh spent. He was tortured by thirst; his tongue was parched and his throat was swollen. Greatly he suffered, and he moaned to himself: 'Now I begin to taste of death'. Yet he struggled on in his despair, and suddenly his heart was cheered by the sound of a man's voice and the sweet lowing of cows.

He had arrived among the Bedouins. One of them spoke to him kindly, and first gave him water to drink and then some boiled milk. The man was a chief, and he perceived that Senuhet was an Egyptian of high rank. He showed him much kindness, and when the fugitive was able to resume his journey the Bedouin gave him safe conduct to the next camp. So from camp to camp Senuhet made his way until he reached the land of the Edomites, and then he felt safe there.

About a year went past, and then Amuanishi, chief of Upper Tonu, sent a messenger to Senuhet, saying: 'Come and reside with me and hear the language of Egypt spoken.'

There were other Egyptians in the land of Edom, and they had praised the prince highly, so that the chief desired greatly to see him.

Amuanishi spoke to Senuhet, saying: 'Now tell me frankly why you have ed to these parts. Is it because someone has died in the royal palace? Something appears to have happened of which I am not aware.'

Senuhet made evasive answer: 'I certainly ed hither from the country of the Libyans, but not because I did anything wrong. I never spoke or acted treasonably, nor have I listened to treason. No magistrate has received information regarding me. I really can give no explanation why I came here. It seems as if I obeyed the will of King Amenemhet, whom I served faithfully and well.'

The Bedouin chief praised the great king of Egypt, and said that his name was dreaded as greatly as that of Sekhet, the lioness goddess, in the time of famine.

Senuhet again spoke, saying: 'Know now that the son of Amenemhet sits on the throne. He is a just and tactful prince, an excellent swordsman, and a brave warrior who has never yet met his equal. He sweeps the barbarians from his path; he hurls himself upon robbers; he crushes heads and strikes down those who oppose him, for he is indeed a valiant hero without fear. He is also a swift runner when pursuing his foes, and he smites them with the claws of a lion, for they cannot escape him. Senusert rejoices in the midst of the fray, and none can withstand him. To his friends he is the essence of courtesy, and he is much loved throughout the land; all his subjects obey him gladly. Although he extends his southern frontier he has no desire to invade the land of the Bedouins. If it happens, however, that he should come hither, tell him that I dwell amongst ye.'

The chief heard, and then said: 'My desire is that Egypt may ourish and have peace. As for yourself, you will receive my hospitality so long as you please to reside here.'

Then Senuhet was given for wife the eldest daughter of the chief of Upper Tonu. He was also allowed to select for himself a portion of land in that excellent country which is called Aia. There was abundance of grapes and figs; wine was more plentiful than water; the land owed with milk and honey; olives were numerous and there were large supplies of corn and wheat, and many cattle of every kind.

The chief honoured Senuhet greatly and made him a prince in the land so that he was a ruler of a tribe. Each day the Egyptian fared sumptuously on cooked esh and roasted fowl and on the game he caught, or which was brought to him, or was captured by his dogs, and he ever had bread and wine. His servants made butter and gave him boiled milk of every kind as he desired.

Many years went past. Children were born to him and they grew strong, and, in time, each ruled over a tribe. When travellers were going past, they turned aside to visit Senuhet, because he showed great hospitality; he gave refreshment to those

who were weary; and if it chanced that a stranger was plundered, he chastised the wrongdoers; he restored the stolen goods and gave the man safe conduct.

Senuhet commanded the Bedouins who fought against invaders, for the chief of Upper Tonu had made him general of the army. Many and great were the successes he achieved. He captured prisoners and cattle and returned with large numbers of slaves. In battle he fought with much courage with his sword and his bow; he displayed great cunning on the march and in the manner in which he arranged the plan of battle. The chief of Tonu loved him dearly when he perceived how powerful he had become, and elevated Senuhet to still higher rank.

There was a mighty hero in Tonu who had achieved much renown, and he was jealous of the Egyptian. The man had no other rival in the land; he had slain all who dared to stand up against him. He was brave and he was bold, and he said: 'I must needs combat with Senuhet. He has not yet met me.'

The warrior desired to slay the Egyptian and win for himself the land and cattle which he possessed.

When the challenge was received, the chief of Tonu was much concerned, and spoke to Senuhet, who said:

'I know not this fellow. He is not of my rank and I do not associate with his kind. Nor have I ever done him any wrong. If he is a thief who desires to obtain my goods, he had better be careful of how he behaves himself. Does he think I am a steer and that he is the bull of war? If he desires to fight with me, let him have the opportunity. As it is his will, so let it be. Will the god forget me? Whatever happens will happen as the god desires.'

Having spoken thus, Senuhet retired to his tent and rested himself. Then he prepared his bow and made ready his arrows, and he saw that his arms were polished.

When dawn came, the people assembled round the place of combat. They were there in large numbers; many had travelled from remote parts to watch the duel. All

the subjects of the chief of Tonu desired greatly that Senuhet should be the victor. But they feared for him. Women cried 'Ah!' when they saw the challenging hero, and the men said one to another: 'Can any man prevail over this warrior? See, he carries a shield and a lance and a battleaxe, and he has many javelins.'

Senuhet came forth. He pretended to attack, and his adversary first threw the javelins; but the Egyptian turned them aside with his shield, and they fell harmlessly to the ground. The warrior then swung his battleaxe; but Senuhet drew his bow and shot a swift arrow. His aim was sure, for it pierced his opponent's neck so that he gave forth a loud cry and fell forward upon his face. Senuhet seized the lance, and, having thrust it through the warrior's body, he raised the shout of victory.

Then all the people rejoiced together, and Senuhet gave thanks to Mentu, the war god of Thebes, as did also the followers of the slain hero, for he had oppressed them greatly. The Chief Ruler of Tonu embraced the victorious prince with glad heart.

Senuhet took possession of all the goods and cattle which the boastful warrior had owned, and destroyed his house. So he grew richer as time went on. But old age was coming over him. In his heart he desired greatly to return to Egypt again and to be buried there. His thoughts dwelt on this matter and he resolved to make appeal unto King Senusert. Then he drew up a petition and dispatched it in the care of a trusted messenger to the royal palace. Addressing His Majesty, 'the servant of Horus' and 'Son of the Sun' Senuhet wrote: –

I have reposed my faith in the god, and lo! he has not failed me… Although I ed away from Egypt my name is still of good repute in the palace. I was hungry when I ed and now I supply food unto others; I was naked when I ed and now I am clad in fine linen; I was a wanderer and now I have many followers; I had no riches when I ed and now possess land and a dwelling… I entreat of Your Majesty to permit me to sojourn once again in the place of my birth which I love dearly so that when I die my body may be embalmed and laid in a tomb in my native land. I, who am a

fugitive, entreat you now to permit me to return home. . . Unto the god I have given offerings so that my desire may be fulfilled, for my heart is full of regret – I who took ight to a foreign country.

May Your Majesty grant my request to visit once again my native land so that I may be your favoured subject. I humbly salute the queen. It is my desire to see her once again and also the children so that life may be renewed in my blood. Alas! I am growing old, my strength is diminishing; mine eyes are dim; I totter when I walk and my heart is feeble. Well, I know that death is at hand. The day of my burial is not far off... Ere I die, may I gaze upon the queen and hear her talk about her children so that my heart may be made happy until the end.

King Senusert read the petition which Senuhet had sent unto him and was graciously pleased to grant his request. He sent presents to his fugitive subject, and messages from the princes, his royal sons, accompanied His Majesty's letter, which declared:

These are the words of the King... What did you do, or what has been done against you, that you ed away to a foreign country? What went wrong? I know that you never calumniated me, but although your words may have been misrepresented, you did not speak next time in the gathering of the lords even when called upon... Do not let this matter be remembered any longer. See, too, that you do not change your mind again... As for the queen, she is well and receives everything she desires. She is in the midst of her children...

Leave all your possessions, and when you return here you may reside in the palace. You will be my closest friend. Do not forget that you are growing older each day now; that the strength of your body is diminishing and that your thoughts dwell upon the tomb. You will be given seemly burial; you will be embalmed; mourners will wail at your funeral; you will be given a gilded mummy case which will be covered with a cypress canopy and drawn by oxen; the funeral hymn will be

sung and the funeral dance will be danced; mourners will kneel at your tomb crying with a loud voice so that offerings may be given unto you. Lo! all shall be as I promise. Sacrifices will be made at the door of your tomb; a pyramid will be erected and you will lie among princes... You must not die in a foreign country. You are not to be buried by Bedouins in a sheepskin. The mourners of your own country will smite the ground and mourn for you when you are laid in your pyramid.

When Senuhet received this gracious message he was overcome with joy and wept; he threw himself upon the sand and lay there. Then he leapt up and cried out: 'Is it possible that such good fortune has befallen an unfaithful subject who ed from his native land unto a hostile country? Great mercy is shown unto me this day. I am delivered from the fear of death.'

Senuhet sent an answer unto the king saying:

Thou mighty god, what am I that you should favour me thus?... If Your Majesty will summon two princes who know what occurred they will relate all that came to pass... It was not my desire to ee from Egypt. I ed as in a dream... I was not followed. I had not heard of any rebellious movement, nor did any magistrate receive my name... I ed as if I had been ordered to ee by His Majesty... As you have commanded, I will leave my riches behind me, and those who are my heirs here will inherit them... May Your Majesty have eternal life.

When he had written this to His Majesty, Senuhet gave a great feast and he divided his wealth among his children. His eldest son became the leader of the tribe, and he received the land and the corn fields, the cattle and the fruit trees, in that pleasant place. Then Senuhet turned his face towards the land of Egypt. He was met on the frontier by the officer who commanded the fort, who sent tidings to the palace of Senuhet's approach. A boat laden with presents went to meet him, and the fugitive spoke to all the men who were in it as if he were of their own rank, for his heart was glad.

A night went past, and when the land grew bright again he drew nigh to the palace. Four men came forth to conduct him, and the children waited his coming in the courtyard as did also the nobles who led him before the king.

His Majesty sat upon his high throne in the great hall which is adorned with silver and gold. Senuhet prostrated himself. The king did not at first recognize him, yet he spoke kindly words; but the poor fugitive was unable to make answer; he grew faint; his eyes were blinded and his limbs were without strength; it seemed as if he were about to die.

The king said: 'Help him to rise up so that we may converse one with another.'

The courtiers lifted Senuhet, and His Majesty said: 'So you have returned again. I perceive that in skulking about in foreign lands and playing the fugitive in the desert you have worn yourself out. You have grown old, Senuhet... But why do you

not speak? Have you become deceitful like the Bedouin. Declare your name. What causes you to feel afraid?'

Senuhet found his tongue and said: 'I am unnerved, Your Majesty. I have naught to answer for. I have not done that which deserves the punishment of the god… I am faint, and my heart has grown weak, as when I ed… Once again I stand before Your Majesty; my life is in your hands; do with me according to your will.'

As he spoke, the royal children entered the great hall, and His Majesty said to the queen:

'This is Senuhet. Look at him. He has come like a desert dweller in the attire of a Bedouin.'

The queen uttered a cry of astonishment, and the children laughed, saying: 'Surely it is not him, Your Majesty?'

The king said: 'Yes, it is Senuhet.'

Then the royal children decked themselves with jewels and sang before the king, each tinkling a sweet sistrum. They praised His Majesty and called upon the gods to give him health and strength and prosperity, and they pleaded for Senuhet, so that royal favours might be conferred upon him.

Mighty thy words and swift thy will!
  Then bless thy servant in thy sight –
With air of life his nostrils fill,
  Who from his native land took ight.
Thy presence fills the land with fear;
  Then marvel not he ed away –
All cheeks grow pale when thou art near;
  All eyes are stricken with dismay.

The king said: 'Senuhet must not tremble in my presence, for he will be a golden friend and chief among the courtiers. Take him hence that he may be attired as befits his rank.'

Then Senuhet was conducted to the inner chamber, and the children shook hands with him. He was given apartments in the house of a prince, the son of the king, in which he obtained dainties to eat. There he could sit in a cool chamber; there he could eat refreshing fruit; there he could attire himself in royal garments and anoint his body with perfumes; and there courtiers waited to converse with him and servants to obey his will.

He grew young again. His beard was shaved off, and his baldness was covered with a wig. The smell of the desert left him when his rustic garments were thrown away, and he was dressed in linen garments and anointed with perfumed oil. Once again he lay upon a bed – he who had left the sandy desert to those accustomed to it.

In time Senuhet was provided with a house in which a courtier had dwelt, when it had been repaired and decorated. He was happy there, and his heart was made glad by the children who visited him. The royal children were continually about his house.

King Senusert caused a pyramid to be erected for Senuhet; his statue was also carved at His Majesty's command, and it was decorated with gold.

'It was for no ordinary man,' adds the scribe, who tells us that he copied the story faithfully, 'that the king did all these things. Senuhet was honoured greatly by His Majesty until the day of his death.'

THE STORY OF THE SHIPWRECKED SAILOR

Our next story requires a little bit of explanation to begin with. It was found on an old papyrus roll which is now in one of the museums of Petrograd, and perhaps part of the story has gone amissing, for at present it begins very abruptly; but we can quite well picture what must have gone before. The story is told by one of the officers of an exploring vessel to his chief, the Prince in command of the expedition. The Egyptians, you know, were really the first African explorers. So long ago that we can scarcely realize it, they sent their ships away down the Red Sea to the country which we now call Somaliland. Of course they didn't call it Somaliland then; they called it The Divine Land, or The Land of Ghosts, and they got all sorts of wonderful things from it – incense, and gold-dust, and giraffes and apes.

But besides that, they sent expeditions both by land and river southwards into the Land of Ethiopia and the Soudan. They called that land The Land of Wawat, and their expeditions were often quite big affairs, lasting many months, and sometimes running great risks. More than once a whole exploring party was cut off by the natives and never returned, and sometimes the Egyptians had to send a ying column of armed men down into the south country to bring back the bodies of the explorers who had perished, so that they might have honourable burial in their own country.

Well, then, you are to imagine one of these expeditions coming home by river. The great galley, gorgeous with scarlet and green and gold, comes ashing round the bends of the river between the stony Nubian hills, the rowers bending lustily to their oars because they know that every stroke is bringing them nearer home. In the waist of the great ship is piled the cargo – gold-dust in bags, ivory, ebony – perhaps a prisoner or two, one of them, maybe, a little dwarf, whom they are bringing down as a present to the Pharaoh. By-and-by he will be made a jester in the Court, and the King and his courtiers will laugh at his uncouth dances and his quaint foreign ways.

Mile after mile the galley swings on, and now the great rock of Abu Simbel is passed. Some day a famous Pharaoh will come up here himself and order that rock to be made into a huge temple. The Egyptian architects will hew away at it till they have hollowed out the very heart of the cliff, and left it changed into the most wonderful of temples, in front of which four great statues of the Pharaoh, hewn from the solid rock, sit with their hands on their knees, looking solemnly across the river. But that will not be for many a long day yet, and meanwhile there is nothing but the great rock, bare and frowning and grim.

Still northward the galley swings day by day, until at last the Island of Philae can be seen in the distance, and the sailors know that they are almost at their journey's end. Behind the island lie the docks of Shellal, where their ship will moor, and the familiar thunder of the First Cataract is already in their ears as the vessel rushes onwards with a line of foam at her bows.

On board the vessel everyone is wild with excitement and delight at seeing Egyptian soil again after so long a journey – everyone except one man. He lies under the awning in the gaily decorated little cabin at the stern of the ship, and his heart is very heavy. Today his men will reach home and be at the end of all their toils and troubles; but his are only beginning. He has still to make a long journey down the river to Pharaoh's Court, and at the end of it he will have to make his report to the

King. Perhaps he knows that the report is not too favourable; for some think that one of the ships of the expedition had been lost, or perhaps the cargo is not so good as was expected.

But even if he can report a most successful journey, he knows perfectly well that he will have no peace till the terrible interview with Pharaoh is over, for Pharaoh is God; to enter his presence is a terror. If he is angry with his servants, his anger is a consuming fire; and the Prince, as he lies in his cabin, feels that he would rather face the Nubian bows and spears a dozen times over than face 'the good God' who is waiting to hear his story. So he lies tossing to and fro on his couch in the cabin, wondering whether his fate will be favourable or the reverse. If he makes a good impression with his report, or finds Pharaoh in a good humour, he may get promotion, and have a gold collar put round his neck by the King's own hand; but if he does not

happen to please the King, well, he knows what the upshot of that is likely to be – banishment to some miserable frontier-station on the eastern desert will be the least of it. Oh, if it were only all over, and he knew what his fate was to be!

In the midst of all his misery there comes in the ship-captain to make his report. He is an old sailor who has grown grey in the royal service, and has himself commanded smaller expeditions both on the river and on the Red Sea; so, when he saw his chief looking utterly miserable, he knew perfectly what was the matter. He had been there himself, and knew what it was to have the report to Pharaoh hanging over one's head. So it came into his mind that he would try to cheer up his chief by telling him a story of his own adventures, and of the wonders that had befallen him. I dare say the Prince was in no great mood to listen to stories; but he might as well let the old sailor talk as lie there eating his own heart out. So he signed to the captain that he could speak, and this is what the old man said:

'Good luck, Prince! Behold, we have reached home. They have taken the mallet and driven in the mooring-post, and the ship's cable has been passed ashore. The crew is shouting and praising God, each man embracing his neighbour, and the crowd is shouting "Good luck" to us. Without any loss among our soldiers we have reached the end of the Land of Wawat, we have passed the Island of Sen-mut, and now, see, we have come back in peace, and are in our own country. Listen to me. Prince, for I am talking simple sense without exaggeration. Pluck up heart, wash yourself, and pour water on your fingers. Then, when you are called to speak, answer the King like a man with a good heart in you. Reply to him without losing your head; for a man's speech either saves him or condemns him. Follow your own good sense, and may your speech be pleasing in the ears of Pharaoh.

'Hearken, now, to me, and I shall tell you the story of a similar adventure which happened to myself. I was going to the Royal Mines, and I went down on the Great Green Sea in a vessel of one hundred and fifty cubits long and forty cubits broad.

She carried one hundred and fifty sailors, the very pick of all the land of Egypt, men who were both weather-wise and war-wise, and who were bolder than lions. They were sure that there would be no storm, and that no harm would come to us; but the tempest burst upon us while we were in mid-ocean, and before we could sight land the increasing wind had raised enormous waves. Our ship went down, and not one soul of the crew was saved except myself.

'I managed to seize a plank, and by good fortune a great wave washed me ashore upon an island. I passed three days alone, with no other companion than my own heart. Night by night I slept in the fork of a tree, and day by day I sallied out in search of something to eat. I found figs and grapes, magnificent pears, berries and grain, melons in abundance, fish and birds – there was nothing wanting that heart could desire. I satisfied myself, and left lying on the ground what was over of the abundance with which my hands had been filled. I made a fire-drill, I lighted a fire, and I made an offering to the gods.

'Suddenly I heard a voice like thunder, and I thought, "It is a great wave of the sea." The trees groaned, the earth trembled, I uncovered my face, and looked round. Behold, a great serpent was drawing near! He was thirty cubits long, and had a beard more than two cubits in length; his body was overlaid with pure gold, his eyebrows were of true lapis-lazuli, and his form was even more perfect than his face. I ung myself on my face and made salaam before him, and, towering over me, he opened his mouth and spoke, saying: 'What has brought thee here, what has brought thee here, little one, what has brought thee? If thou dost not tell me speedily what has brought thee to this isle, I shall quickly show thee, by burning thee to ashes, what it is to become invisible.

'So he spoke, and I hearkened without understanding; I was before him like a man without sense. Then he took me up in his mouth, he carried me to his lair, and he set me down there without any hurt. I was safe and sound, and no harm had been done to any of my limbs.

'Then once more he opened his mouth while I lay on my face before him, and this is what he said to me: "What has brought thee, what has brought thee, little one, to this isle of the sea, whose two shores are washed by the waves?"

'With my hands hanging down before him, I replied: "I was going to the Royal Mines on a mission of the King in a ship of one hundred and fifty cubits long by forty cubits broad. She carried one hundred and fifty sailors, the pick of the Land of Egypt; they were both weather-wise and war-wise, and they were bolder of heart than lions. They were sure that there would be no storm, and that no disaster would happen to us; each one was stronger of arm and braver of heart than his neighbour, and there were no cowards among them. But the storm burst upon us while we were on the open sea, and before we could reach the land the gale increased, and raised enormous waves. I snatched a plank; but, as for the ship, she perished, and of the crew not one survived but myself alone, who am now here before thee. And as for me, it was only by the good fortune of being washed up by a wave that I got to land."

'He answered me: "Fear not, little one, fear not, and do not wear so sad a face! If you have come to me, it is because the gods have allowed you to live, and have brought you to this Island of the Blest, where nothing is lacking, and which is filled with all sorts of good things. Now, behold, you shall pass month after month, until you have spent four months on this island. Then a ship will come, with sailors of your own people; you will go home with them, and you will die in your own town."

'"Now, it is a pleasure to talk about one's own experience, when once the sadness is past; so I shall tell you the exact story of what is in this isle. I was here with my brethren and my children, in the midst of them; we numbered seventy-five serpents, my children and my brethren, without counting a young girl who was brought here by art magic. For, a star having fallen from heaven, those who were in the fire with the girl perished, even all my companions; and, though I could not come near to the fire lest I should be destroyed, I found her afterwards among the dead bodies.

But now she is dead, and all my brethren are dead, and I am alone. Now, if you are brave and of a stout heart, you shall yet clasp your children to your bosom, you shall embrace your wife, you shall see your own house; and, best of all, you shall return to your own land and live among your own people."

'Then I cast myself on my face and made salaam, and I said to him: "I shall describe your Highness's being to my Sovereign; I shall make him understand your greatness, and I shall send to you ointment, holy oils, perfumes, cassia, and the sacred incense with which men seek the favour of the gods. I shall recount what has happened to me, and what I have seen of thy wonderful nature, and they shall adore thee in my town in presence of all the mighty men of the earth. I shall slay for thee bulls in burnt-offering, I shall slay birds for thee, and I shall send thee ships laden with all the treasures of Egypt, as one would do to a god who is the friend of man in a distant and unknown land."

'He laughed at what I said, and, chuckling at his own thought, he answered me: "Is there not plenty of myrrh under your eyes, and abundance of incense on every hand? For, as for me, I am Lord of the Land of Ghosts, and I have myrrh in plenty; only this holy oil which you talk of is not common in this island. But do not think that you will ever see this isle again; for, as soon as you have left it, it will be transformed into waves once more."

'Now, behold, even as he had predicted, the vessel came after four months: and when I saw her in the distance I ran and climbed a high tree, and I recognized the sailors. Then I went to tell the news to my good friend, the serpent; but I found that he knew of it already, for he said to me: "Good luck, good luck, little one! Return to your dwelling-place, behold your children, and may your name be good in your town; these are my wishes for you."

'Then I cast myself on my face, and made salaam before him, and he gave me gifts of myrrh, of perfume, of ointment, of cassia, of pepper, of antimony, of cypress,

much incense, courbashes of hippopotamus-tail, ivory, greyhounds, apes, giraffes, and all excellent treasures. I loaded the whole upon the ship; then once more I cast myself upon my face, and adored the serpent. He said to me, "Behold, in two months you will arrive at your own land, you will press your children to your heart, and, afterwards, in a good old age you will go to inherit new life in your tomb."

'So then I went down to the shore where the ship lay, and I called the soldiers who were on board. I rendered adoration on the shore to the master of the island, and those who were with me on the ship did likewise. We returned to the north, to the palace of the King, arriving there the second month, even as the serpent had said. I obtained audience of Pharaoh, and I offered to him the presents which I had brought from the enchanted island, and he honoured me in presence of the mighty men of the Double Kingdom. Behold he made me his personal attendant. Look upon me now that I have come back to the land of Egypt, having passed through such hazards; and take my advice, for it is a good thing for men to hearken unto wise counsel.'

But the Prince would not listen; he said wearily: 'Do not be a fool, my friend; does anyone give water to a goose the night before it is killed?'

Thus it is finished, from the beginning to the end, as it has been found in the writings. He who has written it is the swift-fingered scribe, Ameny-Amenu (life, health, strength!).

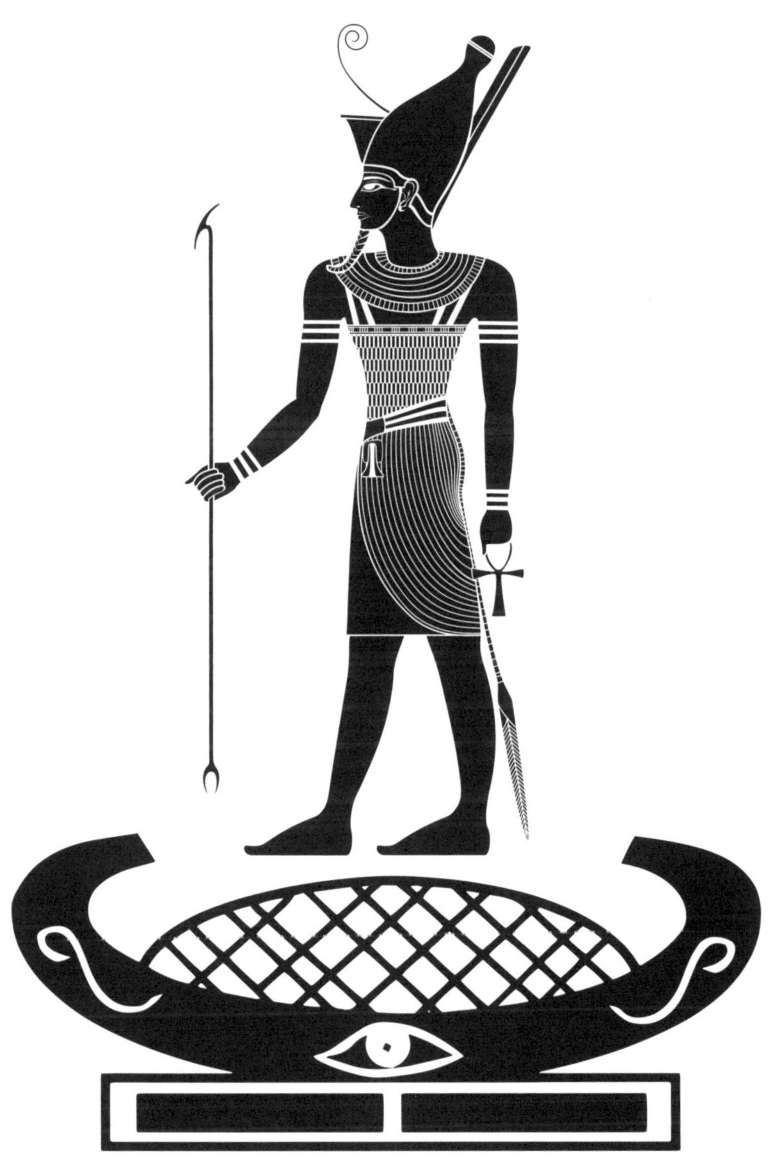

HOW TAHUTI TOOK THE TOWN OF JOPPA

Now, it came to pass that in the land of Egypt there reigned a great King whose name was Menkheperra. He ruled in great power and glory over the Two Lands, and when he went forth to war, either against the Asiatics or the sons of Kush, they fell down in heaps before the chariot of His Majesty. Now, among the soldiers of Menkheperra, whose hearts were braver than lions, there was a general of infantry called Tahuti. He followed King Menkheperra in all his wars, whether in the North or the South; and everywhere he approved himself an excellent soldier, strong and of a good courage in the day of battle, and cunning to bring skilful devices to pass against the enemy. More than once His Majesty, with his own hand, gave to Tahuti 'the gold of valour' before the whole army; for he was a mighty man of valour, who had not his equal in all the land.

Now, behold, it came to pass in those days that a messenger came from the land of Kharu (Palestine), and brought an evil report unto His Majesty, saying: 'The Governor of the North-land has sent me unto thy Majesty, saying, "The Foe in Joppa has revolted against His Majesty, and has slain the spearmen and the charioteers of His Majesty, and, behold, we are not sufficient to fight against him."'

Then His Majesty, when he heard these words, became furious as a panther of the South, and he called together the chief of the whole land – his Princes, his rulers, and his mighty men of valour. Then said His Majesty to them: 'Behold, how this vile Asiatic has arisen against my Majesty! Whom shall we send, and who will go for us, that he may cause the Foe in Joppa to smell the ground before my Majesty, and may destroy his city?'

Then the General Tahuti arose and made salaam, and spoke on this fashion to His Majesty: 'O thou who art the Good God of Both Lands, in whose beams Upper and Lower Egypt rejoice every day, I will go for thee to bring down the pride of the high looks of this vile Asiatic; only let it be done unto me on this wise: Let the great leading staff of Menkheperra, in whose name is power, be given unto me for a season; let there be given unto me also spearmen and bowmen and charioteers, the best of the mighty men of the army of Egypt; then shall I slay this Foe in Joppa, and I shall take his city.'

Then said His Majesty: 'What thou hast spoken is good in mine eyes; be it done according as thou hast said.'

Now, after many days, Tahuti came with his host unto the land of Kharu; neither at this time did he purpose to fight against the Foe in Joppa, but rather to take him by guile. Therefore he made ready a great sack of leather, large enough to hold a man, and he caused the smiths of the army to make many fetters for the feet and manacles for the hands; he caused them also to make one great set of irons with four rings, and many wooden stocks for the necks of men, and, chief of all, two hundred great earthen vessels. Then, when all things were now ready, he sent a messenger unto the Foe in Joppa, saying: 'Now, when this is come unto thee, know that I am Tahuti, Captain of the host of the land of Egypt, and I have followed the King of Egypt in all his wars. But now, behold, the King Menkheperra hath indignation and jealousy towards me because of my great deeds; therefore I have ed

from before his face, and I have carried away the great leading staff of His Majesty, in whose name is power, and I have hidden it in the forage of my horses. Now, therefore, let us speak with one another face to face in the field, and if thou wilt, I will give thee the leading staff of Pharaoh; and I, and all the men who are with me, even the best of all the mighty men of valour in Egypt, will fight for thee.'

Now, when the Foe in Joppa heard this saying, he rejoiced exceedingly because of the words which Tahuti had spoken. Therefore he sent unto Tahuti, saying: 'Let it be as thou hast said, and the gods do so unto me and more also if I make thee not as my brother, and give thee not the best of the land of Joppa!'

So the Foe in Joppa came out from the city with his charioteer, and with many of the women and children of the city; and he came face to face with Tahuti. Then Tahuti took him by the hand, and embraced him, and caused him to enter into his

camp; but in his guile Tahuti had pitched his tent at a distance from the tents of his men, that so the companions of the Foe in Joppa might not see nor hear what befell their Prince. And while the Foe in Joppa ate and drank along with Tahuti, the men that were with him drank and were drunken along with the soldiers of Egypt.

Now, when they had well drunk, then said the Foe in Joppa unto Tahuti: 'Now, as touching this great leading-staff of Menkheperra, of which thou hast spoken unto me, where is it? For my heart is set upon seeing it, and if thou showest it to me thou shalt do well.' Now, Tahuti had hidden the leading-staff of Menkheperra in the forage of his horses, and the forage was in baskets, even as the forage of the chariot-horses of the host of Egypt was wont to be carried. Therefore, when the Foe in Joppa had spoken on this wise, Tahuti answered him: 'If thou wilt, I shall cause my men to bring in the baskets of forage, and thou shalt see the great leading-staff of His Majesty the King of Upper and Lower Egypt, Menkheperra.' Then the soldiers of Tahuti came in, bearing the baskets of forage; and the eyes of the Foe in Joppa were blinded by his heart's desire, so that he could not see how he was falling into the pit which Tahuti had digged.

Now, it came to pass that they searched in the baskets of forage, and Tahuti found the great leading-staff; and the Foe in Joppa said: 'By the soul of Menkheperra, show it unto me, for my heart desires to see it.' Then Tahuti rose and stood erect, the leading-staff of Menkheperra in his hand. He seized the Foe in Joppa by his robe, and he cried with a terrible voice; 'Look on me, thou Foe in Joppa, behold the leading-staff of the King Menkheperra, the terrible lion, the son of Sekhet, to whom Amen, his father, gives might and strength!' Then, raising the staff in his hand, he struck the Foe in Joppa on the temple, and stretched him senseless on the ground. Meanwhile his trusty soldiers had seized and bound the men of the Foe with the fetters which Tahuti had provided, and their chief was now thrust into the leathern sack, bound hand and foot in the irons with four rings.

Now, behold, Tahuti caused his men to bring the two hundred great earthen vessels which had been made, and into each vessel he put a soldier, a mighty man of valour, with his harness and his weapons. Then he slung the jars on poles, each jar between two stout soldiers, and in the sides of the jars with the soldiers were other fetters and collars of wood; and to the men who bare the jars he said: 'When you have entered the town, you shall break the jars and let your companions out, and you shall seize upon all the dwellers in the town and put them in irons immediately.' Then Tahuti went forth, and spoke to the charioteer of the Foe in Joppa. 'Behold, O miserable one, thy master is fallen! Now, therefore, go, say to his wife, 'Rejoice with me, for Sutekh our god has given into our hands Tahuti and all that is his!' Then shalt thou show to her as the spoil of the Egyptians these two hundred earthen vessels which are full of men of war, of fetters and of manacles.'

Then in that great hour the heart of the charioteer melted within him for fear, and he hearkened unto the voice of Tahuti to do according unto his commands. So he went before the Egyptian soldiers, and cried to the Princess as she stood upon the wall over the gate: 'Rejoice, for we are masters of Tahuti!' Then were the bars of the gate undone and the soldiers entered bearing the vessels. And when they were within the city they broke the jars, and their companions came forth, and they took possession of the city and all that were therein, both great and small, and bound them with fetters of iron and collars of wood.

And when the army of Pharaoh had taken the city, and Tahuti had refreshed himself, he sent a message even unto Egypt, to the King Menkheperra his master, saying unto him: 'Rejoice! Amen, thy father, hath given into thine hands the Foe in Joppa, with all his subjects and his city. Send, therefore, thy people to lead them into captivity, that thou mayest fill the house of thy father Amen Ka, the King of the gods, with men-servants and maid-servants, who shall be under thy feet for ever and ever.'

SETNA AND THE MAGIC ROLL

Once upon a time there was a great King of Egypt named User-maat-Ra (Ramses II.), to whom be life, health, and strength. He had a very large family, and one of his sons, whose name was Setna-Khaemaus, was a very wise and learned man. He used to spend nearly all his time studying the sacred books, or reading the inscriptions engraved upon the walls of the temple and the tablets in the cemetery of Memphis. Moreover, he was a great magician, there was none like him in all the land of Egypt. He knew all kinds of charms and spells, and could speak and write words of power that made all creatures and spirits do his bidding.

Now, it happened one day that Setna was standing in the court of the temple of the great god Ptah, reading the inscriptions on the walls, when a man of noble appearance who stood near him began to laugh loudly. Setna turned angrily to him, and said: 'Why are you laughing at me?'

The man answered: 'I am not laughing at you, but I am laughing to see you wasting your time reading these senseless words when I can tell you where to find a book which the god Thoth wrote with his own hand. To read it will make you only a little lower than the gods. There are two spells in it. When you repeat the first, you will charm heaven and earth, sea and sky, mountains and rivers; you will understand

what the birds say as they fly, and the serpents as they crawl; and when you call to the fish, a divine power will bring them up to the surface of the water. When you repeat the second spell, though you were in your grave you will come back to life again as you were before; and you will see the sun in the sky, and the moon in her changes, and all the company of the gods.'

'By my life,' said Setna, 'show me where this book is, and I will give you anything you like to ask.'

'The book is not mine,' said the stranger. 'It lies in the tomb of Prince Na-nefer-ka-ptah, son of King Mer-neb-ptah (to whom be life, health, and strength). Only I advise you not to meddle with it, for Na-nefer-ka-ptah will make you bring it back again, with a forked stick in your hand and a firepan on your head.'

As soon as Setna heard where the book was, he cared for nothing else on earth. He hastened away, as fast as his feet would carry him, to the King his father, told

him everything that had been said, and asked his permission to go down into the tomb of Prince Na-nefer-ka-ptah, and bring back the magic book. So he took with him his foster-brother An-he-hor-eru, and for three days and three nights they searched the cemetery of Memphis, reading all the inscriptions on the tombs, that they might find the tomb of Prince Na-nefer-ka-ptah. When at last, on the third day, they found it, Setna recited a spell over it; the earth opened, and he went down into the long rock-hewn passage that led to the chamber of the tomb, leaving his foster-brother to wait for him above. A vulture and a crow apped slowly on before him down the passage till they came to the door of the chamber, where they perched, one on either side. A great stone closed the door of the tomb; but Setna, putting out all his strength, rolled it aside, and went boldly into the chamber.

At first his eyes were dazzled, for a great light shone from the magic roll, and the whole chamber was as bright as day. After a little he looked round, and there was Prince Na-nefer-ka-ptah sitting in his chair, and beside him were the ghosts of his wife Ahura and his little boy Merab. Their bodies were buried far away up the Nile at Coptos; but, by the power of his magic book, Na-nefer-ka-ptah had brought their spirits back to Memphis to keep him company in his grave.

So, when Setna came in, the Princess Ahura sprang up and cried: 'Who art thou?'

And Setna answered: 'I am Prince Setna-Khaemaus, son of King Ramses' (to whom be life, health, and strength), 'and I am come to carry away this book of Thoth which I see between you and your husband. Give it to me, or I will take it by force.'

Then said the lady Ahura: 'Do not take it away, I beg of you; but listen first to the story of all the evils which it has brought upon us, and how the getting of it shortened our days upon earth.'

So Ahura began, and told to Setna the story of the magic book.

'My name is Ahura, and when I was alive I was the daughter of King Mer-neb-ptah (to whom be life, health, and strength), and Na-nefer-ka-ptah, my husband, was my brother, and we loved one another very dearly. When I grew old enough to be married, the King my father said to the Queen my mother: 'See, Ahura our daughter is quite grown up, and it is high time that she was married. To whom shall we marry her?' Now, I had told my mother that I loved Na-nefer-ka-ptah, and would have none other but him for my husband. So my mother said to my father: 'Ahura loves Na-nefer-ka-ptah; let us marry them, the one to the other, according to the custom.' But my father said: 'We have only these two children, why should they marry one another? Let us marry the one to the daughter of a General, and the other to the son of a General; for this will be far better for the family.'

'That night there was a banquet in the palace, and I had to appear before Pharaoh my father; but I was grieved at what he had said, and was not so gay and bright as usual. So Pharaoh said to me: 'Little stupid, what folly is this that you have said to your mother about marrying your brother?' 'Oh, well,' I said, 'do what you like – marry me to the son of a General, and marry my brother to the daughter of a General, and let us be a happy family.' Then I laughed, and Pharaoh laughed, for he saw that I should never be happy without Na-nefer-ka-ptah. And he said to his Chamberlain: 'Marry Ahura to Na-nefer-ka-ptah this very night, and send to their house treasures of gold and silver, and all sorts of good things.' So we were married, and were very happy together for a while; and we had this one son, little Merab, whom you see.

'But after a time my husband began, like you, to think of nothing but reading the sacred books, and the inscriptions in the temples and the tablets on the tombs of the Pharaohs. Now, one day, when he was reading the writings on the walls of the Temple of Ptah, an old man who was standing by laughed at him. "Why are you laughing at me?" said Na-nefer-ka-ptah.

'"I am not laughing at you," said the old priest, "but I am laughing to see you wasting your time in reading this nonsense. If you really wish to see something worth reading, come to me, and I shall show you a book which Thoth wrote with his own hand. There are two spells in it. When you repeat the first you will charm heaven and earth, sea and sky, mountains and rivers; you will understand what the birds say as they y, and the serpents as they crawl; and when you call to the fish, a divine power will bring them up to the surface of the water. When you repeat the second, though you were in your grave, you will come back to life again as you were before; and you will see the sun in the sky, and the moon in her changes, and all the company of the gods."

'"By the life of Pharaoh," said my husband, "tell me anything you wish, and I will give it you, if only you will bring me where this book is."

'Then said the priest: "If you wish me to show you where the book is, you must give me one hundred pieces of silver, and cause two coffins to be made for me, that so 1 may be buried as a rich priest."

'So the money was handed over, and the coffins were made, and then the priest said: "The book you wish is in the middle of the River Nile at Coptos, in an iron box. In the iron box is a bronze box; in the bronze box is a sycamore box; in the sycamore box is an ivory and ebony box; in the ivory and ebony box is a silver box; in the silver box is a gold box; and in the gold box is the book. Round about the box are snakes and scorpions, and all sorts of crawling things; and a deathless serpent keeps guard over all."

'When my husband heard this he was so glad that he scarcely knew where he was. He came and told me all about it, and said: "I am going to Coptos to bring back this book, and then I will never leave you anymore." But when I knew what was in his mind, I was very angry with the priest for what he had said, and I threatened him; for I was sure that if my husband went up the Nile to look for the

book, harm would come of it. Then I besought Na-nefer-ka-ptah not to go to Coptos; but he would not listen to me. He went to Pharaoh and told him everything, and Pharaoh said to him: "What do you really want, then?"

'"Give me your royal barge, with the crew and tackle," said he, "and I shall take my wife and my son, and go south and bring back this book; and then I will never leave this place anymore."

'So we embarked on the royal barge and came to Coptos. When we arrived, the High-Priest and the other priests of Isis at Coptos came down to meet us, bringing their wives to salute me. We offered sacrifice and stayed there for five days, the priests making holiday with Na-nefer-ka-ptah, and their wives making holiday with me. On the morning of the sixth day my husband caused a great quantity of pure wax to be brought to him. Out of it he made a boat with rowers and sailors. He recited a spell over them, which gave them life and breath, and then he launched the boat in the river, filling it with sand. Then he went on board, and I waited by the bank of the river, saying: "I must see what will happen to him."

'So Na-nefer-ka-ptah cried to his waxen sailors: "Oarsmen, row me to the place where the book of Thoth lies;" and they rowed day and night, till in three days they came to the place. Then he threw sand into the river, and the water parted this way and that way, and lo! in the midst of the riverbed there was a great tangle of serpents and scorpions and all sorts of creeping things over the box. He recited a spell over them, and in a moment all their wriggling and twisting ceased, and they were held motionless by the power of his magic. Then he came to the deathless snake, and, as it reared its fiery crest against him, he struck it a mighty blow, so that it fell dead before him; but immediately it came to life again. A second time he slew it, and a second time it came to life. But the third time he filled his left hand with sand and drew his sword, and as the serpent reared up against him, he smote it so that it fell in two halves, and then in a moment he cast the sand between the writhing pieces

of the creature's body, so that they could not come together again. The deathless snake was dead.

'Na-nefer-ka-ptah took the iron box out from the midst of the stiffened coil of serpents and scorpions, and opened it. Within it was a bronze box, and inside that a sycamore box, and inside that an ivory and ebony box, and inside that a silver box, and inside that a golden box, and in the golden box lay the book. He took it out, broke the seals and undid the knots, and unrolled it. When he had read the first spell, he charmed the heavens and the earth, the sea and the sky, the mountains and the rivers: he understood what the birds say as they y and the serpents as they crawl; and when he called to the fish, a divine power made them come to the surface of the water. Then he recited another spell, and the river closed again over the place where the box had been.

'So he went on board the waxen boat once more, and said: "Oarsmen, row me back again to the place where Ahura waits for me;" and they rowed day and night for three days, till they found me sitting by the river-bank at Coptos. For all the time he was absent I had tasted neither food nor drink, but had sat like one dead.

'After we had welcomed one another, "By the life of Pharaoh," said I to him, "let me see this book for which we have taken so much trouble." He put the roll into my hand, and when I had read it, I could enchant everything just as he could. Then he made a copy of the whole book, washed off the ink with beer, and drank the beer; and so he knew everything that had been written in the roll of Thoth.

'So we embarked once more on the royal barge, and rowed northwards from Coptos. But the god Thoth had learned what we had done, and he went to Ra, the chief of the gods, and complained to him that Na-nefer-ka-ptah had robbed him of his book and killed its guardian serpent. Then said Ra: "He is in your hands, he and all that is his." Then Thoth sent a curse from heaven, saying: "Forbid that Na-nefer-ka-ptah should ever return to Memphis safe and sound with his family." In that very

moment when the curse descended the little boy Merab came out from under the awning of the barge, and lo! he fell into the river. As he fell, all who saw him cried out, and his father came swiftly from the cabin. Swiftly, too, he spoke with words of power, and Merab rose to the surface of the water and was drawn on board. Then, as they laid him down on the deck, Na-nefer-ka-ptah recited another spell, and Merab opened his cold lips and told him all that had happened and how Thoth had accused him before the gods; but no spell could bring our little boy back to life again.

'So we returned sadly to Coptos, and there we embalmed little Merab, and laid him in the tomb with such honour as becomes a Prince of the house of Pharaoh; and we hastened northwards again, lest the King our father should hear first from others of what had happened, and should be troubled. But when we came to the place where Merab had been drowned, the curse wrought once more, and as I came out from under the awning of the barge, I too fell into the river. My husband brought me to the surface again by his spells; but he could not bring me back to life. So he returned with me to Coptos, embalmed my body, and buried me beside our little son with the state that becomes a Princess.

'Then with a sad and lonely heart he embarked once more for Memphis; but as the barge passed the place where the curse had fallen upon us, he said to himself: "Would it not be better to die, and to be buried with them both? How shall I face Pharaoh and say to him: 'I have taken your children with me; I have slain them, and now I come back alive to you?" He took a long piece of fine royal linen, and fastened the magic roll tightly round his waist; and then he went out from under the awning of the barge, and cast himself into the river. And all who saw it cried out: "Woe and lamentation! He is gone, the good scribe, the wise man who had no equal!"

'So at last the barge of Pharaoh finished its voyage, in very different guise from that in which it went forth, and no one knew what had become of Na-nefer-ka-ptah. But when the galley came to Memphis, Pharaoh and his courtiers, the garrison

of the city, and all the priests came out in mourning garments to meet it; and, behold! they saw the body of Na-nefer-ka-ptah, which, by his spells, had entangled itself with the steering-oars. They lifted it up, but none dared to take from his bosom the magic roll for which he had paid so dearly; and when they had embalmed him and mourned him for many days, they buried him in this tomb.

'Behold, therefore, Setna, I have told you all the sorrows which have come to us because of this book which you covet, and would fain take by force. You have no right to it, but we have; for because of it our days of life on earth have been cut short....'

So said Ahura; but Setna would not listen to her pleading.

'Give me the book,' he said roughly, 'or else I take it by force,' for he knew that the ghosts could not withstand a living man.

Then said Na-nefer-ka-ptah, and he spoke craftily: 'If you are so hard-hearted, let us stake the book upon a game of draughts. I will play you for it, the best of fifty-two points.'

'Done,' said Setna. So the board was taken from the funeral furniture; and the two magicians, the living and the dead, sat down to play for the magic roll. Na-nefer-ka-ptah won the first game. Triumphant, he recited a spell; then he struck Setna on the head with the board, and Setna sank into the earth up to his knees. The pieces were arranged once more, and the second game began. It ended like the first, and Setna sank to his waist. Then the third game, Setna's last hope, went as the first and second had done, and the defeated wizard sank to his neck.

In despair he called for his foster-brother, An-he-hor-eru, and said: 'Hasten to Pharaoh, tell him what has happened, and bring here my book of incantations and the talisman of Ptah.' An-he-hor-eru hastened to the palace, and came back with the talisman. He placed it upon Setna's head, and Setna immediately rose out of the earth again. Then, stretching out his hand, he took the magic roll from between the two helpless ghosts; and as he went forth from the tomb, light went before him, and darkness was behind him. Ahura wept as he went, crying: 'Glory to the King of Darkness! Glory to the King of Light! All power is gone from our tomb.' 'Do not trouble yourself,' said Na-nefer-ka-ptah, 'I will make him bring back the book before long, with a forked stick in his hand and a firepan on his head.' So Setna went forth from the tomb, and it closed behind him, even as it was before, so that no man might know of the entrance. Then he went to Pharaoh, and told him all that had happened; and Pharaoh said to him: 'If you are a wise man, you will put the book back in the tomb of Na-nefer-ka-ptah: otherwise he will make you bring it back, with a forked stick in your hand and a firepan on your head.' But Setna paid no heed to Pharaoh's warning; he could think of nothing but unrolling the book and reading it to everybody whom he met.

Then it happened one day that, as he walked in the court of the temple of Ptah, he saw a very beautiful girl. There was not a woman in all the land to match her in beauty; she was richly dressed and bedecked with golden ornaments; a number of young girls walked behind her, and she had fifty-two servants in her train. When Setna saw her, he was enchanted with her beauty. He sent his page to inquire her name, and found that she was Tabubua, daughter of a priest of the cat-goddess Bast. So eager was he that he followed her to her house, and there pled hard with her that she would marry him. Really, he was in a dream which Na-nefer-ka-ptah had sent upon him by enchantment, and Tabubua was an evil spirit sent to torment him; but this he did not know. Before she would consent to marry him, Tabubua insisted, first that he should give her all his estate as her marriage portion, next that he should disinherit his own children, and at last that he should cause his children to be slain. So in his madness he granted her wishes; the children were slain, and their bodies were cast to the dogs and cats, and Setna heard the hungry brutes crunching their bones while he sat drinking wine with Tabubua. Then he claimed her promise; but, as he stretched out his arms to her, she gave a dreadful cry and vanished; and Setna awoke, and found himself lying in a miserable hovel, without a stitch of clothes to cover him.

Terribly ashamed and frightened, he hurried back to Memphis, and when he got to the palace he found his children, to his great joy, not as he had seen them in his dream – all mangled and bleeding – but safe and sound. Everyone marvelled to see the wise Prince in such a state, and Pharaoh his father looked upon him and said: 'Setna, have you been drunk, that you come here in such a miserable condition?' So Setna told him the whole story of his evil dream, and Pharaoh said: 'Well, I warned you already that you would come to a bad end unless you gave back the book. Now take it back to Na-nefer-ka-ptah, with a forked stick in your hand and a firepan on your head.'

So Setna took the book, and with a forked stick in his hand and a firepan on his head, he went down again into the tomb. When she saw him, Ahura said: 'Setna, you may thank the great god Ptah that you are here alive.'

But Na-nefer-ka-ptah chuckled and said: 'What did I tell you before?' And while they talked, behold the whole tomb was filled with light.

Then said Setna very humbly: 'What penance do you put upon me, Na-nefer-ka-ptah?'

And Na-nefer-ka-ptah answered: 'You see, Setna, that the bodies of my wife Ahura and my son Merab are still at Coptos, though by my arts their ghosts are here with me. I order you to go to Coptos and bring them here, that we may be all united in one tomb.'

So Setna took the royal barge and went to Coptos, and there he searched vainly for three days and three nights in the cemetery, moving the tombstones and reading the inscriptions upon them, but nowhere could he find the tomb of Ahura and Merab. At last he found an old, old man, and asked him if he knew where they lay. The old man thought for a while, and then said: 'My father's father's father once said to my father's father: 'The tomb of the Princess Ahura and her son Merab is under the southern angle of the priest's house.'

'Has the priest done you any harm,' said Setna, 'that you want me to knock down his house?'

'Keep me under guard,' said the old man, 'while you knock down the house, and if you do not find the tomb, you may punish me as a rogue.' So they put him under guard, and pulled down the priest's house, and under its southern corner they found the tomb with the bodies of Ahura and Merab. Then they built up the house exactly as it was before, and taking Ahura and Merab on board the barge, Setna went back to Memphis. Then Pharaoh (to whom be life, health, and strength) caused the dead Princess and her son to be carried with honour to the tomb of Na-

nefer-ka-ptah, and when the family had been united once more, the tomb was sealed, and they were left in peace.

THE TRUE STORY OF SETNA-KHAEMAUS AND HIS SON SENOSIRIS

Once upon a time there was a great King of Egypt, called User-maat-Ra (to whom be life, health, and strength). He had a son named Setna-Khaemaus, who was the wisest of all scribes in the land of Egypt; but Setna had no child, and his heart was very sad, and so was the heart of his wife. Now, it fell out that one night when Setna's wife was sleeping, the god Imhotep appeared to her in a dream, and promised her that a son should be born to her and her husband, and that he should work great miracles in the land of Egypt. When the little boy was born, they called him Senosiris, and he grew so fast that when he was one year old people would have said he was two, and when he was two they would have said that he was three. His father was so fond of him that he could not bear to let him out of his sight even for an hour. When he grew big he was sent to school, but in a very short time he knew more than his teacher. Then he began to read spells with the scribes of the Double House of Life of the temple, so that all who heard him were filled with wonder; and Setna delighted to take him before Pharaoh on festival days, that he might see him striving with his magic against the magicians of Pharaoh, and holding his own with the best of them.

Now, after this it happened one day when Setna was bathing on the terrace of his house and Senosiris with him, that they heard a loud lamentation. They looked down, and behold there was a rich man being carried to his burial in the Mountain of the West with great mourning and honour. And while they looked, behold, a poor man was carried also to his grave, wrapped in a mat, and with no one to follow him or to weep over him.

Then said Setna: 'By the life of Osiris, Lord of the Underworld, may my lot in Hades be like that of the rich man for whom they make mourning, and not like that of the poor man whom they bury without honour!'

But Senosiris, his little son, said to him: 'Father, may your lot in Hades be like that of the poor man, and may there never happen to you that which is happening to the rich man in Hades.'

When Setna heard these words, he was greatly grieved, and said: 'Are these the words of a child who loves his father?'

Then Senosiris said to him: 'If you wish it, I shall show to you, each one in his own place, the poor man over whom no one wept, and the rich man over whom such lamentation was made.'

So Senosiris, the little boy, recited his spells. He took his father by the hand, and led him to a place which he did not know, in the mountain of Memphis. Here were seven great halls, and in them were people of all sorts. They passed through the first three, no man offering to hinder them. In the fourth they saw a number of men toiling hard, while behind them asses devoured all the fruit of their labours. Beside them were men over whose heads hung bread and water. Every now and then they sprang up to seize the food, but as fast as they sprang, others dug away the ground from beneath their feet, so that they were no nearer the bread than before.

When they came to the fifth hall, behold the pivot of the great door turned in the eye socket of a man who lay beneath it, beseeching the gods for mercy, and uttering

terrible cries of pain. When they came to the sixth hall, Setna saw the forty-two gods of the jury of the other world, sitting to try the causes of the souls of men, while the ushers of the court called the causes. When they came to the seventh hall, Setna saw the great god Osiris sitting on his throne of pure gold, and crowned with his diadem with its double plumes. Anubis, the great god, stood on his left, and Thoth, the great god, on his right, while all around sat the jury of the gods. In the midst of the hall stood a balance, and there the hearts of men were weighed. Those whose sins were more than their virtues, their souls and bodies were cast to the Devourer of the Unjustified; but he whose virtues were more than his sins, was led in among the gods, and his soul went up to heaven among the souls of the blest.

Then Setna saw a distinguished person, clothed in garments of fine linen, standing in a place of honour close to the throne of Osiris ; and while he marvelled at all this that he was seeing, Senosiris said to him: 'My father, do you see this noble personage, clothed in fine linen, standing close to the throne of Osiris? This is the poor man whom you saw being carried to the grave, wrapped up in a mat, with no one to mourn over him. When he came here to judgment, it was found that his virtues were more than his sins, and that on earth he had not had the good fortune and happiness that he deserved; and so it was ordained that all the treasures of the rich man whom you saw carried with honour to his grave should be transferred to him, and that he should be placed among the souls of the blessed, near to the throne of Osiris. As for the rich man, his sins were found to be more than his virtues, and punishment has fallen upon him. It is he who lies beneath the door of the fifth hall, with the pivot of the door turning in his eye socket, while he prays for mercy and utters cries of pain. By the life of the great god Osiris, was not I right when I said to you on earth, 'May your lot be like that of the poor man, and not like that of the rich?'

Then said Setna: 'My son Senosiris, many are the wonders I have seen in Hades. Now may I know who are the men who toil while the asses devour behind them,

and who are they who leap to grasp the bread hanging over their heads, while others dig the ground from beneath their feet?'

Senosiris replied: 'My father, the first are men who on earth were cursed of the gods, and who toiled day and night for their living, only that their extravagant wives might devour all that they earned. When they came to Hades, it was found that their sins were more than their virtues, and so their punishment here is the same as it was on earth. As for those whose bread hangs over their heads, and who yet can never reach it, these are men who on earth seemed to have prosperity in their grasp, but God's providence, no man knew why, never allowed them to attain it. When they came here, it was found that their sins were greater than their virtues, and so their punishment here is the same as that which had begun for them on earth.'

So when Senosiris had spoken thus, he and his father returned to Memphis, and Setna could not tell what was the way by which he had descended into Hades. Therefore Setna marvelled greatly because of the things which he had seen in the other world, and when the little boy Senosiris was twelve years old, there was not a scribe or a magician in Memphis who could equal him in the reading of spells.

Now, after this, it fell out on a day that Pharaoh was seated in the audience-chamber of his palace at Memphis, while all the Princes, the chief officers, and the great men of Egypt, stood before him, each according to his rank at Court. Then came there an usher to the King and said: 'Thus and thus says a vile Ethiopian, even that he carries with him a sealed letter unto Pharaoh (to whom be life, health, and strength).'

So the man was brought unto the Court, and he made obeisance, saying: 'Is there any man here who can read the sealed letter which I bring to Pharaoh without opening it or breaking the seals? If there is no man in Egypt, scribe or magician, who can do this, then I will proclaim Egypt inferior to the Land of the Ethiopians – my country.'

When Pharaoh and his servants heard these words, they were greatly troubled, saying: 'By the life of Ptah, where is there a wise scribe or a magician clever enough to read a letter without opening it or breaking the seals thereof?'

Then said Pharaoh: 'Call to me Setna-Khaemaus, my son.' When Setna came, he bowed to the ground and adored Pharaoh; then he arose and stood upright, blessing and praising Pharaoh. Then said Pharaoh to him: 'My son Setna, have you heard the words wherewith this filthy Ethiopian has spoken before my Majesty, saying, 'Is there a good scribe or a wise man in Egypt who can read the letter which is in my hand without opening it or breaking the seals?'

The moment Setna heard this he was troubled and said 'Mighty Lord, who is there that can read a letter without opening it? Nevertheless, let me have ten days' grace, that I may see what I can do.'

Then answered Pharaoh: 'So be it, my son Setna.'

So they appointed a lodging for the Ethiopian messenger, and Pharaoh arose from his throne heavy and displeased exceedingly, and went to bed without eating or drinking.

Setna went to his house, scarcely knowing whither he went. He wrapped himself in a mantle from head to foot, and lay down upon his bed in great perplexity. His wife heard of it and came to his room. 'Setna, my husband,' she said, 'you have no fever, your limbs are whole, your sickness is nothing but sadness of heart.'

'Leave me, my wife,' he answered; 'the business that troubles me is not a matter to tell to a woman.'

Then came the little boy Senosiris. He bent o'er his father and said to him: 'My father, why have you lain down, heavy at heart? Tell me the troubles that weigh upon you, that I may take them away.'

'Leave me, my son Senosiris,' he answered; 'you are too young to understand the matters that grieve my heart.'

'Tell me them, all the same,' said Senosiris, 'that I may calm your heart with regard to them.'

Then said Setna to him; 'My son Senosiris, it is a vile Ethiopian who has come into Egypt, carrying with him a sealed letter, and saying: "Is there anyone here who can read this letter without opening it? If there is no good scribe or wise man able to read it, I will proclaim Egypt inferior to my country, the Land of the Ethiopians." I have lain down grieved and heavy of heart over this business.'

When Senosiris heard this he laughed in his father's face.

'Why are you laughing?' said Setna.

'I am laughing to see you making such a to-do over such a trie. Rise up, my father, for I will read everything that is written in the letter without opening it or breaking the seals.'

'But what proof can you give me, Senosiris, my son, that you can do this?'

'My father,' said he, 'go to your library in the basement of the house, and I will tell you the name of each book that you choose as you take it out of its case, remaining here myself all the time.'

So Setna went to his library, and Senosiris read for him every book that he took out, without its being opened. Setna came up from the basement the happiest man on earth. He lost no time in going to the palace where Pharaoh was; he told him all that Senosiris had said, and Pharaoh rejoiced exceedingly.

When the morrow came, Pharaoh came into the audience-chamber in the midst of his nobles; he sent for the vile Ethiopian, who was brought into the hall with the sealed letter upon him, and stood in the midst of the Court. The child Senosiris also came and stood in the midst, beside the vile Ethiopian. Then he spoke thus against him, saying: 'The curse of Amen thy god be upon thee, Ethiopian. Thou hast dared, then, to come to Egypt, the sweet pool of Osiris, saying, "I shall proclaim the inferiority of Egypt to the Land of the Ethiopians." May the anger of Amen thy god fall upon thee! Listen to the words which I shall recite unto thee, and which are written in the letter, and do not dare to deny them falsely before Pharaoh thy sovereign.'

When the vile Ethiopian saw the child he bowed his head to the ground and said: 'I will say nothing false concerning what thou sayest.'

Here beginneth the story which Senosiris recited in the midst of the Court before Pharaoh and his nobles, the people of Egypt listening to his voice, while he read all that was written in the letter which the vile Ethiopian carried. Thus he spoke:

'It happened one day, in the prosperous times of the King Siamen, that, as the King of the Land of the Ethiopians took his siesta in the pleasaunce of Amen, he heard three vile Ethiopians talking in a house behind him. One of them spoke

loudly, saying, among other things, "If Amen would keep me safe from the anger of the King of Egypt, I would cast my spells upon Egypt, so that for three days and three nights there should be thick darkness, and no one should see the light." The second said, "If Amen would keep me safe from the anger of the King of Egypt, I would cast a spell upon Egypt, and bring Pharaoh of Egypt to the Land of the Ethiopians, give him publicly, before the King, five hundred blows with the courbash, and carry him back to Egypt in exactly six hours." The third said, "If Amen would keep me safe from the anger of the King of Egypt, I would cast a spell upon Egypt so that nothing should grow in the fields for three years."

'Then the King of Ethiopia caused the three vile Ethiopians to be brought before him, and said to the second of them: "Execute by your magic spells that which you have said, and, by my god Amen, if you do it well, I will make you rich."

'So the wizard, whose name was Horus, made of wax a litter with four bearers; he recited a spell over them, and breathed hard upon them; he gave them life, and said: "You will go to Egypt; you will bring back Pharaoh to this place where the King is; you will give him a good beating, five hundred blows with the courbash, before the King, and then you will carry him back again to Egypt, all in six hours, and not a minute more."

'They answered, "We will leave nothing undone of what you have ordered." So the familiars of the Ethiopian hastened to Egypt; they made themselves masters of the night; they took possession of the Pharaoh Siamen; they brought him to the Land of the Ethiopians where the King was; they gave him a good beating, five hundred blows of the courbash, in public before the King, and then they carried him back to Egypt, all in six hours, and not a minute more."'

Thus spoke Senosiris before Pharaoh and his nobles and the people of Egypt; and then he said to the Ethiopian: 'The curse of Amen thy god be upon thee! Are not my words the words of the letter which is in thy hand?'

The vile Ethiopian answered: 'Go on reading, for all your words are true, so far as you have gone.'

Then said Senosiris: 'After all this had happened, Pharaoh awoke, sore all over with the blows which he had received. In the morning he said to his courtiers, "What evil thing has happened to Egypt that I have been obliged to leave it?"

'Ashamed at their own thoughts, the courtiers said one to another: "Has Pharaoh gone mad?" Then they said aloud: "What is the meaning of the words which thou hast spoken before us, O great Lord?" Then Pharaoh arose; he showed them his back, all scarred with blows, and he said: "By the life of the great god Ptah, someone has carried me to the Land of the Ethiopians during the night. They have given me a good beating, five hundred blows with the whip, before the King of the Ethiopians, and they have brought me back, all in six hours, and not a minute more."

'When his courtiers saw the scarred back of Pharaoh, they uttered loud cries of astonishment. Now, the Pharaoh Siamen had a head librarian named Horus, son of Panehsi, and he was very wise.

'When he came before the King, he gave a great cry, saying: "My lord, this is the magic of the Ethiopians. By the life of your royal house, I will make them come to your house of torture and execution!"

'Then said Pharaoh: "Be quick about it then, lest I be carried to the Land of the Ethiopians another night."

'So the chief scribe Horus went at once. He took his magic books and charms to the palace, and put a charm upon Pharaoh, so that the spells of the Ethiopians should not take hold upon him. Then he went to the temple of Thoth, the nine times great god, and prayed for his help.

'The image of the great god spoke to him, saying: "Go tomorrow morning to the library of the temple; there you will find a shrine, closed and sealed; open it, and you will find a box in which is a book which I have written with my own hand. Take

it, copy it, and put it back again; for it is the spell which protects against evil, and it will protect Pharaoh, and save him from the sorceries of the Ethiopians."

'The wise scribe Horus therefore did as the god had told him, and wrote a charm for Pharaoh; and the next night, when the familiars of the Ethiopian came, they could not master Pharaoh, because he was guarded by the spell which Horus had made for him.

'Next day Pharaoh told the chief scribe Horus all that he had seen during the night, and how the familiars of the Ethiopian had failed.

'Then Horus the son of Panehsi got a quantity of pure wax; he made a litter with four bearers out of it; he spoke a spell over them; he breathed hard upon them, and gave them life, and he said to them: "You will go to the Land of the Ethiopians;

you will bring back the King of the Ethiopians to Pharaoh's palace; you will give him a sound beating, five hundred blows with the courbash in public before Pharaoh, and you will carry him back to the Land of the Ethiopians all in six hours, and not a minute more."

'They answered: "Truly we will perform all that thou hast commanded."

'The familiars travelled swiftly by night on the clouds of heaven to the Land of the Ethiopians. They took possession of the King; they brought him into Egypt; they gave him a sound beating with the courbash, five hundred blows before the King of Egypt; then they carried him back to the Land of the Ethiopians, all in six hours, and not a minute more.'

Thus spoke Senosiris in the midst of the Court before Pharaoh and his nobles, with the people of Egypt hearkening, and then he said: 'The curse of Amen thy god be upon thee, wicked Ethiopian. Are the words that I speak those which are written in this letter?'

Bowing to the ground, the Ethiopian answered: 'Continue to read, for all that thou hast said is as it is written.'

Then Senosiris went on: 'After all this had happened, and the King of the Ethiopians was back in the palace again, he awoke, sore all over from the blows which he had received in Egypt. He said to his courtiers, "What my sorceries did to Pharaoh, the sorceries of Pharaoh have done to me. I have been carried into Egypt, beaten before Pharaoh, and brought back again." He turned his back to the courtiers, and, seeing his scars, they made a great outcry. The King sent for Horus the Ethiopian magician, and said: "Beware of the anger of Amen my god! Let me see how you will save me from the enchantments of your Egyptian rival." The Ethiopian wizard made charms and fastened them upon the King to save him; but the next night he was carried to Egypt and beaten once more, and the same thing happened the third night. Then the King was very angry, and said to his wizard:

"Bad luck to you, enemy of Ethiopia! You have humbled me before the Egyptians, and have not been able to save me from their hands. By the life of Amen, unless you can save me from the spells of the Egyptians, I shall deliver you over to a cruel and lingering death!"

'"My lord the King," said he, "let me go into Egypt, that I may see this Egyptian wizard, and work my magic against him, and punish him for all that he has done."

'So the King gave him leave to go, and he went first to his old mother, and told her all that had happened, and how the King had threatened him with a cruel and lingering death unless he was able to conquer the wizardries of the Egyptian magician. "My son," said she, "be wise, and do not go near the place where Horus of Egypt dwells. If you go to Egypt to work magic, beware; for you cannot conquer the Egyptians, and you will never come back again to the Land of the Ethiopians." "It is of no use to talk in such a fashion," said he, "for I must go." Then said his mother: "Since you must go into Egypt, let us fix upon signals between us, so that if you are conquered I may come to help you." "If I am beaten," he said, "whenever you drink or eat the water will change to the colour of blood, the food will change to the colour of blood, and the sky will change to the colour of blood before you."

'So when they had agreed upon these signals, the Ethiopian wizard journeyed into Egypt. When he came into the hall of audience before Pharaoh, he cried with a loud voice, saying: "Ha! who is this that works sorcery against me in the presence of Pharaoh, King of Egypt, and has brought the King of Ethiopia into Egypt against his will?" Then Horus the Egyptian wizard stood forth and cried: "Ha! thou vile Ethiopian! Is it not thou who hast carried Pharaoh my master to the land of Ethiopia and beaten him there? Yet thou comest to Egypt saying, 'Who works sorcery against me?' By the life of the god of Heliopolis, the gods of Egypt have brought thee here to punish thee! Gather thy courage, for I come against thee!" Then said the Ethiopian wizard, "Is this dog who barks at me he who works magic against me?"

'So saying he spoke a spell; and lo! a ame burst out in the audience-chamber, and Pharaoh and the chiefs of the land of Egypt cried aloud: "Help us, O Horus, chief of the scribes!" Then the Egyptian wizard spoke a spell, and lo! a great rain from the south fell upon the fire, and it was extinguished in a moment. Then the Ethiopian spoke another spell, and lo! a huge black cloud came over the audience-chamber, so that no one could see his neighbour. But the Egyptian wizard recited a spell towards the sky, and it became clear once more. The Ethiopian spoke a third spell, and lo! a great vault of stone – two hundred cubits long and fifty cubits wide – rose up over Pharaoh and his Princes to separate Egypt from its King. Pharaoh looked up; he saw the immense vault hanging over his head, and he and all that were with him uttered a great cry of fear. But Horus the Egyptian spoke another spell, and behold! a papyrus boat appeared, and loaded itself with the great vault of stone and sailed away with it to the Lake Moeris.

'Now, when the vile Ethiopian saw that he could not contend with the Egyptian wizard, he made himself invisible by art magic, thinking to go back to the Land of the Ethiopians, his own country. But the Egyptian wizard cast a spell over him, and, behold! Pharaoh and all his Court saw the vanquished wizard like a loathly bird, ready to y away. Horus recited another spell, and cast him down upon his back with a falconer over him, his knife in his hand, ready to kill him. Then away in Ethiopia the signals which the Ethiopian wizard had agreed upon with his mother came to pass, and her food and drink changed to the colour of blood.

'At once she changed herself into the form of a goose, and ew towards Egypt, where she hovered over the palace of Pharaoh, calling loudly to her son. Horus, the Egyptian wizard, looked up to the sky; he saw her there, and knew who she was. He spoke a spell, and threw her down to the ground with a falconer standing over her, and threatening her with his knife. Then she changed her shape once more, and became again an Ethiopian woman, and besought the Egyptian wizard, saying:

"Slay us not, O Horus, son of Panehsi! but pardon our crime. Only give us a boat to travel in, and we will never return to Egypt." Horus refused to reverse his spells unless the wizard and his mother swore by the gods never to return to Egypt. She raised her hand and swore, and her son also swore, saying: "I will not return to Egypt until 1,500 years have passed." Then the Egyptian reversed his spells; he gave a boat to the Ethiopian wizard and his mother, and they hastened back to the Land of the Ethiopians.'

Thus spoke Senosiris before Pharaoh, while Setna his father and all the people listened. Then, turning to the Ethiopian, who bowed with his head to the ground, he cried to Pharaoh: 'By thy life, my mighty lord, this wretch whom thou seest here

is Horus the Ethiopian wizard, whose wicked acts I have recounted. He has not repented him of his evil; but now that the 1,500 years have passed he has returned to work sorcery upon Egypt again. And I! I am Horus the Egyptian! When I learned in Hades that this vile Ethiopian was coming to bewitch Egypt, knowing that there was no scribe in Egypt strong enough to contend with him, I besought Osiris to let me return to earth again that I might hinder him from humbling Egypt before Ethiopia. I was born again as the son of Setna for this one end, that I might work wizardry against this filthy Ethiopian who stands here.'

So saying, he spoke a spell against the Ethiopian, and he wrapped him in fire, which straightway consumed him in the sight of Pharaoh and all his Court. Then Senosiris himself vanished like a shade from before Pharaoh and his father Setna, and they saw him no more. Pharaoh and all his nobles marvelled exceedingly at what they had seen, saying: 'Never was there a good scribe or wise man like Horus, the son of Panehsi; neither will there ever be another like unto him again.' But Setna mourned, and made great lamentation, because his son had vanished like a shadow. In the fulness of time his wife bore him another son; but he never ceased to make offerings to the spirit of Horus the son of Panehsi, who had also been his little son Senosiris.

THE PEASANT AND THE WORKMAN

A tale of the Ninth Dynasty, which from the number of copies extant would seem to have been very popular, relates how a peasant succeeded in obtaining justice after he had been robbed. Justice was not very easily obtained in Egypt in those times, for it seems to have been requisite that a peasant should attract the judge's attention by some special means, if his case were to be heard at all. The story runs thus:

In the Salt Country there dwelt a sekhti (peasant) with his family. He made his living by trading with Henenseten in salt, natron, rushes, and the other products of his country, and as he journeyed thither he had to pass through the lands of the house of Fefa. Now there dwelt by the canal a man named Tehuti-nekht, the son of Asri, a serf to the High Steward Meruitensa. Tehuti-nekht had so far encroached on the path – for roads and paths were not protected by law in Egypt as in other countries – that there was but a narrow strip left, with the canal on one side and a cornfield on the other. When Tehuti-nekht saw the sekhti approaching with his burdened asses, his evil heart coveted the beasts and the goods they bore, and he called to the gods to open a way for him to steal the possessions of the sekhti.

This was the plan he conceived. 'I will take,' said he, 'a shawl, and will spread it upon the path. If the sekhti drives his asses over it – and there is no other way – then

I shall easily pick a quarrel with him.' He had no sooner thought of the project than it was carried into effect. A servant, at Tehuti-nekht's bidding, fetched a shawl and spread it over the path so that one end was in the water, the other among the corn.

When the sekhti drew nigh he drove his asses over the shawl. He had no alternative.

'Hold!' cried Tehuti-nekht with well-simulated wrath, 'surely you do not intend to drive your beasts over my clothes!'

'I will try to avoid them,' responded the good-natured peasant, and he caused the rest of his asses to pass higher up, among the corn.

'Do you, then, drive your asses through my corn?' said Tehuti-nekht, more wrathfully than ever.

'There is no other way,' said the harassed peasant. 'You have blocked the path with your shawl, and I must leave the path.'

While the two argued upon the matter one of the asses helped itself to a mouthful of corn, whereupon Tehuti-nekht's plaints broke out afresh.

'Behold!' he cried, 'your ass is eating my corn. I will take your ass, and he shall pay for the theft.'

'Shall I be robbed,' cried the sekhti, 'in the lands of the Lord Steward Meruitensa, who treateth robbers so hardly? Behold, I will go to him. He will not suffer this misdeed of thine.'

'Thinkest thou he will hearken to thy plaint?' sneered Tehuti-nekht. 'Poor as thou art, who will concern himself with thy woes? Lo, I am the Lord Steward Meruitensa,' and so saying he beat the sekhti sorely, stole all his asses and drove them into pasture.

In vain the sekhti wept and implored him to restore his property. Tehuti-nekht bade him hold his peace, threatening to send him to the Demon of Silence if he continued to complain. Nevertheless, the sekhti petitioned him for a whole day. At

length, finding that he was wasting his breath, the peasant betook himself to Henen-ni-sut, there to lay his case before the Lord Steward Meruitensa. On his arrival he found the latter preparing to embark in his boat, which was to carry him to the judgment-hall. The sekhti bowed himself to the ground, and told the Lord Steward that he had a grievance to lay before him, praying him to send one of his followers to hear the tale. The Lord Steward granted the suppliant's request, and sent to him one from among his train. To the messenger the sekhti revealed all that had befallen him on his journey, the manner in which Tehuti-nekht had closed the path so as to force him to trespass on the corn, and the cruelty with which he had beaten him and stolen his property. In due time these matters were told to the Lord Steward, who laid the case before the nobles who were with him in the judgment-hall.

'Let this sekhti bring a witness,' they said, 'and if he establish his case, it may be necessary to beat Tehuti-nekht, or perchance he will be made to pay a trie for the salt and natron he has stolen.'

The Lord Steward said nothing, and the sekhti himself came unto him and hailed him as the greatest of the great, the orphan's father, the widow's husband, the guide of the needy, and so on.

Very eloquent was the sekhti, and in his orid speech he skilfully combined eulogy with his plea for justice, so that the Lord Steward was interested and attered in spite of himself.

Now at that time there sat upon the throne of Egypt the King Neb-ka-n-ra, and to him came the Lord Steward Meruitensa, saying:

'Behold, my lord, I have been sought by a sekhti whose goods were stolen. Most eloquent of mortals is he. What would my lord that I do unto him?'

'Do not answer his speeches,' said the king, 'but put his words in writing and bring them to us. See that he and his wife and children are supplied with meat and drink, but do not let him know who provides it.'

The Lord Steward did as the king had commanded him. He gave to the peasant a daily ration of bread and beer, and to his wife sufficient corn to feed herself and her children. But the sekhti knew not whence the provisions came.

A second time the peasant sought the judgment-hall and poured forth his complaint to the Lord Steward; and yet a third time he came, and the Lord Steward commanded that he be beaten with staves, to see whether he would desist. But no, the sekhti came a fourth, a fifth, a sixth time, endeavouring with pleasant speeches to open the ear of the judge. Meruitensa hearkened to him not at all, yet the sekhti did not despair, but came again unto the ninth time. And at the ninth time the Lord Steward sent two of his followers to the sekhti, and the peasant trembled exceedingly, for he feared that he was about to be beaten once more because of his importunity. The message, however, was a reassuring one. Meruitensa declared that he had been greatly delighted by the peasant's eloquence and would see that he obtained satisfaction. He then caused the sekhti's petitions to be written on clean papyri and sent to the king, according as the monarch had commanded. Neb-ka-n-ra was also much pleased with the speeches, but the giving of judgment he left entirely in the hands of the Lord Steward.

Meruitensa therefore deprived Tehuti-nekht of all his offices and his property, and gave them to the sekhti, who thenceforth dwelt at the king's palace with all his family. And the sekhti became the chief overseer of Neb-ka-n-ra, and was greatly beloved by him.

THE VISIT OF OUNAMOUNOU TO THE COAST

On the sixteenth day of the thirteenth month, the harvest month, Ounamounou, the chief priest of the temple of Amen-Ra, departed on a voyage to procure wood for the fashioning of the sacred barque of the god.

'When I arrived at Tanis,' he says, 'I gave them the edicts of Amen-Ra, which they read and decided to obey. I stayed at Tanis till the fourteenth month of Shomou, when I embarked to voyage upon the Syrian sea. When the ship arrived at Dora, city of Zakkala, the Prince of the place, Badîl, sent bread, meat, and wine unto me.

'While in this place a man of the vessel deserted, carrying with him much gold and silver. Thereupon I went to the Prince and made my complaint to him, saying that the gold belonged to Amen-Ra. And the Prince answered and said he knew naught of it, but if the robber were of his country, he would reimburse me out of his own treasury; if, on the other hand, the robber were of my own company, I must stay there for some days and he would search for the thief. I stayed nine days in that port. Then I went again to the Prince, saying, 'You have not yet found the stolen gold. But

now I must go. If you should find it in my absence, then keep it against my return.' This was so arranged between us.

'Then I embarked again and reached Tyre, to whose Prince I recounted my loss, and complained that the Prince of Dora had not found my gold, but, being a friend of Badîl, he would not listen – indeed, threatened me. At break of day we set out in the direction of Byblos, and on the way a vessel of Zakkala overtook us with a coffer on board. On opening this coffer I discovered money, and took possession of it. I said to them that I would keep and use it until my stolen gold was restored to me. When they saw I was firm they accepted the situation and left me, and we at last reached Byblos.

'I disembarked, carrying the naos containing the statue of Amen-Ra, having put therein the treasure. But the Prince of Byblos bade me begone. I said to him, "Is this because the men of Zakkala have told you that I took their money? That money is my own, for in their port the gold of Amen-Ra was stolen. Besides, I come from Herihor to procure wood for the sacred barque of the god Amen-Ra." I stayed in this port for nineteen days, and each day the Prince sent this message bidding me begone.

'Then one eve when the Prince of Byblos sacrificed to his gods, and one danced before them, he mocked me and bade me bring my god to life. That night I met a man whose vessel was bound for Egypt, and I charged him with all concerning me. I said to him that I would embark and depart unknown to any, and surely the gods I trust would watch over me. While so debating the commander of the port came to me, saying, 'Stay; it is the will of the Prince.' And I answered him, 'Are you not the one who brought me the message each day bidding me begone, and never bade me stay? Now why is it that you bid me rest?'

'He turned and left me and went to the Prince, who this time sent a message to the captain of the vessel bidding him wait till the morrow. The next morning he sent for me to be brought to the palace in which he lived beside the sea. I was taken

to his chamber, and there he asked me how long it was I had been on this journey. I answered five months, but he doubted me, asking where were the edicts of Amen-Ra which ought to be in my hands, and where was the letter of the high-priest? I told him that I had given them to other princes. He was angered, and said that I came with no proofs, and what was there to hinder him ordering the captain of the vessel to kill me? Again I answered that I had come from Egypt for wood for the sacred barque. And then he told how formerly those from Egypt had come in state to visit his city. After a long altercation with the Prince, and when I had told him that if he executed the commands of Amen-Ra much good would be his, he still hesitated. Then I asked for a messenger to take a letter from me to the other Princes, Smendes and Tantamounou, and he would see how they would do my bidding and succour me.

'It seemed that the Prince had changed his mind, for after he had given my letter to his messenger he ordered a ship to be loaded with wood, seven pieces in all, and to be taken to Egypt.

'His messenger went to Egypt and returned to me in the first month of the winter. And soon the Princes Smendes and Tantamounou sent me ships laden with many gifts. Seeing this, the Prince was rejoiced, and soon he commanded much wood to be hewn for me. And when it was finished he came saying that he had done as his fathers had done before him, and giving orders that the wood should be loaded on a vessel. He also said that I had not been treated as were the envoys of Khamoîs, who had lived seventeen years in the country and died there. Turning to his courtier, he bade him show me their tomb. But I had no desire to see it, and said so. I also said, 'The envoys of Khamoîs were but men of his household; I came as the messenger of the great god Amen-Ra.'

'Then I bade him erect a stele and this inscription to be engraved thereon: "Amen-Ra, the great god of the gods, sent me a divine messenger, together with Ounamounou as his human ambassador, for the wood wherewith his sacred barque should be fashioned. I cut down trees for this and loaded them, furnishing the vessels by which it was carried into Egypt. I did this that I may obtain immortal life from the great god Amen."

'"And," I continued, "a messenger shall come from the land of Egypt who shall read your name upon the stele, and you shall receive the water of Amenti even as the gods."

'He said, "This is a wonderful thing you tell me." Then I told him that when I returned I should acquaint the high-priest of Amen of how he, the Prince, had done all as he was commanded, and that he should assuredly receive the gifts.

'When I went down to the shore where the wood was loaded I beheld eleven vessels sent from Zakkala to seize and imprison and prevent me from reaching

Egypt. Then I was distressed and cried out, and a messenger from the Prince approached me, saying, "What troubles you?"

'I explained to him what menaced me, and he went and told the Prince, who was much distressed. To cheer me he sent gifts of food and wine, and an Egyptian singer, Tantnouit, whose songs he thought might chase away my sorrow. His message was, "Eat, drink, and be not troubled. You shall hear my plans in the morn."

'And when the day was come the Prince called his men, and they set out and spoke to the men of Zakkala, asking them the object of their coming. They answered that they had come to seize the vessels and their rascally crews. He answered, "I have not the power to take prisoner the messenger of Amen-Ra in my country. I shall let him go, and after you can do with him as you please."

'I embarked and left the port, and the wind drove me into the country of Alasia. There the people of the town came to put me to death, dragging me to the presence of Hatibi, the Princess of the city. I looked at the men around, and asked was there not one who could understand Egyptian? One came forward saying that he understood it. I said that I had heard that if justice was to be found anywhere it was in Alasia, and yet here were they ready to work an injustice. The Princess inquired what I had said.

'Again I spoke, and pleaded that as the storm had driven me into their country they should not slay me, for in truth I was a messenger of the great god Amen-Ra. Then I pointed out that if harm came to me I would be avenged. In a little while the Princess called her people and caused them to relinquish their evil designs, saying to me, "Be not troubled...."

Here the papyrus ends. It is tantalizing not to know how Ounamounou managed to return to Egypt, but we may be sure a person of such infinite resource and determination, not to say doggedness, accomplished all he desired.

THE REIGN OF THE TWELVE KINGS

There was a certain king of Egypt named Sethos, who sprang from the priestly class, and had gained the throne because of dissension among the people. One of his first acts was to take away all power from the military class, for they were to be feared more than all others beside, and he deprived them of the land allotted to each member by former kings. These indignities greatly estranged the warriors, and when Sennacherib of Assyria marched with his forces into Egypt they refused to fight against him. In this calamity King Sethos went into the inner sanctuary of the temple and called upon his god to come to his help. As he bewailed his hapless state he fell asleep, and dreamed that the god appeared to him and told him to be of good cheer, for he would send help when the time was meet.

Then Sethos marched out against the Assyrians at the head of an army consisting of farmers, artisans, and traders, and camped near Pelusium, a town on the eastern branch of the Nile that commanded the entrance into Egypt. Thither came the forces of Sennacherib; and during the night, as the two armies lay waiting for the dawn, the one in fear and trembling, the other singing and vaunting their proud strength, countless multitudes of mice came up from the fields hard by into the Assyrian camp, and ate the bowstrings of the soldiers, and gnawed in twain the thongs of their shields. When they arose next morning they were helpless, and ed

incontinently; and great numbers fell at the hands of the Egyptians. Wherefore King Sethos, on his return to Memphis, set up before the temple of Ptah a statue of himself with a mouse in his hand, and underneath was this inscription, 'Look on me, and learn to reverence the gods.'

But as years rolled on Sethos grew ever more disliked by his people, and on his death they resolved never more to allow themselves to be ruled by one man. This resolve they failed to keep in later years, but for the moment they were filled with zeal for their new plan. Wherefore they chose twelve kings, dividing the whole country into twelve districts and setting over each a king. The twelve were bound together by intermarriage, and they also took a solemn vow not to depose any of their number nor to seek aggrandizement at the expense of the rest. They were, you see, jealous of one another, and their distrust was heightened by the declaration of an oracle, which said that he among them who first poured out in the temple of Ptah a libation in a cup of bronze should become sole ruler of all Egypt.

As a means of strengthening their bond of union, the twelve resolved to build a monument which should serve both as a common memorial to them and as a burial-place for their remains. To this end it was said they constructed a wonderful building known as the Labyrinth, in the fertile spot of land called the Fayoum. This Labyrinth had twelve courts with gates exactly opposite each other, six facing north and six south. Round each court ran a colonnade of white stone, from which opened off chambers, and these led into other courts, and thence by fresh colonnades into other houses until the stranger was lost as in a maze. The total number of rooms was 3000, half of which were built underground, and the other half above ground and resting upon them. The upper rooms were for the use of the priests who attended to the temple worship and the many servants who ministered to them; the lower chambers were the tombs of the twelve kings and of the sacred crocodiles that were held in honour there.

Now it came to pass that on a certain day the twelve kings had met together for worship in the temple of Ptah at Memphis. All went well until the time for pouring out the libations, when it was found that by some mischance the high priest had brought out only eleven goblets instead of twelve. Psammetichus, who stood last in the line of kings, was thus without a goblet; but, not wishing the ceremony to be stopped, he took his bronze helmet from his head, saying, 'This will do for my cup. Pour the wine within.' As he spoke the other kings looked quickly at one another, remembering the saying, 'He that first among you poureth out in the temple of Ptah a libation from a cup of bronze shall be King of all Egypt'; and after the service was over, they met together in secret to consult what should be done.

'He is worthy of death,' said one. 'He hath taken an unfair advantage, seeking his own glory in spite of the oath we swore.'

'In sooth,' said another, 'he was ever ambitious, and, knowing the oracle, he seized the opportunity, hoping to be made King over us.'

Then arose a grey-headed old man, bent with years, and wise beyond all the rest. 'Hearken, my brothers,' he said. 'Psammetichus hath indeed fulfilled the words of the oracle, but how know ye that it was with guilty intent? Had not all of you helmets of bronze on your heads, even as he had, and would ye have done otherwise had ye stood last? But call him in and examine him, and learn wherefore he used his helmet, knowing what the oracle had spoken.'

So Psammetichus was called before them and they questioned him closely; but to all he stoutly protested that he had no thought of the oracle, and sought only to allow the religious service to go on uninterrupted.

'It was even as I told you,' said the old man, when Psammetichus had been removed. 'The finger of Fate is in this. Kill him an ye will, and the gods will exact a terrible vengeance from you. As for me, I lay no hand on him whom Heaven befriendeth.'

At these words there arose much discussion in the council, some still cleaving to the wish to kill him, but the greater part inclining to the words of the wise old King. At last it was agreed that Psammetichus should be stripped of his kingship and banished to the marshes of the Delta, and forbidden to hold intercourse with any other part of Egypt.

For the second time in his life Psammetichus went into exile, he having been a fugitive when erstwhile the usurper Sabacos seized the throne and put his father to death. Now he ed into the marshes, where he lay hid for several years, hoping that a means would be found whereby he might return to his dominion. But, wearying of the loneliness, he sent to the town of Buto, where was the oracle of Latona, to inquire how he might take vengeance upon his enemies and regain his rights.

This oracle of Latona at Buto was the most celebrated in all Egypt, for never had it been known to err. Hence it was consulted from far and wide and its wealth increased daily. A magnificent temple was built in honour of the goddess, surrounded by a high wall, the entrance being through a massive gateway sixty feet in height. Rich sculptures decorated the walls, and gold and silver ornaments were there in great profusion. But the greatest marvel was a shrine dedicated to Latona, cut out of a single stone, each side measuring sixty feet in length and the same in height. The roof was formed of another at stone, so large that it projected at the eaves six feet on every side.

Hither then did Psammetichus send his inquiry, and the answer came forthwith. 'Vengeance shall come from the sea,' said the oracle, 'when brazen men shall appear.' The cryptic answer puzzled the exile exceedingly; for never, thought he, could brazen men come to his aid, and from the sea withal.

Howbeit, not long afterward it came to pass that a number of soldiers, men of Ionia and Caria, were driven by stress of weather out of their course, and put in, perforce, to a small harbour on the Egyptian coast, where they disembarked and,

being in want of food, began to harry the land. Tall and fierce were they, and, clad in armour of bronze, they inspired deep dread in the defenceless peasants and fishermen of the coast regions. One of these, who had ed on their approach, brought the tidings of their arrival to Psammetichus, and, as the rustic had never before seen men so clad, he said that brazen men had come up out of the sea and were plundering the land.

The King pondered on the news, and then light came to him. ‘’Tis the word of the oracle,’ he said. ‘The brazen men from the sea! I will haste to meet them.’ And without delay he set forth to find the strangers.

He had little difficulty in this, for the tale of their evil doings was bruited far and wide. On coming up with them Psammetichus entered into conversation, and found out whence they came and how they chanced to be there. After long parley it was agreed that they should return to their own land and bring back a large force of warriors, and aid Psammetichus to gain his kingdom once more; in return wherefore they should have rich rewards and a city in Egypt to dwell in.

In a few months all was ready, and placing himself at the head of his new allies Psammetichus marched south. The conict was short, for his enemies had received no tidings of the power which was being brought against them; and, after one or two engagements in which they were defeated, Psammetichus entered Memphis and was crowned King of all Egypt. Thus were the two oracles fulfilled.

In gratitude to the gods Psammetichus built a large gateway in the south wall of the temple of Ptah in Memphis, and also a court for the Apis bull. This court was adorned with a number of statues, and surrounded with a colonnade, resting upon statues each eighteen feet in height.

He reigned fifty-four years in Memphis, doing much to restore Egypt to her ancient prestige among the nations, and died full of years and honour; and his son Necho reigned in his stead.

THE SHADOW OF THE END

Hophra, the great-grandson of Psammetichus, was the last of the mighty kings of the ancient line of Egypt, for soon after his reign the country was conquered by the Persians and ruled by them. He carried the arms of Egypt into far distant lands, bringing under his sway kingdoms that had long since thrown off the Egyptian yoke; but, although he did so much for the glory of his land, he was put to death at last by his own subjects. And his untimely end came about in this wise.

Hophra had sent an army to subdue Cyrene in Libya, a rebellious town and a stubborn. Instead of gaining an easy victory as they expected, the Egyptians suffered a terrible reverse, so many being killed that the survivors and the relatives of those who were slain declared the King had sent them thither in the hope that they would be destroyed, when he could rule Egypt without fear, and inict whatsoever measures of oppression he would. So, far from home, they broke out into open revolt.

When the tidings came to Hophra, he called Amasis, one of his most able men and a tried warrior, and bade him go see if he could win the people back to their allegiance by fair words and promises. Amasis thereon set forth, and on his arrival in the rebel camp he summoned the leaders before him.

'Wherefore do ye gather thus together, and set the King at defiance?' he said. 'Is it for this that he hath raised you to be the chosen warriors among his people and given you lands and honour?'

'He gave us over to death,' cried one; 'for that he sent us to fight against Cyrene.'

'Nay, friend, 'tis not so,' replied Amasis. If ye suffered defeat and loss, 'twas not the King's wish. Rather did he think to yield you the greater glory, trusting to your known valour to carry you to victory against any odds.'

'Hark to my lord Amasis,' said a voice. 'Verily he would make a splendid wooer.' And at the words there was a loud laugh.

'Thou speakest sooth, I hope,' answered Amasis, 'for I come hither to woo thee and these others to your faith. Lay down your arms and go to your homes, and I promise you the King's forgiveness for your treason here made manifest. No harm shall come to you, and the remembrance of your misdeeds shall be wiped out.'

While he spoke one of the soldiers had come behind him with a shining brass helmet in his hand, and at this moment he placed it on the envoy's head and cried, 'Long live King Amasis! Hail to our King!' The cry, begun in jest, was taken up in earnest, and soon the men were beseeching Amasis to claim the crown himself, promising to go with him and support him against the forces of Hophra. At first Amasis demurred; but secretly he was pleased at the offer of a crown, and afterwards he agreed to march at their head and urge their claims on the King.

'If he refuse to hearken to your just complaints,' said Amasis, knowing full well that it would fall out so, 'then perchance I will give ear to your request.'

While pretending to act for Hophra, Amasis travelled in royal state, and news of these doings being brought to the King, he sent Patarbemis, one of his most trusty friends, to bring the traitor alive into his presence. Having come to where Amasis was encamped, Patarbemis bade him return with him to Court; but the rebel leader, aware that his plans were known and realizing that he could expect no mercy of the King, only gave the messenger a rude answer. Patarbemis, however, who had known Amasis of old and would have helped him if he could, exhorted him to obey the King's commands and trust to his clemency.

'Thou wouldst have me put a noose about my own neck,' said Amasis; 'but if I must suffer, it shall not be thus tamely. Go back to thy royal master and tell him that I hasten to come into his presence, bringing others with me.'

Then Patarbemis could not fail to understand his meaning, and had any doubts lingered in his mind of his friend's faithlessness, the preparations going on around would have dispelled them; so, turning away, he rode swiftly back to the King to tell him of these things. But when Hophra saw him coming without Amasis he fell into a terrible fury, and commanded that he should be seized and bound, and his ears and nose cut off. Then the rest of the Egyptians who had hitherto espoused the King's cause, shocked by such shameless outrage toward a noble Egyptian and a faithful servant, went over to the rebels, and put themselves and all they had at the disposal of Amasis.

Thus abandoned by his own people, Hophra quickly mustered his Greek troops, to the number of 30,000 men, and marched out from Sais against the rebel host. The two armies met near the city of Momemphis, and though the Greeks fought bravely they were worsted in the battle, overcome by the multitude of their enemies. Hophra himself fell prisoner to Amasis, and was led back a captive to the palace whence he had fared forth so proudly. The new King, however, did not treat him harshly, allowing him full freedom in his goings-out and comings-in, and showing all honour and respect to his former master. But the followers of Amasis murmured against him, saying he was wrong to show mercy to one who had been his bitter enemy and who had sought to enslave them also; wherefore he delivered Hophra into their hands to do with him as seemed good to them. And they took him out and strangled him, and buried him in the tomb of his fathers in the great temple at Sais.

So the ancient line of the Egyptian kings came to an end, and a man of the people sat upon the throne. Because he was of humble origin the Egyptians were not disposed to show him the honour and reverence due to a king; and Amasis, who

was both witty and clever, determined to convict them by their own words of their inconsistency. He took a large golden bath, in which many of his guests had been wont to wash their hands and feet, and he made of it an image of one of the gods, which he then caused to be set up in a public place in the city; whereupon the Egyptians ocked thither in great numbers and worshipped the image with all reverence. Seeing this was so, Amasis assembled all the chief men of the city and thus questioned them.

'The statue that is newly set up in the city, wherefore do ye all run to worship it?' he asked.

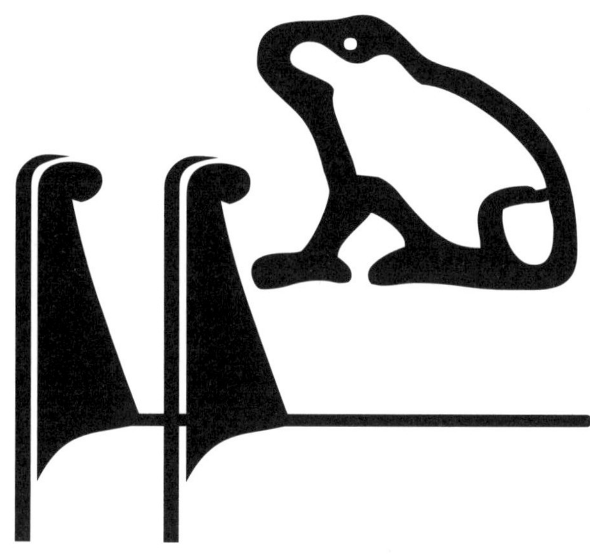

'Because it is the semblance of our god to whom reverence is due,' said the spokesman of the assembly.

'But know ye not that this image was once the bath into which ye washed off impurities from hands and feet?'

'We know it, O King,' was the reply. 'But, now it is changed and is an image of the god, it is meet that worship be paid to it.'

'It matters not then what a thing was before,' said the King; 'even that which was put to the basest uses is worthy of the highest honours when its station is changed. Is it so?'

'O King, you read our hearts,' said the courtier.

'Out of your own mouths do I condemn you,' said the monarch. 'Lo, I, who erst was one like you am now raised to be King over you, yet I receive not the honour due to my rank. Go now, and see to it that I am treated henceforth as your King and master.'

With these words he dismissed them, nor had he again to complain of lack of reverence from his subjects.

On another occasion certain of his courtiers, who disliked the way he passed his time, ventured to remonstrate with him. It was the King's custom to transact business and attend to affairs of state from sunrise until the market-hour, when the people went abroad in the streets to buy and sell; the rest of the day he spent in feasting and merrymaking, or otherwise diverting himself. These courtiers came to him and said it was not proper that the King should waste so much time in levity; he ought to sit upon the throne and occupy the whole day in attending to state matters, as had done the kings before him.

Amasis heard them to the end in silence, and then said: 'When the archer hath used his bow and would lay it aside, he unstringeth it; for were it always kept taut the string would fray and the bow lose its suppleness, and fail him in time of need.

So it is with men. If they are always at work and their minds fretted with carking cares, they grow moody and depressed, and lose vigour of both mind and body. For this reason I divide my time between work and pleasure.'

Although the Greek troops in Egypt had fought against Amasis, he bore them no ill will for that, and even cultivated acquaintance with the lands whence they came. In this way he came to know a king named Polycrates, ruler of one of the Greek islands, and the two monarchs became fast friends. Polycrates was a man of great ability, and he quickly conquered all the neighbouring islands, making himself king over them. Wherever he went victory attended him, and his successes were so remarkable that Amasis grew alarmed. So one day he wrote his friend a letter; and this is what he said.

'Amasis to Polycrates King of Samos, Greeting! The news of thy successes hath been brought to me, and for a time I, as thy friend and ally, rejoiced thereat. But no tidings of any reverse, be it even a triing one, having been reported, I joy no longer, for I know the gods are envious of thee. My wish for myself and for those whom I love is to be now prosperous, now unfortunate, thus preserving the balance 'twixt good and ill fortune. Never yet have I heard of anyone being always successful who did not in the end suffer some terrible calamity, and come to utter ruin. Now, therefore, give ear to my words, and meet thy unfailing good luck in this wise. Bethink thee which of thy possessions thou prizest most and art most loath to part with; then take it and cast it far from thee so that it may never come to thee again. And if thy good fortune thenceforward be not chequered with ill, keep thyself from harm by doing again as I have counselled.'

When Polycrates read this letter he pondered over what his friend had written, and came to the conclusion that the advice was good; so he thought upon all the valuables he possessed, considering which it would grieve him most to lose. After long reection he decided that his best-loved treasure was a signet-ring he was wont

to wear, an emerald set in gold, of exceeding cunning workmanship. Thereupon he bade a boat be manned, in which he was rowed out into the sea, and when he was far from the land he took the ring, and, in the sight of all there, cast it into the deep. This done, he returned home and gave vent to his sorrow.

Now it came to pass some six days later that a fisherman caught amongst other fry a fish so large and beautiful that he deemed it a fit present for a king; so he took it up to the royal palace, where he happened to meet Polycrates himself. On being asked what he sought there, he knelt before the King and said, 'O sire, this morning I caught a splendid fish, and though I am a poor man who live by my trade, I did not take it to market, for I said to myself, "This fish is truly worthy of the table of the King," and straightway I brought it here to give it to your Majesty.'

Polycrates, on seeing the fish, replied, 'Thou didst well, friend, to bring it hither. Nothing shalt thou lose by thy gift. Take it to the kitchen, and come and sup with me tonight.'

The poor man, overjoyed at this great honour, carried the fish to the cook, and then hurried home to prepare for the coming feast.

Meanwhile the servants took the prize and began at once to clean it; but judge of their surprise when, on cutting it open, they found within its belly the very ring their master had cast into the sea. With shouts of joy they seized upon it and, hastening to Polycrates, told him how the ring had been found; but, instead of showing delight as they had expected, the King received their news in silence and with troubled mien. For in this accident he saw the hand of Fate, refusing to allow him to juggle with his lot; and forthwith he wrote a letter to Amasis of Egypt telling him all that he had done and what had come of his schemes.

Amasis was grieved on hearing what had chanced, for he believed that the gods were conspiring against his friend's happiness. He therefore wrote a second letter to Polycrates and sent it by a trusty messenger.

'Amasis to his well-beloved friend Polycrates, Greeting! The account of the ring which thou didst send to me I have read with unfeigned sorrow, for, in sooth, I see in these things the finger of Fate directed against thee. Wherefore I break off the bonds of friendship that have hitherto united us, and pray I may never hear of thee again. This I do, not because I would desert thee, but that I may escape the bitter grief which the news of the sad end in store for thee would cause me; for I would fain think of thee always as I do now, in the heyday of health and prosperity. Fare thee well!'

Many years afterward that which Amasis foreboded came to pass, for Polycrates, who had been beguiled into Asia by the fair promises of a Persian officer, was shamefully done to death and his body hung upon a cross.

Like the kings of Egypt before him, Amasis sought to glorify the gods by adding to the temples built in their honour. The temple of Neith at Sais was the one that received his greatest gifts, and before it he built a huge gateway with lofty towers that looked far out over the plain. To it also he gave a number of colossal statues and several sphinxes like that near Memphis, only smaller. But the most wonderful of all his works was a chamber made of a single block of stone. This stone had been quarried at Elephantine in the far south of the country, and had taken three years to convey from the quarry down the river to Sais, no less than 2000 labourers, all of whom were skilled boatmen, being engaged in the task. Its length outside was thirty-three feet, its breadth twenty-two feet, and its height twelve feet; and inside the length measured thirty feet, the breadth nineteen feet, and the height eight feet, a wondrous piece of work indeed when it is remembered that the roof formed part of the one block of stone, the chamber being hollowed out of the solid mass.

At last it arrived without mishap at the city of Sais, and a great festival had been arranged for the day when it should be transferred from the raft on which it had oated downstream to the sanctuary in the temple. The King himself was to be present and perform the ceremony of anointing. But without the temple wall an accident happened. The block was being pushed along on rollers, when one of the levers slipped, and before the man who worked it had time to escape, the mighty mass rolled back, crushing him beneath it. So overcome was the King at the sight that he gave orders for the great stone to be left where it stood.

During the reign of Amasis Egypt was more prosperous than the country had ever been before; the river was more liberal of its ood, and the land more abundant in crops. Amasis, too, gave many useful laws to his people, among them one which bade every man appear once a year before the governor of his district and tell his means of living, failing which and to prove he got an honest livelihood, he should be put to death.

Toward the end of his life he came to variance with the King of Persia; but before that monarch invaded his land Amasis died, and was buried in the temple at Sais that he had so richly adorned.